NPCs

By Drew Hayes

Copyright © 2014 by Andrew Hayes
All Rights Reserved.
Edited by Erin Cooley (cooleyrevision.com) and Kisa Whipkey (http://kisawhipkey.com)
Cover by Clay Kronke

No part of this publication may be reproduced, stored in a retrieval system, or transmitted in any form or by any means electronic, mechanical, photocopying, recording or otherwise without the prior permission of the author.

This is a work of fiction. Names, characters, places and incidents either are products of the author's imagination or are used fictitiously. Any resemblance to actual events or locales or persons, living or dead, is entirely coincidental.

Acknowledgements

I feel it is only appropriate to dedicate this book to my college tabletop group. To Matt, Dan, Neil, Alex, Jenny, Alaric, Kendra, and Biggie; the people who made those dice-based adventures into the fond memories I still carry to this day.

I also want to thank my beta readers for all their input and assistance. To E Ramos E, Priscilla Yuen, Bill Hammond, and Chad; whose time and energy helped make this book the best it could be.

Prologue

The halls stank of death, a sour mixture that cobbled together the worst parts of time, neglect, and rot. With every step, he was certain something would spring from the shadows, show its visage in the dim light of the glowing runes on his staff, and then tear his throat out. He was desperate to run, to turn and flee from this strange labyrinth they'd uncovered, but he dared not. Any moment of cowardice would be his last, for when word reached the king, there could only be one outcome.

Moving carefully past the broken door housed in an ancient arch, he entered a room different from the others he'd encountered so far. It was circular and compact, where everything else had been sprawling. There were accoutrements for living: bookshelves and a stove, both long ago ravaged by time. They started to call to him, for he'd been walking over a day now and hunger gnawed at his belly, but then he saw the pedestal.

It sat in the center of the room, a dusty, white material that might have once gleamed in a different life. Atop it, without any grandeur whatsoever, sat a strange object that reflected the enchanted light from his staff. He moved toward it, and as he did, he felt a strange pulse of magical energy ripple forth. The strange item gleamed now, fully illuminated by the staff's mystical glow.

He knew better than to reach out and pick up a clearly enchanted object. Even as a lowly court wizard, that lesson had been beaten into his head by all of his teachers. He did know better… and yet, he was still unable to stop himself as his slender elven fingers curled around the object and plucked it from its perch.

The glow intensified; no longer was it reflecting his staff's light. Now, the object generated illumination of its own. Around him, sounds filled the air as the dungeon began to come alive. Traps re-armed, monsters stirred, and magic poured from every surface. He paid no heed to any of it, however.

All he saw, all he could see anymore, was the curious object clutched tightly in his hand.

1.

"Your party finally makes it into town sometime past midnight. The streets are vacant, save for the occasional guard making rounds, and the only light seems to be emanating from the local tavern." Russell took care describing the sleepy hamlet of Maplebark, determined to get all of the details just right.

"About freaking time," Mitch grumbled. "That took forever."

"I told you, I want to do more realism in our games. That includes dealing with physical travel time," Russell said, letting out a heavy sigh.

"Whatever; I say we hit the tavern. Boys?" Mitch asked.

"Hells yeah," Glenn echoed.

"I'm in," Terry agreed.

"I'm not sure if paladins are supposed to drink," Tim said quietly.

"Oh, would you relax? The oath of purity isn't that big of a deal. Besides, you're a level one character. If your god abandons you, then just re-roll," Mitch said. "We're going to the bar."

"Fine," Russell said. "Roll me Vision checks."

"How does that work again?" Tim flipped through the character sheet in front of him, trying to make sense of the various numbers. This was his first time playing *Spells, Swords, & Stealth*, a tabletop RPG, and there was a lot to remember.

"You roll the die, in this case a D-Twenty, and add your skill bonus. For you, that bonus should be four." Having helped make Tim's character, Russell was quite familiar with Tim's skills and stats. It was the duty of every Game Master, or GM as they were informally called, to help the new players get acclimated to the system. "If you roll a twenty, that's an automatic success and you pull off whatever you're trying. If you get a one, that's a critical failure and you screw it up, no matter what your bonus is. Those rules also apply when you're trying to attack someone, only the repercussions are worse. You have to re-roll on a one, and if it's not above five, then you hurt yourself. If you ever get three ones in a row, your character has failed so badly they accidently kill themselves."

"We can do that?" Tim's already pale face seemed to lose a few shades.

"Unbunch your panties, it almost never happens," Mitch said. "That's as rare as getting three twenties in a row, which auto-kills your opponent. Now, hurry up and roll; my character's got a thirst only ale can slake."

Once the dice were thrown and the results had been tabulated, Russell described the scene that met their characters' eyes. "You see two humans sitting at the bar—one, a man who appears to be a local guard, and the other, a woman dressed in slightly more noble clothing. Drinking alone at a table in the back is a shadowy figure, small and crooked. You notice him glance at each of you carefully as you walk in."

"Yeah, he better be scared," Terry declared.

"Right. Sure. Anyway, tending the bar is a half-orc. Once you've all entered, he cocks an eyebrow," Russell said.

"Oh, he is so trying to start something." Glenn almost giggled. "Destructive wizard time."

"No way, he hasn't provoked us. Can I roll a Read Motive?" Tim asked. He'd finally found the page with his various abilities and was anxious to be of use.

"Sure," Russell told him. Tim's roll was sufficient, so Russell explained the gesture. "You understand this is his way of inquiring what you all want to order."

"Oh," Tim said. "I step up to the bar and say 'A round of mead for myself and all my friends', then put a silver piece on the bar."

"He gives you back several coppers as change, along with four mead-filled, metal mugs."

"Damn paladin, stopping us from fighting the bartender," Glenn grumbled.

"I know. I wanted to loot all of his cash. But at least Tim's drinking with us," Terry pointed out.

"Oh, crap! I forgot." Tim cringed. "Is it rude not to drink something I ordered from him?"

"Who cares? He's just an NPC," Mitch said. He turned to Tim, who had already halfway opened his mouth to ask a question. "That means Non-Player Character, someone who doesn't matter. They're background scenery, like the buildings and trees. But you're still drinking the damn mead. Bad enough we have a paladin in the party. If you're a fucking buzzkill too, then we'll stab you in your sleep."

"You know that would lead to an alignment shift, Mitch," Russell warned him.

"Whatever, it's not like alignment affects my stats," Mitch countered. "Okay, boys, hoist them mugs. To the quest!"

"To the quest!" echoed the other three players.

"So, you all toasted with your mead, does that mean you all drink?" Russell asked.

"Duh," Mitch said. "I drain my mug in one sip."

"The rest of you ingest alcohol too, I assume?" Russell kept probing.

"Sure," Terry confirmed.

"Yup," Glenn added.

"Against my better judgment, yes, I take a deep draw from the mug," Tim sighed.

"You should trust your judgment more, Tim," Russell said. Behind his screen, he rolled several dice. After what seemed like a very long amount of time rolling given the fact that nothing had been done other than drink, Russell looked back up at the group. "So, let's recap for a moment. Does everyone remember when I warned you this whole week that the new module I bought was going to be more realistic, and that meant accounting for weight and food and the like?"

The other players nodded, confused looks spreading across their faces.

"And do you remember how no one bought rations or water when making their characters, so you all wound up starving in the forest earlier?"

"Until yours truly stepped in and found us some food," Mitch declared.

"You found mushrooms. And you found them when you rolled a critical failure. Didn't you think that was mildly odd?" Russell asked.

"Whatever, it's just a Foraging check. Barbarians are made for ass-kicking, not flower picking," Mitch said.

"Right, but then you brought the mushrooms back to camp and made a soup that everyone ate. That was about four hours ago, in game time, giving the mushrooms ample time to digest and enter your system—a system you just introduced alcohol into."

"You have a point here?" Mitch asked.

In response, Russell pulled one of his books from behind the screen. It was the module he'd referenced—a pre-made campaign that saved a Game Master from having to create every detail in the imaginary world and instead, handed him one ready to use. The book was already turned to a page with a picture of a mushroom and several paragraphs about said fungi. Russell handed the book to Mitch. "Read the third paragraph."

"The Drunken Devil is a nickname assigned to this mushroom because of its peculiar effects. It is easily recognized by anyone with the Naturalist skill, and is therefore avoided due to its danger. While The Drunken Devil usually only causes sickness and vomiting six hours after ingestion, if at any point in the twenty-four hours following ingestion the character consumes alcohol, it reacts with the mushroom, causing severe damage and often . . . death," Mitch said, his voice trailing off near the end.

"Do we get saves?" Glenn asked hopefully.

"I had you make them when you ate the soup. You all failed. And given the damage I just rolled, I'm afraid all of your characters' heads slump over, slamming into the table," Russell said.

"So . . . we're dead?" Tim asked.

"Yes, you are. Consider this an object lesson in listening when I give you fair warnings about changing up the game style. This is also why I had you make backup characters. I figured you guys might blunder into something like this."

There was the sound of shuffling paper as his players produced new character sheets, tossing away the old ones and leaving them forgotten. To others, though, the deaths of those four characters were anything but forgettable.

*   *   *

"Damn, Grumph, you slipping whiskey into the mead again?" Gabrielle asked as the four strangers dropped their mugs and collapsed onto the table.

"No," Grumph replied, his half-orc voice like two stones scraping together.

"Then I guess these boys just can't hold their mead," Eric ventured, adjusting his armor for the umpteenth time that night and taking another sip of ale. Russell hadn't mentioned it, but both Eric and Gabrielle were good-looking humans, with Gabrielle more of a classic, blonde beauty, and Eric dark-haired with vibrant eyes. The next voice to speak most certainly did not emanate from an attractive being, though. Not even by gnome standards.

"I suppose the proper procedure here is to loot their purses and dump them outside," the shadowy-looking gnome said, working his way across the bar. Thistle's black clothes didn't quite conceal the crooks in his bones or the strange gait with which he moved.

"Thistle, you know I'm a guard. I can't just let you loot drunk people randomly," Eric sighed.

"What if I were to put them up in a room? Then removing their gold would simply be them paying for that service, and since they are not awake to haggle, they can hardly complain later if they feel it was a poor deal. Once services are rendered, there are no refunds."

"I'm not sure …" Eric wavered.

"The other option is to toss them in the street, and you know how a vulnerable adventurer draws the monsters," Thistle pointed out.

"Okay, okay, you win. Just gold, though. Stealing equipment would be going too far," Eric warned.

"Aye, I am fully abreast of general propriety. Gabby, come give me a hand here," Thistle called.

"Yeah, sure," Gabrielle agreed. For the daughter of the local mayor, she was oddly undisturbed by carrying out acts less savory than a proper lady of society should be comfortable with, hence why she and Thistle had not quite a friendship, but at least a familiarity with one another.

Together, they went over to the party's table and began removing the gold pouches from the fallen adventurers. Gabrielle was on the heavily-armored one when she smelled something familiar. It took her a moment to place, but as soon as it registered, she jerked back up to a full standing position and began backing away slowly.

"Shit," Gabrielle swore.

"What's wrong?" Eric asked her, rising to his own feet in concern.

"They're dead," Gabrielle said simply.

"What do you mean 'dead'?" Eric asked.

"What do you think I mean? Dead, gone, no longer with us, passed on, moved on, bugbear food, are you getting this?"

"But, I mean, how? All they did was walk in and drink Grumph's mead," Eric said.

"Yes. That's what killed them," Gabrielle confirmed.

"WHAT!" Eric shakily drew his sword and turned around to face the half-orc that loomed at least a foot taller than his own thin form. "Grumph, why would you poison some innocent adventurers?"

"Way to go there, Lord Shaky of Valiantville, but that's not what I meant," Gabrielle clarified. "They ate Drunken Devil in the woods at some point and then had alcohol. That will kill most people quicker than an axe to the gut."

"How can you be so sure?" Eric asked.

"The smell coming from their mouths. It's very distinctive. It's one of the deadly plants my parents had a tracker teach me about, since I end up kidnapped in the woods a lot. This was right near the top of the list; they showed me victims as well, so I would recognize the symptoms and scents in case it was ever slipped to me. It's sickly-sweet and yeasty — the same smell coming from their open mouths right now," Gabrielle explained.

"This is... this is bad," Eric said, sheathing his sword. "I mean, this sure looks like Grumph poisoned them."

"Oh, don't be such a wench," Gabrielle chastised him. "It's not that big of a deal. We throw the corpses in the woods and let the monsters take care of the rest. Look at their equipment; these four are nobodies. No priest will be calling their spirits, or checking on why they died if they vanish. Easy fix."

"Not quite, I'm afraid," Thistle said, shambling over with a scroll in his hand. "I discovered something while scouring their belongings that complicates matters."

"Great," Eric said. "More trouble."

"That's putting it lightly. According to this writ, these four were on their way to the court in Solium to receive a quest from King Liadon himself," Thistle said.

"Wait, so they were summoned to appear before the king in order to receive a quest?" Gabrielle asked.

"Correct, which means from the minute they received this scroll, they have technically been emissaries in the employ of The Mad King, the one who is known to burn whole villages at the slightest perceived offense," Thistle confirmed.

"So, we have four corpses in royal employ, who are expected in court soon, and who, to an untrained or careless eye, it looks a lot like we've poisoned," Eric said. "That about summing it up?"

"Perfectly so, though you could have mentioned that it isn't just royal employ, but royal employ that loathes inconvenience and is more than happy to investigate the death of every person who has failed him in any way in hopes of exacting more torture on them, or at least on the people nearby their corpses," Thistle added.

There was a moment of silence, and then the sound of a stony half-orc voice eloquently summarizing the situation in a single syllable:

"Fuck."

2.

"Okay, we can handle this, we just have to think. There must be a solution here," Eric rambled, trying desperately, and still failing, to stay calm.

"That would depend greatly on your definition of a solution. Technically, the entire town being laid siege to and everyone we know being killed qualifies as a solution. It just isn't a solution that we find favorable," Thistle pointed out.

"Thank you for the cheer, Thistle," Gabrielle snapped. "We're looking for more constructive feedback, if you don't mind."

"I'm looking over this scroll; searching for anything we might be able to use to swing the blame off of us. Does that not qualify as constructive?"

"It does, and we greatly appreciate it. We're just trying to think of other options in the event you don't discover anything of use," Eric placated.

"Now who's the pessimist?" Thistle grumbled before turning his attention back to the scroll.

"Maybe we can still just dump the bodies in the woods," Gabrielle ventured. "I mean, we're the only ones who know they came through here. If they just die on the way, then the king might swing by, but he wouldn't have any reason to launch a full inquisition."

"This is less of a 'the king needs a reason' thing and more of a 'the king loves burning shit and killing people' thing," Eric corrected. "If we hide the bodies, and if they don't find them, and if they don't manage to use magic to contact the departed souls, then our best case scenario is still royal forces cutting a swath through a huge chunk of land, searching for those answers. It happened last harvest over in Furgrer."

"Why does he keep employing random adventurers who can be so easily killed?" Gabrielle wondered.

"Again, because he seems to like leaving a trail of destruction in his wake," Eric reminded her.

"Right. Awesome."

Gabrielle and the others had heard terms like these from the various adventurers who wandered through their little hamlet from time to time. It struck the townsfolk as curious that these bands of warriors seemed to have a vernacular all their own, but language is infectious, and over time, they had taken to using such slang as well. Some phrases were more popular than others, though, and no one had discerned a standard meaning for the word pronounced as "pone" despite its recent surge in usage.

"So, the bottom line here is that we're dead," Eric said, a not-so-subtle hint of despair creeping into his voice.

"If only," Thistle corrected him. "That would be far more preferable. Instead, we're looking at the potential death of everyone in town, including friends and family, as well as the burning of our lands and homes to the ground."

There was a sound like muted cannons firing as Grumph cracked his knuckles. "They'll earn it."

"Of that, old friend, I have no doubt," Thistle agreed. "But while you lot were bemoaning your fate, I discovered something fascinating about the quest this scroll charges them with."

"Please let it be something good," Eric said.

"Not on its own, no. It is simply what it is. There is potential in how it can be used, though. You see, it seems this scroll charges the adventurers with appearing before King Liadon in three weeks' time. It details that they won the honor to serve him by the bravery shown when they stopped a kobold invasion in their own town."

"They killed some small monsters. What does that do for us?" Gabrielle asked.

"Very little, if not nothing. If you had let me finish, however, I would have made my point. This scroll details their exploits and their orders to meet the king, but at no point does it ever refer to them by name, only as the Kobold Slayers of Bluefall."

"That seems strange," Eric noted.

"Indeed. My money says the king is gearing up for some big hubbub and is recruiting every adventurer who can swing a sword, or cast a spell. Likely, he never knew the names of these four, only heard of their small success and decided to add them to whatever he has planned." Thistle paused, then tacked on, "That is, of course, mere speculation."

"If you're right, it would mean they were summoned to see the king, but they haven't met, or interacted with him yet." Eric said.

"That would be my deduction," Thistle confirmed. "The scroll merely requests that the team of a paladin, a barbarian, a wizard, and a rogue, known as the Kobold Slayers of Bluefall, attend audience with the king to receive a quest."

"Sorry, but I'm still not seeing how this helps us at all," Gabrielle said.

It was Grumph who clarified the point. He stepped out from behind the bar and walked over to the corpse-laden table. "One," he rumbled, pointing to the armored body. "Two, three, four." He gestured to each corpse in turn. He then turned to face the group and thrust his massive grey finger in Gabrielle's direction. "One." He pointed next at Eric. "Two." He moved his hand to the direction of the already-nodding Thistle. "Three." At last, he jabbed in his own direction, pressing his finger against his tremendous sternum. "Four."

"My thoughts exactly, old friend," Thistle agreed.

"Whoa whoa whoa, let's just hold on a second here," Eric protested, raising his hands and waving frantically. "Are you saying what I think you're saying?"

"Do you think I'm saying our best bet is to don their equipment and carry out the mission ourselves?" Thistle asked in return.

"Yes."

"Then, yes."

"But that's suicide!" Eric all but shrieked. "We don't have any of their experience; we can't just start masquerading as them."

"Experience is gained through adventure, and we still have three weeks of traveling to gain the prerequisite necessary," Thistle pointed out. "They clearly weren't very strong, given how easily they died. It could well be possible to achieve a level of skill comparable to theirs given our training and a few weeks of effort."

"You're insane," Eric said, advancing on the gnome. "You have finally lost your damn mind. There is no way we can pull this off. Back me up here, Gabby."

"Actually," Gabrielle said slowly. "I think I'm on board with this."

"What?"

"If you think about it, it's basically certain death versus probable death. If we do nothing, we know the crazy king will do some murdering, and he has the resources to track their death to this tavern. On the other hand, if we pick up the equipment and give it a whirl, we'll still probably die, but at least we have a sliver of hope."

"Not to mention, if we should fall further up the road, then the king will direct his murderous tendencies elsewhere," Thistle said.

Eric had been about to raise another round of objections, but that pulled him up short. Thistle was saying what he should have already realized: their fates were likely sealed regardless of what they did, but it needn't be so for their village. Eric had grown up here; he had friends here; his mother still lived and worked here. Thistle wasn't proposing this plan because he truly believed it would give them a better chance of survival, he was doing it because he believed it would give one to the people they loved.

Eric's shoulders slumped as the wind flew out of his proverbial sails.

"You're right," he admitted softly. "We have to do this."

"Glad you're with us," Thistle said. "Now we come to the next part: division of roles. As the scroll stated, we will need a paladin, a rogue, a wizard, and a barbarian."

"I guess I'm probably the best choice for wizard," Gabrielle said, stepping forward. "I have more formal education than the rest of you, and I doubt how much use I'd be in a fight. I'm already always getting kidnapped by goblins."

"True, and despite my crooks and hobbles, I'm likely the best choice for the rogue. I am, after all, not unfamiliar with shady dealings, since I have served as a henchman for many a tyrannical madman," Thistle said.

"But you did that so you could sabotage them and give away their secrets to the warriors trying to take them down," Eric countered.

"Knowledge is knowledge. How it was acquired is of no consequence, only how it is used," Thistle said. "That leaves the barbarian and the paladin."

"The paladin wears the armor, right?" Eric asked.

"Yes," Gabrielle confirmed for him. "They also wear ardent moral standards and the divine blessing of goodness."

"I'm not sure about the other stuff, but I know how to maneuver in armor. It takes some practice, so I'm probably the best choice for that one," Eric said.

"Which leaves only barbarian on the table. Grumph, you possess the raw strength and boot-quaking level of intimidation to play that part well," Thistle said.

Grumph gave only a nod to signal his agreement.

"All right then. Everyone sleep tonight, and say your goodbyes tomorrow. Grumph and I will move the corpses, then tend to our own farewells. Meet back here at this same time tomorrow night," Thistle told them. "We'll loot the bodies and be on our way."

"The words that start every great adventure," Gabrielle quipped sarcastically.

She might have been surprised to discover how accurate that statement truly was.

3.

Eric packed a small bag of essentials from the modest farmhouse where he lived. He'd only had it for a few years, finally earning enough money as a guard for the local mayor to move out from under his mother's roof. He wasn't a particularly adept guard, in truth; the goblins had slipped by and taken Gabrielle no fewer than three times on his watch. In fact, were it not for his and Gabrielle's childhood friendship, the mayor likely would have dismissed him long ago. Thankfully, the mayor knew his daughter had few friends, so he'd deigned to keep Eric on the payroll, quasi-ineptitude and all.

Eric slung the knapsack over his shoulder and adjusted his armor. He was already exhausted; sleep had eluded him the night before thanks to his bone-quaking levels of worry. Eric slipped his father's old sword into its sheath and checked his reflection in the mirror. When he'd become a guard, Eric had expected to see himself the way he saw them: heroic and stalwart, warriors in their shining armor. Instead, he thought he looked like a child playing dress up, his ill-fitting armor cinched tightly around his narrow frame. Eric's mother often spoke of his father, the great paladin and unconquerable swordsman. Eric supposed he must take after her side of the family, though, a line of not-unimpressive seamstresses and tailors.

He looked around his home one last time, then set out to bid farewell to his mother. He hoped that the next time he came upon this cottage, it would not be mere ashes under the king's heel.

* * *

Gabrielle didn't bother with goodbyes, since her parents wouldn't have let her go anyway. It was all well and good for men to strike out alone, but there was no way her family would tolerate a lady leaving her father's homestead before marriage. She packed a sack of rations and changed into her horse-riding outfit once morning broke over the horizon. After breakfast, she gave her mother a hug and her father a kiss and told them she was going to spend the day riding the horses. Gabrielle adored riding, and she often went late into the night with her equine friends. When she didn't come home, they'd be annoyed, but not worried. It wouldn't be until the next morning that they'd suspect she might not be returning.

A stray tear may have slipped from Gabrielle's eye as her steed broke into a gallop. Despite their meddling, she truly did love her parents greatly. She hated having to make them worry as they would when she vanished. Still, it was that same love for them that spurred her on, away from the comfortable life she'd known since birth. This was the only chance she had to protect them.

She urged her horse to run faster. Gabrielle was not one to linger on sadness, or hard decisions, so she raced forward as fast as she could to meet her future.

* * *

The grave on the hill was small and simple, yet painstakingly maintained. It was marked by a modest headstone and overlooked a brook that was about an hour's walk from town. It had been one of her favorite spots; Thistle had dug the grave himself so that his wife might have a pleasant view for eternity.

"I'm afraid I won't be able to visit again for some time," he said, voice rising over the gentle lap of the water on the bank. "The winds have begun to blow again, it seems." Thistle adjusted his stance in a vain attempt to find a comfortable way to stand on the hill's sloping surface.

"I don't want you to worry about me; I'll be safe. Grumph is coming along, and so are the human pair I've told you about before. They're green as a dryad's hair, but good kids overall. Who knows, we might just pull off this little charade."

The small gnome paused and looked out at the scenery. It was truly lovely here; he had hoped to be buried on this hill alongside her when his god called him home. Sadly, it wasn't looking too likely now. The only one he'd have trusted with the burial task was Grumph, and Thistle had a feeling that if he fell on their journey, Grumph and the others wouldn't be far behind.

"And if we don't," Thistle added, "then I suppose I'll be seeing you soon, anyway."

Thistle gently touched his fingertips to the headstone, then shambled down the hill and began the long trek back toward town.

*   *   *

Grumph didn't have a family in Maplebark. He didn't have graves to visit either. The only person he truly counted as a friend was Thistle, and that wily gnome was coming with him. Grumph did have his tavern, though. He ran his hands along the wooden planks of the bar, remembering how long it had taken him to get the measurements just so. He sipped the mead, savoring its flavor, thinking of all the careful testing and calculations required to get his brew perfect. Grumph sat at one of the many tables he had constructed, in one of the chairs he had carved, and simply took it all in. He had built this bar with love and considerable strength. It had taken the Maplebark residents time to adjust to a half-orc in their midst, but eventually, Grumph had been accepted, doing business with all manner of citizens.

Grumph hadn't just built a business here, he'd carved a home. And he'd come to love this hamlet of Maplebark, plagued by the occasional weak monsters and villains though it was. Grumph was under no illusions: much as he loved his bar, his creation, it wasn't a building that made a place home. It was the people. As Grumph poured the lamp fluid on the floor and the tables, he was struck by the poignancy of it all, destroying his house to protect his home. There was a knock on the door, signaling the first of his companions' arrivals. Perhaps it would be Thistle and there would be time for one last drink.

The last drink, as it were.

*　　　*　　　*

Grumph's tavern burned at their backs as they trekked slowly through the forest.

"I still don't get it," Eric said as he checked his footing in hopes of avoiding another impressive tumble. "Why did he burn the bar?"

"Let me put it to you this way. What usually happens to abandoned taverns and inns?" Thistle asked him.

"They get inhabited by monsters, or bandit gangs," Eric replied. It was common knowledge, after all. Adventurers often sought out such locations when hunting for a good fight.

"Precisely. Now, setting aside the logistical concerns of creating a temptation like that in our little town, Grumph built that tavern himself. He poured a piece of himself into its frame and foundation. He cared for it with more affection than I've seen some show their children. The idea of some ruffians wrecking it, or kobolds shitting on its floor… it's too much. Just try to understand that sometimes it is better to see a thing destroyed, rather than ruined." Thistle hopped lightly along the path in hope of keeping up with his larger companions. It was a difficult proposition, but one he had managed for many years now.

Gabrielle patted the half-orc lightly on his muscular arm. "Sorry about your bar."

Grumph replied with little more than a grunt, a sound that spoke to both his profound sadness and his appreciation of the heartfelt sentiment. Or it meant he was hungry. Orcish didn't have many unique sounds, so there was a lot of room for misinterpretation.

The party, for that is what they were whether they liked it or not, had set out at dusk into the woods. They had chosen to walk and avoid main roads for two reasons. First was that Gabrielle's family would send people looking for her and they needed to make a clean break into their new identities if they hoped to succeed. The other reason was because they hoped to encounter some weak monsters. They might have the tools and garb to pass in their new professions, but none of them had the skills. For that purpose, they would travel at night, when the most monsters were loose, leaving study and rest for the days. It would take them longer to reach the city of Solium; however, it also provided the greatest opportunity for being prepared when they arrived.

To their rear, the smoke billowed into the empty night sky. Despite their hopes, they encountered no animal or monster worth fighting through the evening. In fact, they made such good progress that only Eric heard the fire when it reached the liquor tanks in the basement, sending a fresh fireball into the night and a loud boom across the land.

*   *   *

Despite their fears and the sense of dread lingering over them, the group made it through the night without being killed or discovered. When they rose after a few hours of unrestful sleep, each set about attending to the task they felt most important, using the daylight to its fullest.

Eric took a few swings with his new blade, managing to accidently hack off some tree branches in the process. The previous paladin had possessed fine taste in steel; there was no doubt about that. The long sword was well-crafted and perfectly balanced. It was also unnecessarily ornate, a gold-plated design worked along the guard and onto the hilt. Unfortunately, its previous owner had also possessed thicker arms than Eric, leading him to struggle with wielding the blade effectively. Back in his guard position, he'd gotten away with using his father's old short sword, its status as an heirloom saving him from merciless teasing by the other guards.

Thistle was also adapting to his new equipment. The rogue had kept a pair of long, wickedly-serrated daggers that nearly looked like swords in Thistle's small hands. Still, he was at least proficient with his weapons, twirling them about and practicing a few of the defensive moves he'd learned in his younger, more ambitious days. Testing the heft of his left dagger, Thistle cradled it carefully before whipping his arm suddenly and hurling it into a nearby tree. The dagger struck true, cleaving a few inches deep before wobbling to a rest. Thistle sighed. Accuracy, he still had; power, it seemed, he would need to work on.

Gabrielle was seated cross-legged on the ground a safe distance away from the whirling pieces of steel wielded by her comrades. She focused on the wizard's book, picking through its open pages and trying to piece together the art of weaving a spell. Gabrielle turned a piece of worn parchment and began to appreciate the reason wizards spent so much time in school learning their craft. While she could comprehend some of the concepts being put forth, it seemed like grasping the whole would take far more than a quick perusing.

Of the four, only Grumph was attending to a more immediate concern rather than training. He had gathered up some berries and tough meat scraps, along with the water from a local brook, to concoct a soup. It certainly wasn't his finest culinary achievement; however, in the wild one had to make do with what was available. Grumph's new axe rested near him, relatively untouched. Grumph knew how to swing and knew how to aim. He had faith he would learn the rest through action, rather than practice. Besides, they would need to eat, then rest, if they wanted to continue on their way with the setting of the sun.

It was Eric who heard the first rustling, which was unfortunate. Gabrielle had spent enough time in nature, Thistle had enough experience, and Grumph was simply smart enough to know a rustling bush should always be looked at with suspicion. Eric, on the other hand, merely dismissed it as the wind and continued as he had been taught, blocking out all distractions and focusing on the training at hand. By the time the gentle movement of the leaves reached Thistle's ears, it was too late to implement any plan aside from bracing for impact.

"Boys and girl," Thistle said softly, yet firmly. "I believe we are soon to have company in our clearing."

Gabrielle kept her book open, but seized the quarterstaff at her side while rising to her feet. Grumph kept his eyes trained on the soup. His hands, however, moved deftly and certainly as they wrapped around his axe. Eric pulled his sword up to a fighting stance, eyes darting around nervously as he searched for the threat.

"A word of encouragement," Thistle said, just before the commotion erupted. "Don't die. We aren't nearly far enough away yet."

"I'll try to keep that in mind," Gabrielle said through clenched teeth.

After that, there was no time for words or banter.

4.

The wheels of the sturdy cart-cages absorbed the bounces from the multitude of uneven drops in the road, making the trip back to camp surprisingly pleasant for the prisoners. Gabrielle sat in one cart-cage at the front of the convoy, speaking to her captors in a series of loud growls and clicks. Behind her was a cart containing Eric and Thistle, both silent. Eric was nursing a nasty blow he'd taken to the head. At the rear of the convoy was the best-built of all the cages, this one dedicated only to the task of holding Grumph.

To call what had taken place a "battle" would be an overstatement; even "skirmish" would be giving the new adventurers too much credit. Goblins, while physically weaker than humans, were experienced in dealing with stronger opponents, and skilled in using the environment to their advantage. By the time the party had braced for battle, twenty archers had emerged from the bushes, followed immediately by ten warriors with polearms. Making a snap decision, Thistle had immediately called out their surrender. Five arrows apiece was more than he felt confident most of them could endure, and those who did survive wouldn't be in any shape to fight off a polearm.

Once they'd thrown down their weapons, a goblin runner had been dispatched, returning less than an hour later with some other goblins riding ponies, and of course, the cage-carts. While getting inside, Eric had managed to slip on the step and strike his head against one of the rear planks, resulting in the one and only injury from their "battle."

"I've got good news and bad news," Gabrielle called from her cart in the front. She'd been gibbering with the goblins since their capture, greeting them with such familiarity that the others found it somewhat disconcerting. "Bad news is that, now that they know I'm here, they're going to send a runner into town to announce it and lure out adventurers. The good news is that it's almost sunset, so they won't do it until morning."

"Gabby, pray tell, when did you learn to speak the goblin language?" Thistle asked, his restrained voice as polite as he could make it.

"Gobleck isn't hard to learn, if you have a decent teacher," Gabrielle replied. "I learned it years ago from one of the goblin commanders who can speak the Proper Kingdom Language."

"I think Thistle was more asking about why you speak it," Eric clarified.

"Because things would be really boring if I didn't? Sometimes, it's two or three weeks between when they kidnap me and when the adventurers would arrive for the rescue. That's a lot of downtime, and the goblins only let me pack so many books when they would kidnap me."

"They let you pack?" Eric asked, certain his ears had deceived him like the vile villains they were.

"They did once I explained to them that it would make my downtime more pleasant. Don't get me wrong, they make a point of teaching me things about the forest and taking me on hunts, but they've got real things to do and can't spend all day defending me from boredom."

"It's pleasing to know we have such kind hosts," Thistle said, jumping in before Eric asked any more questions that might ultimately give the young man a stroke. "Any chance they'd let us out of the cages once we arrive at their war camp?"

"I don't think so. If it were just me, certainly, but since they don't know you all, I get the feeling they're trying to keep up appearances. They didn't even bring my usual horse for me to ride."

"She has her own horse," Eric muttered, slinking down against the firm, yet pliable, wooden bars of his moving cell. "I once stayed up for thirty hours straight to guard her door because we heard goblins were in the area, and she has her own horse she rides away on."

"Riverjump is not *my* horse," Gabrielle defended. "She's just one I like, and who knows me. Bringing her makes the whole process easier on everyone."

"Gabby, I think perhaps we should let Eric be for a bit," Thistle encouraged. "About how far would you say we are from their camp?"

"With no monster encounters, we'll be there within the hour."

"Very well. And you, old friend, how are you faring back there?" Thistle called.

Grumph let out a harrumph, which indicated either that he was unharmed and waiting patiently for a new opportunity to arise, or that a sparrow had shit in his porridge.

Thistle nodded that he understood and took a seat across from Eric in the cart. His crooked little mind was already working on a plan for escape; however, it would do no good if his crooked little body was too worn out from standing through the ride. Now was the time to play patient. They would have at least a few days before any more adventurers happened through town. Opportunity would come eventually.

As it turned out, Opportunity had far less patience than Thistle.

*   *   *

The goblin camp was somewhat homier than Thistle had imagined. Certainly, there were bulwarks of defense: archer stations, barriers to trip horses, even a few oddly-colored patches of earth Thistle suspected to be traps. But there were also things that made no sense in this setting, things like goblin children racing around, goblin cooks tending to the night's evidently sizable dinner, and several goblin musicians warming up their strange instruments as the last valiant rays of sunlight dotted the landscape.

"Gabby, is the camp always so domestic?" Thistle asked. Their cages had been parked next to one another, while Grumph's sat on the other side of the fire that was the center point of the camp. The goblins had clearly dealt with half-orcs enough to minimize the damage he'd have the opportunity to do.

"No, this is how it is when they aren't baiting adventurers," Gabrielle replied. "Once the runner goes out in the morning, they'll move everyone but the warriors to some other site. Then, once it's over, they'll all come back."

"To what? Corpses?" Eric asked. "Won't the warriors be dead after they fight the adventurers?"

"What? Why would you think that? This is their home turf, and they know the adventurers are coming. The goblins almost always win, and even if they lose, they're smart enough to have a retreat plan."

"Then why do you always come back after the adventurers leave to get you?" Eric kept probing.

"Because they let me go. I'm just bait to lure the adventurers in so they can loot them. Once that's done, they let me go until they're ready to trap another party." Gabrielle looked at him, eyes filled with bewilderment that he'd even needed to ask the question.

"Knock off the innocent act, Gabby," Thistle chided. "If you really didn't see anything strange with how you'd been treated, then you'd have told us some of this before."

"Fine, so maybe the kidnappings weren't as bad as everyone assumed." Gabrielle breathed out a heavy sigh and let the faux innocence slide away. "At first, it was scary. But after a while, it's hard not to find some common ground with people you see every day. Honestly, for the last few years, these events have been like vacations for me, trips outside the protective bubble of being the Mayor of Maplebark's daughter."

Eric didn't know what to say to this, his eyes darting about nervously. As they moved, he saw action in another part of the camp and decided a change of subject was in order.

"Hey, what are they doing over there?"

Gabrielle glanced over. "Oh, it looks like they found an abandoned caravan and are sorting the goods."

In front of a large building, easily the most hardily-constructed and well-defended in the camp, stood several goblins wearing makeshift armor. Before them were other goblins leading ponies and a cart filled nearly to the brim with bric-a-brac. In the center of the crowd was an older goblin wearing a dirt-brown robe, examining each item as it came off the cart. Some he sent into the building, others were moved to a different spot in the camp, and a few went back on the cart.

"The one in the middle is an elder; he's tasked with figuring out which pieces of loot have the most value. Those go in the storage building. Bits that are useful, but not expensive, are given out to others in the camp that can use them. The things going back into the cart are for the other scavenger teams to split up, based on who needs what. When they sell the expensive items at market in a few weeks, everyone will get a cut," Gabrielle explained.

"You'd think the ones who found it would get more," Eric pointed out.

"Goblins don't think like that. They regard everyone in the tribe as one big party, and believe in a system of equal treasure sharing," Gabrielle informed him.

There might have been more discussion of goblin economics, had the elder not chosen that moment to open a small box he'd been handed, revealing a glowing red gem the size of Grumph's fist. Excited grunts and clicks filled the area around them, many goblins crowding in to get a closer look. From the vantage point of the cage-carts, the three rookie adventurers could make out the soft radiance of presumably magical light and the dazzling red surface. It was only Eric, however, whose eyes noticed the slight swirls of color within the gem, and he didn't know what to make of it.

"Strange," Thistle remarked. "If they found an abandoned caravan, one would have expected the people who left it to take such a clearly valuable item."

"Maybe it was hit by robbers?"

"Robbers who left this much stuff?" Gabrielle said. "I saw them take in small sets of armor and what I suspect was a magical bow earlier. No bandit in their right mind leaves behind equipment like that."

"They could have been eaten by monsters," Eric suggested.

"At present, that seems like the most likely option," Thistle agreed.

Their conversation was cut short by the sound of the door to Thistle and Eric's cage opening. A pair of goblins stood in the doorway, with several more just outside. The message of "don't try anything" came through loud and clear before a single click was uttered. Another team of goblins opened the door to Gabrielle's cage, motioning her to exit with far kinder expression.

The one nearest to Thistle, tall for a goblin and wearing a red buckler on his arm, spoke up.

"He wants you to take off the armor," Gabrielle translated, looking at Eric as she was escorted over to their cage-cart. None but the paladin corpse had armor that would fit them, and Eric had examined it only to determine it would be more effort than it was worth to try and get accustomed to it. Instead, he'd elected to keep his guard armor on, since that, at least, he was accustomed to dealing with. When they'd been captured, part of him had hoped they'd leave it be, but now, he realized it was merely a matter of waiting for a more convenient time to take it from him.

Red Buckler clicked again.

"He says they will cut it off you, but they'd prefer if you did this voluntarily, since it will damage the armor less."

"Sure, why not," Eric sighed, pulling himself to his feet. "Honestly, I don't even like wearing the stuff. It's heavy, it's loud, and I'm always tripping over myself wearing it." He began carefully removing each piece, a process that grew quicker as the amount of armor he wore lessened. "Still, I don't think I'm much a paladin without any armor."

"Right now, the only identity aspect any of us should concern ourselves with is staying alive," Thistle reminded him.

Eric continued to strip off the metal adornments until they all lay in a pile at his feet. Red Buckler stayed by the door, while the other goblins formed a quick conveyor line to move the armor out of the cage. Once that was done, Gabrielle was sent into the cage with Thistle and Eric. Before the door was closed, a burlap sack was brought in and set before them. Red Buckler made a few goblin sounds and left.

"He thanked us for being cooperative," Gabrielle said.

Thistle opened the sack to reveal a generous amount of bread, cheese, meat slices, and even a bottle of wine.

"I've been held by worse hosts, I'll give them that," Thistle said, helping himself to a slice of bread.

*   *   *

In the transport of the party after the scramble, their equipment had been strapped to the backs of various goblins, since they obviously weren't going to allow prisoners to have weapons. The only item of difficulty had been the spellbook. Goblins understood the value of magic, especially when bargaining, however, they also knew that magical items were unstable, and the less time spent around them, the safer. Spellbooks especially were frequently booby-trapped by wizards to discourage their theft. The result of this knowledge was a healthy disinterest in being the goblin stuck holding onto any items dealing with magic. After five minutes of bickering about who would have to hold the book, they'd ultimately reached the compromise of throwing it in the cage with the half-orc. If it was trapped, it would only hurt him, and the worst thing he would be able to do by reading it was set himself on fire, or turn his feet into pudding.

At first, Grumph had ignored the book, focusing instead on taking in his surroundings and examining his cage for weak points. Once they arrived, and he was stuck away from the rest of his party, boredom teamed up with curiosity to prompt him into flipping through its pages. The vast majority of them were blank; only about five had actually been filled out. The wizard it belonged to truly had been just starting out. Each spell was interesting, a combination of mental images, physical gestures, and specific words; all required to invoke the magic contained within. For most, they would have been very difficult to memorize, especially under pressure. For a veteran bartender who memorized all his mead recipes so they couldn't be stolen, it was relatively easy. Strangely, in all of the specific instructions for how to cast each spell, there was never any mention of what the effects would be. Grumph quickly realized this was likely by design, so that, even if the book was stolen, anyone with a smattering of sense would be too smart to cast a spell they couldn't predict.

The flaw in this strategy was that it failed to take into account a person who was aware they could soon find themselves in a life or death situation. Grumph turned back to the first page and began reading again. He didn't know if barbarians were supposed to cast spells, but he didn't really care. If a spell-casting barbarian was an oddity, then he would simply be the first.

Grumph had never been one to wait for others to clear the trail in advance.

5.

As night fell in earnest, more goblins began gathering in the central area of the camp. Tables were set up, food brought out, and charming melodies filled the air as the musicians started to play. Though the sound wasn't traditional or familiar to anyone but Gabrielle, each of the party members found themselves enjoying it. Warm, peppy, and with an exciting tempo, the music helped make them feel at least somewhat at ease with their situation.

"Do they always party like this?" Eric asked.

Gabrielle shook her head. "This is the celebration they throw the night before trying to bait adventurers. It's partly an offering to Grebspluk, one of the goblin deities of the hunt, but mostly, it's a last meal with the warriors and their families. Some of them probably won't live to see another hunt."

"I've often wondered about that, actually," Thistle piped up. "Why bother luring out adventurers at all? Surely there are safer ways to live."

"I asked that once," Gabrielle said. "They know adventurers would come after them anyway — though they aren't sure why — but this way, they control the circumstances and give themselves the best chance of survival. Evidently, almost no adventurers go goblin hunting when there's a kidnapping to pursue. Plus, they get about thirty percent of their income from looting dead adventurers."

Thistle let out a low whistle that sounded dry despite the ample water available to them. "A not-unhefty sum."

"I'm still stuck on the fact that they have a deity named Grebspluk," Eric admitted.

"It's a rough translation. Gobleck names sound like the rest of the language. Part of why I haven't tried to introduce any of you."

"Still seems silly," Eric replied.

"Don't be too quick to judge another's deity," Thistle cautioned. "I, myself, am a devout follower of a god with an unimpressive name. Yet Grumble is a kind and devoted god to his followers."

"I've never heard of a god named Grumble," Gabrielle said.

"Nor would I have expected you to. His shrines are modest, and off to the side in any temple, but they are abundant if you know how to find them. Grumble is the god of henchmen and minions. Once a former lackey himself, after his deification he chose to look over his own people rather than putting on airs."

"I can see how that guy might get some followers," Eric said. He knew the minions were the lowest on the hierarchy of any organization, regarded as disposable and useless by most commanders. At that thought, he took a long stretch, enjoying the sensation of his muscles' movements now that he was unrestrained by the armor. In truth, he hadn't been much more than a minion himself. Maybe he should drop a prayer to this deity next time he was in a temple.

Around them, the festivities had begun to escalate. As plates were cleaned of food, more goblins transitioned from eating to dancing. There was no established pattern that any of the adventurers could make out, no coordinated effort to create a temporary moment of sublime beauty. Mostly, it was just each goblin going out near the fire, finding a spot clear of others, and thrashing about in whatever way delighted them most. There was no grace or delicacy in their movements, yet it was strangely entrancing all the same. Perhaps it was the way they felt so free to dance in any style that pleased them, with no apprehension, or fear of being judged by the others of their tribe.

The musicians picked up the tempo. This, it seemed, was an unspoken signal, as many more goblins rose from their seats and began to dance. Soon, there wasn't room enough for everyone to move without contacting another, but this didn't dissuade them. Small claws scraped against a neighbor's skin, feet were stomped on repeatedly, and occasionally a pair would end up tangled together, crashing to the ground in a still-writhing heap. None of this seemed to diminish the goblins' enjoyment in the slightest.

No, what it took to kill the party was a massive explosion from the rear of the camp that sent chunks of wood and unknown trinkets flying through the air. The music stopped abruptly, and the dancers immediately crouched into ready positions. Some of the warriors reached for the weapons at their sides, and the archers on the perimeter turned their attention to the smoking husk. It was their storage building, now bathed in a soft red glow from the pieces that were still on fire. For a moment, silence descended upon the camp, save only for the soft crackling of the flames.

Then they heard the clacking of claws and the scraping of feet.

*   *   *

Eric said nothing as he stared at the blade still quivering in the wood less than two inches from his head. There hadn't been time to react, not rationally, when they heard the explosion. Eric had merely glanced at the storage building, seen something coming, and hurled himself to the side. So great was the force from the blast that the axe Grumph had been carrying whipped through one set of the cage's bars with ease, sinking at least halfway into the wooden barriers on the other side. Eric was intimately familiar with that spot; his head had been there only an instant before.

"The fuck?" Gabrielle said at last, eyes trained on the smoldering building uncomfortably close to them. It was strange, the way the flames were cascading through the smoke; it almost appeared that there were shapes moving in the wreckage. It must be a mirage. Her party members were the only ones large enough to make such shadows, and they were all stuck in cages.

"We need to go," Thistle said, grabbing his companions' attention. While the others had been caught up in shock, he'd examined the hole that the axe had carved through the cage's bars. It wasn't too large, big enough for him to fit through without much trouble, though the same couldn't be said for the humans. In this instance, however, the cage's flexibility worked to its disadvantage. While a material that moved made breaking through more difficult, once a hole was carved, it meant areas could be stretched as needed.

"Go?" Eric asked, still unwilling to look away from the axe that tried to behead him.

"Vamoose, escape, do the kobold charge, run away," Thistle clarified. "Someone blowing up part of an entrenched goblin encampment means an attack, and I prefer not to be unarmed and trapped in a cage during such circumstances."

"You're wrong," Gabrielle declared. "These goblins are smart and safe. No one could have surprised them like this. It was probably just some magic item they didn't know was going to blow up. We're in no danger."

"That theory is a good one," Thistle complimented. "But it doesn't explain why the goblins all seem to be braced for attack."

A quick glance confirmed he was right. The children and non-warrior goblins were being herded toward the other side of the camp, while those with armor and weapons slowly advanced toward the remains of the storage shed. It was then that Eric's human hearing finally caught up to what the goblins' large ears had already noticed.

"What is that noise?"

Thistle and Gabrielle cocked their own heads, listening intently. Now that he'd pointed it out, there was a strange clacking sound coming from the burning building. To Gabrielle, it was completely alien; however, Thistle went white as a wight when he heard it.

"We need to get out and get clear, now." Thistle tugged on Eric's tunic. In a motion quicker than one would have suspected his knobby form capable of, the gnome slipped through the hole and landed softly on the ground.

"Why? Do you know what it is?" Eric asked.

Thistle opened his mouth to speak, and as he did, the first of the monsters stepped into view. It was hideous—six feet tall with red, gnarled flesh along its twisted body. Atop its shoulders sat the head of a malformed rat, upper jaw stretched out inches further than its lower. Instead of hands, it had claws like that of scorpion, the clacking sound suddenly making a sickly amount of sense to all in attendance. The legs were birdish, long and lean with feet that spread into four individual claws. Despite all of this, it was the eyes that were most disconcerting, black orbs like midnight dipped in ink. Looking into one, a person couldn't help but feel like they were being sucked into that abyss.

"Demons," Thistle said, his voice scarcely above a whisper.

*   *   *

Grumph had put the book down when the celebration began, and he'd stood up in the cage after the explosion rocked the camp. However, since he was closer to the lines of warriors than the others, Grumph was less impetuous about getting free from his mobile prison. As they began advancing toward the building, Grumph shuffled his position slightly. The goblins had their back to him, and the explosion had dropped his importance in their list of immediate priorities, yet he was patient. Grumph did not move until he saw something that compelled him to. It was not seeing the demon emerge from the smoking ruins, nor was it observing a few of the goblins near the rear drop their weapons and flee. No, the signal that told Grumph things were getting dangerous was when he caught sight of the terror on Thistle's face. He'd known the gnome for many years, and anything that spooked him in such a manner was not to be taken lightly.

The goblin cages were sturdy, well-designed, and built to last. Grumph was impressed by their construction. Had he been a mere mindless brute, the cage would have proved more than a match for his strength. By contrast, had he possessed the knowledge to assess such a contraption, but not the power to act on such information, he would also have been stuck. Thankfully, Grumph was an experienced craftsman with muscles cultivated by centuries of half-orc breeding. In a controlled motion, he seized one of the areas in the corner where a bar had been improperly bound. With a grunt of effort that would have been noticeable in any other situation (demons do tend to steal focus), Grumph tore the bars apart. From there, it was a simple matter to disassemble a few exposed binding cords and knock away a section large enough for him to emerge from.

He landed softly, choosing stealth over speed, the whole process having taken less than a minute. In that time, three more of the creatures had stepped forth from the fire. In the chaos, Grumph couldn't quite make out whether his friends were free from their cage yet. A quick survey of the ground at his feet netted Grumph an abandoned goblin polearm. It felt more akin to a dagger on a stick in his considerable hands, but he would take it over nothing.

With careful steps, Grumph began edging his way around the bulk of the goblin troops and toward his friends' cage. He might have made it unnoticed, too, if the demons hadn't chosen that moment to leap.

The first landed dead center in the mass of the goblin warriors, letting out a horrendous shriek as it seized one in each claw. Another came down on the side of camp where the largest exit was, clacking its claws excitedly. The initial demon to emerge stayed put; evidently it felt no need for relocation. The final demon leapt the furthest, soaring through the air and landing with a muffled thump.

It was less than four sword lengths away from Grumph.

6.

When the demon emerged, the humans had needed very little in terms of convincing to leave the cage. Eric slid out with relative ease, his narrow, lean frame no longer encumbered by the heavy metal burden that had weighed him down. Gabrielle had found the task a bit tougher. Though brought up a proper lady, her love of horse riding and self-defense courses (in a vain attempt to stem her kidnappings) had left her strong and somewhat more muscular than one might imagine. After two unsuccessful tries to squeeze through the cage, she took a new approach.

Seizing the axe wedged on the far side, Gabrielle jerked it free with a solid pull, then slid its head through the hole and set it on the ground. Using the shaft for balance, and with Eric's help, she was finally able to maneuver her way out of the wooden cage and land safely on the ground. Safely, here, was a relative term, since she was still in proximity of a claw-clacking demon and several dozen armed goblins. Still, she wasn't trapped, and that was progress.

Gabrielle's freedom nearly coincided with the demons' leaping; she landed only moments before they took off. For an instant, she thought it was a good thing. After all, fewer demons near them meant a higher possibility of living to see the sunrise, didn't it?

"Dragonshit," Thistle muttered as he watched the horrid creatures crash back down to the dirt.

"What?" Eric asked.

"They're coordinating," Thistle explained. "The one in the center is there to draw focus and stir up chaos among the warriors. Meanwhile, the three on the outside can pick off the ones on the edges of the crowd, while still cutting off the best exit routes. This is very bad. Demons set on a random slaughter are troublesome, but can be outmaneuvered. When they're smart enough to work together, well, let's simply say our survival chances just got lower."

"What do we do?" Gabrielle asked. Without thinking, she pulled the axe up from the ground and brought it to rest on her shoulder. It might not be of much use to her, but better a clumsy weapon than none at all.

"You two get clear," Thistle ordered. "Grab any weapons or armor you see on the way out — it wouldn't do to be picked off by wolves after escaping demons — and get out of camp."

"And what will you be doing while we're turning tail?" Eric asked.

"Someone has to go check on Grumph," Thistle replied. "And I certainly draw far less attention in this crowd than you two."

That part was true. The gnome stood nearly shoulder-to-shoulder with the goblins, meaning he could blend in easily. Two humans would stick out like, well, like a pair of humans in a crowd of goblins.

"I don't want to leave you like that," Eric said.

"Good sentiment; hold onto that later on when we're back to playing our roles. This isn't you abandoning me, though. This is you trusting me to do my job, and not making me worry about you as well. We're a party. We each have our own tasks to fulfill," Thistle explained.

Eric didn't particularly like that answer, but he also didn't foresee changing Thistle's mind, and the longer they were here, the worse their chances of survival grew.

"Fine," Eric agreed at last. "We meet at the clearing we passed on the way in."

"Deal," Thistle said, almost immediately darting off into the crowd.

"Works for me," Gabrielle added.

"Glad we're all agreed. Now, which way should we go to get out of here?"

"I'm going for a gap I know about on the west side of the camp." Gabrielle pointed somewhere past the goblin warriors. "You should probably go another route. I have to pass a lot of goblins on my way. They know me and won't attack in surprise. I can't say the same for you. Plus, it's probably better to go separate ways... just in case."

Eric nodded; there was no need for explanation. They were in a very dire situation and the odds of all of them making it out were slim at best. At least going different ways meant one might find a clear path.

"Be safe," he told her.

"You, too."

With that, each hunkered down and began moving away as quickly and quietly as they were able to manage.

* * *

There are few sensations like staring eye to eye with a demon, nothing between you and it but a polearm that somehow felt even smaller than it had moments ago. Grumph and the beast locked eyes with each other for less than half a second, yet both could feel the weight of a lifetime in that glance. There was no need for pretense: this moment ended with one of them dead. No other outcome was possible.

That sentiment was dispelled when three arrows lodged in the demon's back, earning a sickening twist of its rat-like head in an unnatural angle toward its attackers. Behind it stood three goblin warriors and a quartet of archers, separated from their main force. The warriors were advancing slowly, polearms extended, while the archers nocked fresh arrows into their bows.

With a series of jerking steps, the demon turned its attention toward the goblins. Evidently, it cared more for quantity than size, as Grumph was left largely forgotten, facing its rear. One of the goblin archers met his half-orc gaze and began speaking fiercely at him. Though Grumph didn't speak Gobleck, the "shoo" hand-gestures that the goblin made sent the message quite clearly. They were going to handle this thing; he should run away quickly while the opportunity was there.

Moments earlier, staring down a demon, Grumph might have considered it. But now, watching his captors, small though they were, confront this monster on his behalf, such an idea was ludicrous. He felt no particular love for these goblins; they were merely beings who'd captured him because he was easy prey. Be that as it was, he loathed demons, and he'd be damned to see these four ravage the camp. At the very least, he would assist until the children and non-warriors escaped.

Grumph tightened his grip on the polearm and felt it creak under the pressure. He dearly wished he'd found something more substantial.

*   *   *

Eric, in a show of either cunning or stupidity (the difference between the two being an idea works or not) elected to go the one direction that no one was paying attention to. Creeping along, he made his way to the storage building, which was still burning, but rapidly turning into more of a smolder than an inferno. The first demon had advanced several feet forward, and was now in the process of slicing through a pair of goblins while others of the tribe slashed at it angrily. In the soft light of the fire, Eric slipped through a gap between the storage building and the rubble of what had once been a home.

The heat from the flames was strong; sweat materialized on his face as soon as he was alongside the building's remains. It was slow going, as the gap between the two areas had been designed for only goblins to fit through. Moving through the area at all would have been impossible if the explosion hadn't destroyed large sections of both buildings' walls. Even with that, it took careful footing and balance as, at times, Eric had to climb from gap to gap, getting several feet off the ground. He marveled at the speed of his body, feeling, for the first time in years, the freedom of movement when not confined by that damned armor. He'd only ever taken it off for bathing and bed, activities which rarely offered the chance to stretch his limbs.

He was back on the ground, moving beside a gap in the storage building so large it accounted for at least an eighth of the wall, when he saw it. Sitting there, miraculously untouched by the explosion or the fire, resting on a pile of wrecked chests, was his sword. Not the cumbersome one he'd lifted from the paladin's corpse, but his sword. The one his father had given him when he was a child, meant to be a training blade. The one he'd used as a guard, even though the others had laughed at him for it. The one he'd been unable to leave behind, even when packing light less than a day ago. *His* sword.

Without a thought, Eric reached through the hole and grabbed the hilt of his blade. It was warm, but not as hot as he'd expected, given the environment. The scabbard had melted slightly, however, the blade still pulled free with a little effort. Eric sheathed it once more, tucked it into his belt, and continued his movements toward freedom. In almost no time, he'd passed the final few hunks of rubble obscuring the way and stepped out of the narrow gap.

Eric was surprised by how sweet the night air smelled. The tight goblin perimeter had contained much of the soot and violence, so much so that, once on the other side of the buildings, the world seemed almost peaceful. There were still a few more traps and hurdles to get around, but as Eric looked out into the dark depths of the forest, reality set in.

He'd made it. He was free.

*   *   *

In different circumstances, Gabrielle might have made it. Her idea had been a sound one: sneak behind the bulk of the warriors to a secret get-away path she knew about. It was near the main entrance, obscured enough that one wouldn't find it unless they knew it was there. Her movements were controlled, careful, and precise. She knew this camp well, and if any of the goblin warriors noticed her making for the exit, they did nothing to impede her.

For one thing, she'd been around so much they considered her a friend. For another, they had far bigger problems on their hands.

The demon in the center of the warriors was beginning to show signs of wear. Tough though its hide was, the sheer number of arrows and polearms were beginning to tear away bits of its flesh. The one near the building seemed to be faring better — not enough of the goblins were focused on it — and the monster was dropping their numbers with nearly every swipe of its claws. Gabrielle couldn't make out the one that had jumped across the camp, but she assumed it was probably doing well, too. For a time, she didn't know where the fourth demon had landed. Then she arrived at her exit point.

At first, her heart felt lighter as she saw the swarm of goblins around the demon. This many would end it swiftly and then they could focus on the other two. The tribe might just have a shot at this. Then she noticed how quickly they were falling and realized few of them had armor or weapons. A quick glance toward the area where the secret get-away was located showed that the entrance was blocked.

Blocked with goblin corpses.

The reason there were so many goblins around it was because the demon had caught onto their escape attempt and sealed it. Now it stood between them and escape on the main road. It wasn't being swarmed with warriors, it was cutting a swath of death through the children and peaceful-goblins that had been trying to evacuate.

*   *   *

Thistle moved with all the speed his crooked, gnomish body could muster, which was, unsurprisingly, not a lot. Thankfully, the focus on the incursion of demons made sure he was the last concern on the minds of the goblins he gently moved past. Along the way, he followed his own advice and snagged a pair of mismatched daggers from the corpses of fallen archers. They weren't as well-made as the ones he'd taken from the dead rogue, but they had pointy ends he could stab into people and that was really all that mattered in a dagger.

Of the four, he was the last to reach his destination, both because of the difficulty of what he was moving through and his hobbled size. He did make it without incident, which was more than he imagined the other two would have pulled off. Thistle hoped those two would be safe. Maybe if they survived, they could recruit new people to fill the party's holes and draw the king's ire from their town. It was what Thistle would have done; however, he was less confident in his own survival than theirs. They still had the strength and determination of youth. It was then that Thistle broke through the mass of goblins into the area where Grumph was, and all thought of the humans' safety flitted from his mind.

Seven fresh goblin corpses littered the ground around the demon, their light purple blood already soaking into the dirt. A few feet away, Grumph lay on his side, struggling to get up with the one arm that wasn't covered in blood. A shattered goblin polearm stuck out from the demon's hide, wedged into the shoulder above its right claw.

In an instant, Thistle knew what had happened; he saw the goblin regiment's death, followed by Grumph rushing in and smashing the demon with a weapon not designed to bear his strength, snapping it off in red flesh only to have his own half-orc body savaged by the monster's counterattack. Thistle put it all together, and in the span of a heartbeat, he extended the scene moments into the future, seeing what would play out as plain as a sunlight spell:

Grumph was about to die.

7.

There were surely better ways to die than this. Going down in battle was a point of pride, certainly, but it was supposed to be while making a grand last stand for some important cause. All Grumph had done was whack a polearm against a demon while it was killing several goblins. From the pain in his shoulder and the sizable chunk of missing flesh, he didn't imagine this was going to be a peaceful death. The demon was approaching steadily, but cautiously. Grumph let out a weary sigh that sounded like the wheeze of a broken organ. He'd wanted to be one of the few half-orcs to die out of battle. Oh well.

The knife moved so fast Grumph didn't actually see it fly. One moment, he was staring up at impending death in the form of a rat-faced monster, the next, he was looking at a rat-faced monster with a knife sticking out of one eye. The beast let out a howl that made all who heard it remember times when they sat in the dark, certain something was moving there, coming after them. The demon twisted to the side, searching with one eye for the source of its agony. It did not prove difficult to find.

"Hey, One-eye, that's a good look for you!" called Thistle, twirling the other blade casually in his hand. "Bit uneven, though. Want me to get the other one too? Then you won't have to see how ugly you really are."

The demon snarled, and its clacking grew faster. Whether it understood the words or merely that this small figure had stabbed it in the eye was debatable: what was clear, however, was the effectiveness of Thistle's strategy. Immediately, the demon changed targets, Grumph all but forgotten as it moved toward the gnome.

Grumph felt the bottom of his half-orc stomach drop away as realization hit him. Yes, there were better ways to die, but there were also worse ones. Like watching your only friend be sliced to shreds first.

* * *

Later, when the blood had dried and the dawn had broken, Gabrielle would reflect on how it all happened. She'd face the fact that perhaps this sort of thing had been building in her for years — an inevitable reaction to concealing the life she loved for a duty to the family she had. That would be when she finally faced how much this tribe had meant to her; how she'd loved the way they taught her, hunted with her, and treated her like a capable, functioning person, instead of a delicate doll to be loved and protected. All that would come later, though.

In that moment, when she realized she was watching the indiscriminate slaughter of the weaker goblins, all that existed in her soul was an explosion of incomprehensible fury. There were no thoughts, no fears, no debates: only action. With a primordial scream that none would have believed came from her, Gabrielle gripped the axe at her side and charged forward. It should have been too heavy, her inexperience too much to overcome, yet none of that mattered. The only thing that mattered was the sight of those demon claws tearing through unprotected goblin flesh.

To its credit, the demon did look up when it heard her undisguised charge. Had it been a mindless killer it would have shifted its attention to the new target. These, however, were thinking demons, so it paid almost no heed to the thin woman with the oversized axe. It raised one claw in a purely obligatory blocking maneuver and went back to skewering goblins.

The error of that strategy sank in right around the time it heard a heavy object hit the dirt, looked down, and realized it was its own claw, along with a sizable portion of its arm. The axe had cleaved straight through its tough flesh and bones, so quickly that the pain hadn't even registered yet. It did an instant later, however, and the demon screeched shrilly at the loss of its limb.

"Don't touch my fucking tribe!" Gabrielle screamed back, twirling the axe back to a ready position. She swung again, approaching its now-unprotected right side to go for its head. The demon didn't take her lightly this time, extending its remaining arm at awkward angles to block the blade with its claw.

They danced like this for countless moments, Gabrielle possessing righteous rage, and the demon using honed battle instincts. It seemed a stalemate, but it soon became clear that wasn't the case. With each swing, the axe felt a little heavier in her hands, the ache in her muscles grew more pronounced. She'd gotten its arm, but she wasn't certain she'd get another chance like that. Still, Gabrielle pressed on, because, while she kept it occupied, the children and non-warrior goblins slipped past, making their way to safety and freedom.

Then, with only ten or so left, she swung too far, overextended, and the demon capitalized with a deep slice across her stomach. Gabrielle stumbled back, bringing the weapon up to a defensive position, but only barely. Intense pain from her wound was filling her mind, trying to choke out the anger that had fueled her so far in the battle. From the amount of blood pouring onto her tunic, she suspected that soon she'd be too weak to even stand, let alone keep attacking. It seemed this was as far as she could go.

The demon thought so, too. It snarled in what one could presume was joy, lurching forward a step and preparing to finish the job. With a swift motion, it tried to raise its claw for the killing blow, only to find the appendage unwilling to move. Neither it nor Gabrielle could quite believe what they were seeing.

All of the remaining goblins had, upon seeing Gabrielle injured, changed direction. They rushed forward, all thoughts of self-preservation cast aside, leaping onto the demon's remaining arm and weighing it down. The monster tried once more to lift it, only to find that the goblins who couldn't find a place to grab its arm had latched onto other goblins in an effort to increase the weight. The demon let out a rasp of frustration.

Gabrielle, on the other hand, took a deep breath. She blocked out the pain and focused on the anger. She looked at the goblin corpses that surrounded her, listened to the screams of others dying behind them, and imagined how many of her people had heard that damn clacking as their final memory on this plane. Her rage built upon itself, a fire rekindled, until she could stay still not a moment longer.

This charge was, somehow, clumsier than before, not to mention shorter, given her proximity to the demon. It snarled and tried to raise its arm for defense, only to find the goblins clutching tighter than ever. The awkward bird feet attempted to shuffle backwards; however, their sheer power left little dexterity with which to reorient in battle. Before it had any other chance to react, Gabrielle was upon it.

Her axe moved so quickly that a soft whistle penetrated the carnage-filled night air, a single sound of beauty amid the turmoil. The only thing more pleasing to her ears was the audible thump of the demon's head as it landed on the ground. She surveyed her work with a deep sense of satisfaction and turned to the goblins who were now untangling themselves from a demon corpse.

"Hurry and go; it should be sa—" Gabrielle's next words were lost as the tremendous physical exertion and blood loss struck. Without so much as a staggered step to stop herself, Gabrielle collapsed in the dirt, mere inches away from the remains of the demon.

*   *   *

The battle with the demon by the storage building was still going poorly. Despite more goblins stepping in to help, it was simply too strong, and resistant to their weaponry. They'd managed to push it back, moving it toward the building from which it had emerged, but the effort had cost them several goblin lives.

One of the warriors, midway through stepping over another goblin's corpse to take its place, had the very un-goblin-like thought about the futility of this. He would die soon and another would take his place, as had always been the goblin way. But they were dying so quickly; what would happen if they ran out of goblins? That thought plagued him as he struck the monster with his weapon, barely impacting the beast's thick hide. He tried aiming for a vital spot such as the throat or the eyes, but the demon was protective of those areas, knocking blows away. The efforts weren't helped by the noticeable size difference between the demon and the goblins. With one desperate effort, this warrior leapt up and thrust the blade of his polearm toward the eye of the demon. Its claw swept the weapon away effortlessly, sending the goblin sprawling on his back. He looked upward, waiting for the end to come.

Because of this vantage point, he was the only one not to see the dark shape dart out from the building and swing a short sword into the monster's back. He did, however, hear the earsplitting screech of pain it let out moments later. Taking advantage of the distraction, he rolled away, grabbed another polearm, and retook his position.

The demon turned to search for the attacker, but it found only empty buildings and darkness. Never ones to ignore an opportunity, the goblins struck while its back was turned, managing to gouge a few bits of flesh from its hide.

With a clacking of claws, the demon turned back around, cutting down any goblins it could reach. The figure stepped out of the shadows once more, padding up to it in near silence and delivering another blow. The goblins didn't know why these strikes were hurting the demon so much more than theirs, nor did they care. This time, when the demon whipped about, it stayed that way for several seconds, allowing the goblins to open up more wounds across its back. Eventually, it turned around and renewed the attack, though it was clear that its focus was split.

The stranger came again, but this time, after the strike, the demon jerked its claw behind its back without turning, missing the man while still snagging his dark cloak. As the material came away, the goblins saw it was the male human prisoner they'd taken earlier that day. Now more visible, he retreated slowly, blade close to his body to block the impending claws.

As the demon turned, the goblin warrior saw an opening. One of his fellow polearm wielders had torn away some flesh on the torso, exposing a pair of misshapen ribs. Without a moment to think, the goblin repeated his earlier attempt, only this time, he aimed his thrust between those ribs. He struck true and the former weakness of their weaponry became an immediate strength. Because the polearm was designed for smaller creatures, both the blade and shaft slid through the ribs. The warrior kept pushing as hard as he could until he felt his weapon strike a solid mass somewhere in the demon's chest.

What he'd struck was open to debate; however, its effects were quite apparent. With a blood-spewing grunt, the demon wobbled and collapsed, three inches of polearm shaft still poking out from its ribs. For good measure, and because you can't trust demons, the other goblins immediately took off its head. As for the warrior who'd struck the killing blow, he picked up another discarded polearm and headed off to find more demons.

That was the goblin way.

*   *   *

Thistle had never much focused on how he'd die. A gnome born like he was, with no talent for magic, meant he'd had to accept his mortality very early on. It was only cleverness and the support of good friends that had kept him alive this long, and now, it seemed he would be killed aiding one of those very same friends. Thistle had never thought much about how he would die, but this seemed like a pretty good way to go, all things considered.

The demon advanced slowly, wary of the knife still dancing in Thistle's hand. For all the broken bits of his body, Thistle's hands had always been shockingly nimble. Truthfully, he credited luck, or the gods, for that last throw. He was talented, but that had been spectacular. Thistle moved back slowly and carefully. It wouldn't do much good if he died before Grumph had a chance to pull himself up and escape. Though curious to check on his friend, Thistle didn't dare turn away from the approaching monster. This was why he didn't see Grumph making the strange gestures with his hand, nor hear him muttering something in his deep, half-orc voice.

There are precious few things that can draw the attention of a demon that has just had a dagger planted in its eye, but one of them, it turned out, was a freezing blast of ice magic striking it in the back. The cold was so intense that, for a moment, Thistle's teeth tried to chatter, even being several feet away from the impact. The demon whirled around and Thistle couldn't help but look too.

Sure enough, still slumped over, a swirl of blue magical energy dissipating off his fingers like fog in the sun, Grumph was looking at the demon with an expression of triumph. Thistle didn't even have time to wonder what had his friend so happy as the demon immediately charged. That made it clear: the big idiot was trying to save Thistle, while Thistle had been trying to save him. The futility of it all would have made Thistle stamp his misshapen foot, if there'd been time.

The gnome's brain kicked into high gear, immediately assessing the situation. He had no hope of getting between the half-orc and the demon in time; the monster's back was to him, so another eye shot was out of the question, and he doubted verbal taunts would draw its ire more than the ice spell had. Since he was out of any practical options, all that remained was banking on the impossible.

"Grumble," he prayed, lifting up his remaining blade and taking aim at the moving demon's spine. "Though I know I am not actively henching right now, I would still dearly appreciate any assistance you'd be willing to give." A strange tinkling sound, like bells he'd known in childhood, filled his ears, and Thistle let the dagger fly.

It struck the demon square in the back, though it did not sink in and sever the spine, as Thistle had hoped. Instead, it continued onward, carving through the demon's bones and flesh and exploding out the other the side in a shower of muscle and blood. The goblin knife had somehow left a hole in the demon's chest so large that Thistle and Grumph were able to make eye contact through it. The demon fell down dead, and the knife clattered to the ground some feet away, tendrils of white smoke rising off it.

For a moment, there was only silence between the two, neither one certain of what to say in such a strange situation. Then, a cheer went up from the center of the camp as the goblins killed the final demon. The outpouring of elation was enough to loosen Thistle's tongue, just a bit.

"I might need to buy some of these daggers before we go," he commented, moving toward the blade that was finally beginning to cease smoking. "That is some fine craftsmanship if ever I've seen it."

Grumph snorted in agreement, then set about the cumbersome task of getting himself off the ground.

8.

It was several hours before the chaos finally gave way to some semblance of organization. The warrior goblins conducted a thorough sweep of the perimeter, ensuring no other demons were waiting to ambush them once their guard was down. Non-warriors and children were brought back into camp and immediately herded to the most fortified buildings still standing. The fires were put out, and the corpses of the fallen were gathered in a previously empty building. The reason it had been empty, evidently, was that it was used exactly for occasions like this.

The adventuring party had regrouped quickly, Eric and Grumph spying each other across the sea of short heads. Thistle was still with Grumph, a bloody dagger tucked securely in his boot. Finding Gabrielle had been more difficult. They searched for some time, trying to communicate with the goblins through cross-species charades. Thankfully, one of the non-warriors finally took their meaning and led them into a tent near the center of camp.

Cots dotted the landscape, all filled with beings that had sustained considerable wounds. Most were goblins; however, on the largest bed lay Gabrielle. Several goblins were tending to her: removing her bandages, applying a green salve, and reapplying new bandages. Others were checking her for fever and giving her water. As her friends watched the treatment, one of the goblins noticed the poorly-plugged hole on Grumph's shoulder and motioned him over. After a few minutes, Grumph had been properly tended to as well. Gabrielle's treatment, sadly, was not so easy.

Although they wanted to stay by her side, it soon became apparent that being in the medical tent was hindering more than helping. So, with heavy hearts, the three walked out into the camp, found some unoccupied space, and pulled out their bedrolls. It was certainly possible they'd be recaptured in their sleep, but none of them could hold onto such concerns as the weight of a stressful night came crashing down upon them.

Within a minute of lying down, all three were sleeping soundly.

*　　　*　　　*

Thistle knew he was dreaming as soon he opened his eyes. In part it was because he felt entirely lucid, so much so that he could piece together the impossibility of passing out in a goblin camp and awakening in a church. The other part, however, was because he knew this church very well, and he knew with certainty that if he was here, and no one was yelling at him, then it must certainly be a dream.

Carefully, Thistle pulled himself up from the pew where he'd been lying. It was all the same as he remembered: same large ceiling, causing a breeze; same enchanted glass windows, swirling with ever-changing colors, and same dusty rug running up to the pulpit. That was when Thistle realized that something had changed. Instead of a glowing orb surrounded by mist, the symbol of Mithingow, the gnome god, there was a picture of a broom with a dagger tied to the top. This was the symbol of Grumble, god of the minions.

Thistle had no sooner reached this revelation than he saw a male kobold (at least, male if Thistle correctly recalled how to interpret the number of spines atop their head) hop up onto the pulpit from the front pew. He was scaly and orange, though the bits around his knees and elbows were starting to look ashen. His lizard's head was wide, yet, when it paused to flash a smile, Thistle found it oddly comforting. The kobold walked to the front but didn't take a place behind the altar. Instead, he moved in front of it and looked directly at Thistle.

"Underwhelmed? It's okay if you are. I get that a lot."

"No, nothing like that," Thistle told him. "Just surprised. It's not often one dreams of meeting their god."

"This is a dream, but I think we both know it's not just happening in your head," Grumble informed him. "I've come to have a talk with you."

"Forgive my foreboding, but those words rarely mean good things, coming from deities."

"Well, I guess you're not wrong," Grumble agreed. "I've come to discuss something, and whether it's good, or bad, will be up to you."

"This is about the knife, isn't it?"

Grumble shook his head. "No, this is about the prayer you said right before you threw the knife. I'm not the most popular god in the pantheon — I'm the first to admit it — but I get my fair share of prayers. 'Please, don't let the master beat me tonight' is a big one; right up there with, 'Please, don't let these adventurers find my hiding spot.' Yours, though, that was a rarity: one of my worshippers charging into danger, rather than scrambling away from it, and all to save a friend."

"Your faith does teach the importance of looking out for one another," Thistle said.

Grumble hopped down from the pulpit and landed on the dusty rug. He'd have been shorter than a normal gnome, but Thistle's crooked body left him eye-level with his deity.

"It does teach that, but you went above and beyond. What you did was brave, and selfless, and, dare I say, noble."

Comprehension dropped on Thistle like Grumph after too many shots of dwarven whiskey. "Ohhh, no. No no no no. No way. Look at me, you know this doesn't work."

"I'll admit, you're not exactly what most gods look for, but I don't get a lot of options from my following. Besides, technically speaking, I don't have to ask, you know." Grumble walked forward until he was only a few paces away from Thistle. "I can just give you the calling, and then it's there, and you're stuck with it."

"Aye, you could do that. But I don't think you will," Thistle ventured.

"And why is that?"

"Because you're the god of the minions: those who are already shoved around and controlled by the powerful. If you were the kind of god who did that, you'd never have chosen us to look over in the first place."

Grumble gave a brief nod. "You caught me. I don't force this on anyone. If you tell me your final answer is no, then I'll let it be. You can consider what happened with the dagger a divine boon, and go on your way."

"My final answer is—" Thistle kept mouthing words, but found his voice no longer functioned.

"You could at least hear me out," Grumble said. "That would be the polite thing to do."

Thistle gave no response; however, he did close his mouth and cease his attempts to talk.

"Good enough. Anyway, there are perks to what I'm offering. Increased strength, a significant bump in endurance, and the ability to bless weapons, not quite as extreme as you saw tonight, but still impressive. Plus, there are the non-combat boons: some divine magic, prayer priority when calling your god, and, of course, healing." Grumble leaned forward on the word "healing," so close that Thistle could feel the breath from his snout.

"If you have something to say, please just say it," Thistle urged, glad to hear his voice had returned.

"The woman who was with you, she's not long for this world, and Grumph will only be a few days behind her. Demon claws are nasty things. The damage they do gets in the blood, rots the body from the inside out. Herbs and time won't save them. They need healing magic, the kind powered by a divine backer."

"That's your deal: do what you want, or you let my friends die?"

"Thistle, I'm not the one who attacked them. I didn't unleash those demons. Honestly, if not for your prayer, I never would have known about any of this," Grumble said, his voice surprisingly gentle. "I'm not trying to bully you. I'm offering a way to save them, something you wouldn't have any other way to do. Without this conversation, they'd have just died and that would be the end of it. I'm trying to help."

"I'll grant you that," Thistle said after a moment's consideration. "But it hasn't escaped my notice that you're helping in a way that gets you what you want."

"I am still a god, after all. There's a certain way these things are done."

"Aye. All right then, you win. I'll do it, on one condition." Thistle paused for the barest of instants. "Madroria."

"Your wife?"

Thistle nodded. "As long as serving you won't put me in a place where I can't see her in the afterlife, I'm in."

"My word is given. When your time in my service is done, I will ensure your spirit is reunited with your wife's."

Thistle felt a surge of power, one that rippled out from his god and seemed to pulse all around them. One thing you could say about gods: they always kept their promises. They were bound by them.

"So, how do I do this?"

"You just promise to serve me, and then you wake up," Grumble explained.

"I promise to serve you," Thistle promptly replied.

"Really? That's it? I mean, I don't get many of these, and I thought you'd put a little more theatricality into it," Grumble, well, grumbled.

Thistle choked back a sigh, which was the warning sign of a sarcastic retort. He was going to be working with this deity for some time; it would serve them both better to keep things civil.

"Oh, mighty Grumble, god of minions and henchmen, overseer of them who keep the world running, yet remain overlooked, I pledge myself to your service, and swear to uphold your standards while glorifying your name."

"Much better," Grumble said with a smile. "Welcome to my service, Thistle the Paladin."

*   *   *

When the gnome re-entered the tent, flanked on either side by a bewildered human and a half-orc whose bandages were now removed, the goblins were a touch confused. When he jostled his way to the side of Gabrielle, moving others aside politely, but firmly, they grew concerned. It was only when he pressed his hands on her stomach and the dim glow of golden light began emanating from them that they put everything together. At their capture, the goblins had assumed these folks were searching for a quest, looking to become adventurers, yet not strong enough to actually go by the title. Once the light faded and Gabrielle's eyes flickered open, there was no doubt left.

In the battle, something had changed. One of them, at least, had become a true adventurer.

*   *   *

Despite the divine patch-job, it was several more hours before Gabrielle was cleared by the goblins' medical team and allowed to join her friends. She found them at one of the few tables not destroyed in the previous evening's chaos, eating a few bits of jerky and large amounts of fruit.

"Pull up a seat," Eric welcomed, motioning her over. "There wasn't much meat that survived the fire, but a big gathering party rounded up plenty of apples and berries this afternoon."

Gabrielle nodded and sat down next to Eric. He looked different, somehow. It took a moment for her to realize that he'd yet to re-don his armor. How many years had it been since she'd seen him sans reflective protection? It seemed to have done him good; his back was straighter, and the usual pained expression was nowhere to be seen on his face.

"Not to pester, but I wanted to make sure of something," Thistle said as Gabrielle piled her plate full of various fruits. "I assume they didn't send a runner this morning?"

"Definitely not," she confirmed. "After last night, they aren't ready to take on a band of adventurers. They need time to rebuild and refortify. Besides, they said it didn't seem right, keeping us after we helped them. As far as they're concerned, we're free to go."

"Good," Thistle said, nodding his head. "I'd already chatted with them and gotten that story, but I just wanted to make sure they'd told you the same thing."

Gabrielle's hand froze, a fistful of grapes suspended mid-way to her mouth.

"Thistle, you don't speak Gobleck."

"Correction: I didn't speak Gobleck," Thistle said. "Technically, I still don't. Everything they say sounds to me like it's being said in the Proper Kingdom Language. Presumably, they hear my responses in Proper as if I'd said them in Gobleck."

"That's impossible," Gabrielle pointed out.

"Not really, it makes ample sense. Goblins are one of the most frequent races used as minions, and as such, they are devout worshippers of Grumble. It seems perfectly fitting that a paladin of Grumble should be able to speak with them."

"You're not a—"

"I am," Thistle said, cutting her off. "Unlikely as it sounds, I assure you, I am. Presumably, they told you about your miraculous healing?"

"Yes, but I just assumed they were mistaken, and some other traveler had done it. We all sort of look the same to them," Gabrielle replied.

"It was me. For better or worse, last night changed a few things. I think it best we discuss those, and alter our plans as needed before moving beyond this point. Goblins don't talk much with travelers, but in a few days, we'll reach Appleram up the road. Whatever identities we introduce ourselves as there will then be set in stone, because changing them could end with us coming out as frauds."

"I see," Gabrielle said, finally moving the grapes to her mouth and crunching into them. "Setting aside the 'how' of your paladin-hood, it means that you're now a better candidate to play the part than Eric."

"To be fair, I was never all that good of a candidate to begin with," Eric admitted. "I was just the one who owned armor."

"Aye, and I suppose I'll need to get myself a set of that before we reach Solium," Thistle said, pulling out a quill and parchment, and jotting a few things down.

"Then, who plays the rogue?" Gabrielle asked.

"From what the goblins tell me, it seems Eric was quite nimble last night, darting in and out of battle, hiding in the shadows." Thistle's quill moved deftly and precisely even as he spoke.

Gabrielle raised an eyebrow at Eric, who turned his attention to his food and blushed slightly. "Clumsy Eric did that?"

"I don't really know how," Eric mumbled, moving his berries around his plate. "Everyone else just sort of seemed to be moving slower. I guess I'm used to being weighed down, and when I wasn't, I felt fast."

"You didn't just feel fast, you were fast," Thistle corrected. "Fast, stealthy, and deadly. Just like one would expect a rogue to be."

Eric's blush deepened. "I don't know why my sword worked so much better than everyone else's. It's an old hand-me-down."

"A hand-me-down from your father?" Thistle probed.

"Well, I didn't get it from my mother."

"That might account for it. Paladin weapons are usually blessed; it's possible the one he passed down to you had such magic on it. Demons loathe blessed weapons," Thistle explained.

"A rogue with a blessed sword," Gabrielle chuckled. "What will they think of next?"

"I daresay I might be able to answer that question," Thistle told her. "Grumph, if you please."

Grumph gave a grunt and pulled the spellbook from his pouch, setting it on the table in front of Gabrielle.

"Oh, good, I'd worried we lost that," Gabrielle remarked. She reached forward to take her book; however, Grumph put a thick finger on top, rendering it difficult to move.

"Gabby, were you able to cast any of the spells from that book yesterday?" Thistle asked.

"No, I didn't get much time to look at it before we were attacked."

"Do you think you could have?"

"Maybe. They were tough, but I could have probably gotten through at least one with enough time to practice."

"Grumph has cast three of them. One last night, and two this afternoon while we waited for you," Thistle informed her.

Gabrielle's eyes went up as she stared across the table at the stoic half-orc. It wasn't that she thought Grumph to be stupid, it was just... who'd ever heard of a half-orc wizard?

"If you want to try and play the part, it's only fair that we give you some time to practice," Thistle continued.

"No, Grumph should be the wizard," Gabrielle said immediately. As soon as she'd realized what Thistle was telling her, it became obvious. The one most likely to pull off a role should be the one it was given to. Their task was too important for any other strategy to be considered. "If he cast three spells with less than a day to read that thing, he's better suited to it. The only issue is that now we're short a barbarian."

"That's not what the goblins told Thistle," Eric interjected, his own shyness fading now that he was no longer the subject of discussion.

"It seems you swing a good axe," Thistle added.

"No, that was just one of those things. I like this tribe and seeing them get killed set me off. It was closer to a tantrum than bravery."

"As someone who has traveled with a barbarian before, I assure you, the capacity to turn fury into blood is almost the entire prerequisite checklist," Thistle told her.

"Forgive my lingering doubt," Gabrielle said. "I'll do it, because everyone has roles that fit them better. I'm just saying, don't lean on me during a real fight."

"Concerns have been noted," Thistle said. He could have pushed her harder, but he felt like she was more likely to come around on her own if given time. Now, the better strategy was to pull back and let the idea marinate. "Role changes aside, the plan stays the same from here. We keep heading toward Solium, and do our best not to die along the way. Any objections?"

Only silence and nodding heads met Thistle's question.

"Then, I say we get a good night of rest and set out in the morning," Thistle suggested. "We're not quite running late, but we don't have time to dawdle."

"Plus, we should try and train a little on the way," Eric added. "So we seem somewhat competent in our fake skills."

"Aye, in our 'fake' skills indeed," Thistle said, catching Grumph's eye and giving a light shake of his head. They'd catch on in their own time. For now, there was dinner and sleep to attend to.

9.

The next morning saw the party rising with the sun, having a quick breakfast composed primarily of more fruit, and packing up their bedrolls. The few possessions they'd left Maplebark with had diminished even further, many of their things lost in the fire and chaos of the attack. Their packs, luckily, had been stored below the carts, so their basic necessities were still accounted for. Eric's armor had survived the fire as well; however, he elected to abandon it. It was part of his old life, and any sentimentality he might have held toward it was suppressed by the stomach-turning thought of strapping himself back into the cumbersome apparatus.

The goblins did their best to replace what they could, offering ponies and provisions for the journey ahead. The ponies were mostly declined, because even the hardiest of them would have broken under Grumph's weight; though Thistle accepted one on the grounds that his normal gait would slow everyone else down. The provisions were also taken with thanks. Thistle was offered a set of goblin armor, since he was the only one that was small enough to wear any, but he declined and instead requested a pair of sturdy daggers, a matched set, if possible. The goblins brought forth an array of their weapons, and eventually Thistle selected two that, while not actually a set, were close enough to fool a casual observer.

With one last word of thanks, and a promise to slow any Maplebark citizens that might come through the camp in pursuit, the goblins waved goodbye to the strange party that headed down the road to Appleram.

Once they'd been on the road for some time, Eric broke the silence that had seamlessly settled over them.

"I wanted to ask, why'd you turn down the armor? I thought you said you needed some."

"Aye, I likely do," Thistle agreed. "But right now, we're a rather bedraggled bunch. When we get to Appleram, people will ask what happened. I intend to tell them the truth: we were kidnapped by goblins and we fought our way free."

"That makes it sound like we fought the goblins," Gabrielle pointed out.

"Which is what I want them to infer," Thistle clarified. "People get waylaid by goblins all the time. It won't raise a single eyebrow, or prompt many questions, and that's what we want. Get in, resupply, get back on the road, and remain as unmemorable as possible."

"Why bother?" Eric asked.

"Look, when we get to Solium with the scroll, there might be a bit of curiosity about us; but unless we give them a reason, they won't waste the magic to verify we're really the same adventurers who killed the kobolds. Appleram, however, is close enough to Maplebark that if we make anyone too interested, they might take a leisurely ride back in this direction. A ride that would take them through Maplebark, and it wouldn't require more than one or two questions to piece together who we really are."

"That is, and I say this having known you for years, just amazingly paranoid," Gabrielle commented.

"Better paranoid, than dead," Grumph said, momentarily looking up from the spellbook he'd had his face buried in for hours. How he walked and read at the same time was a mystery to all of them, yet the lack of tripping clearly indicated that he had a system and it worked.

"Precisely, old friend," Thistle agreed. "Anyway, a few daggers and a pony can be explained away as things grabbed hastily in battle. A set of armor is far more conspicuous, hence why I didn't accept the offer. If anyone asks why I'm an unarmored paladin, I'll just tell them a set of armor was one of the things we lost in the capture."

"We lost my set of armor," Eric said.

"What I said is still technically true," Thistle pointed out.

"Oh yeah, now that you're a paladin, does that mean you can't lie?" Gabrielle asked.

"Different gods have different rules. Given that minions constantly have to lie to their master, if only to assuage their egos and assure them they're brilliant and unbeatable, I doubt Grumble objects much to an occasional fib. Still, I find lying to be more dangerous than expertly telling the truth, so I avoid it whenever possible."

"Whatever floats your galleon," Gabrielle said, adjusting the axe strapped to her back for the umpteenth time since setting out. The actual sheath was one of the things lost in the fire, so the goblins had rigged a makeshift sheath from a canvas grain sack and some leather straps. It wasn't pretty, and it wouldn't allow her to draw quickly, but it allowed her to heft the weapon along without tiring out her arms. Grumph had offered to carry it for her, but Gabrielle's own paranoia had reminded her to stick to her role. She was the barbarian; she would carry her own axe.

They continued on in near-silence after that, save for the clopping of Thistle's pony, each lost in the thoughts of what they were trying to do, and how in the names of the gods they had any hope of accomplishing it.

* * *

Two days later, a party of four adventurers wandered into Appleram a few hours before sunset. Three of them were on foot, while the fourth was mounted on a very weary-looking pony. Dust from the road coated their boots and pants, and two wolf pelts were slung over the back of the pony, no doubt the glorious prize from a random encounter on the road.

The quartet made a beeline for the local inn, which was also the tavern, where the pony was hitched and the gear quickly handed out. A blonde woman with a two-handed axe strapped strangely to her back took the wolf carcasses, heading off toward the tannery with her male companion, while the half-orc and the gnome went inside the inn.

On most days, this would have been a sight worth noting. Appleram was a large town, easily the biggest one between Solium and Piro, the next kingdom south, but its townspeople were still interested in hearing tales from adventurers and sometimes in negotiating services from them. That was most of the time. These days, nearly every villager of Appleram who saw them lope through town had, roughly, the same reaction:

"Oh shit, not more of them."

* * *

Grumph and Thistle realized something was amiss as soon as they entered the tavern. This particular establishment, much like

Grumph's and many others throughout the land, utilized the downstairs floor for food and alcohol, while the upper floors were lodging rooms travelers could rent. Years of running an inn had taught Grumph to expect a rush at dinner, a few constant customers at the bar, and occasional clusters of adventurers. Once, during a season where there was rumored to be a dragon in the area, there had been three parties in his tavern at the same time, but that was the most he'd ever seen.

Walking in the door, Grumph counted seven distinct parties, all huddled together at their own tables, many throwing suspicious glances at the others in the room. Any regulars that might have normally dined here had long since abandoned the room to the new patrons.

Grumph and Thistle were both assessed as soon as they walked in and dismissed just as quickly. Neither minded this in the slightest. Making their way to the bar, they passed a set of five humans, all of whom grew silent when they walked by. Whatever was going on, it seemed even those who were deemed not to be threats still weren't allowed within earshot.

Thistle scrambled his way up a bar stool, dearly missing the rungs Grumph had installed on his for the smaller customers, finally coming to a perch with only a minimum of embarrassment. He surveyed the tavern, making note of the strapping human behind the bar serving drinks, as well as the waitresses running to and fro around the tables. From their similar noses and eye color, not to mention the variety of ages, Thistle deduced they were either the bartender's daughters or some other close kin. He filed this away in case it would be of use later and turned his attention to ordering a drink.

"Two meads, kind sir," Thistle called to the sizable fellow behind the bar, a man whose salt-and-pepper hair somehow made him seem more distinguished than aged. It was strange how every bartender seemed to convey a sense of toughness that three-day-old kobold steak couldn't match, but Thistle had always taken it as simply one of those things.

"One silver," the bartender replied, drawing them each a mug from the barrel nearest to him.

Thistle resisted the urge to raise an eyebrow, but only barely. That much, for two drinks, was outrageous. Clearly, this man intended to get all he could from the influx of adventurers that had happened into his bar. With a quick motion, Thistle set a coin on the bar, which the large man promptly scooped up.

"I was also hoping to find some lodging tonight," Thistle added, taking a quick nip from the mug in front of him. It was tolerable; he'd have even thought it good, if not for years of drinking Grumph's homebrews.

"Got two rooms left, going for twenty gold apiece," the bartender informed him.

If getting back up wouldn't have been such an issue, Thistle would have fallen out of his chair just to make a point. Twenty gold apiece was ludicrous, beyond mere gouging and well into outright theft. Before he could voice that opinion, Grumph set the mug he'd been draining on the table with an audible thud.

"Too weak," Grumph announced, meeting the bartender's immediately incredulous eyes. "Good process, poor ingredients. Where you get your hops?"

Thistle quickly noticed that Grumph had affected his "ignorant half-orc" speech pattern. It mostly consisted of growling at the end of sentences, and leaving out unimportant words. Base as it was, the tactic was effective for getting people to underestimate his intelligence. Plus, and Thistle hated to admit this, it would make Grumph less memorable, which was a big priority. Everyone expected half-orcs to be dumb, so this would make him as uninteresting as the tables or stools.

"I'll have you know I buy my hops from one of the top Solium grain merchants and he sells me the Abstanial Silver," the bartender announced proudly.

"No," Grumph rumbled.

"No? 'No' what?"

"Abstanial Silver brew tart, but with undertone of pine. This have undertone of nut. It's Grebthon Silver," Grumph informed him. "Look almost the same. Yours have occasional veins of red in leaves?"

"Actually, yes," the bartender admitted.

"Grebthon Silver. Abstanial has no veins. Merchant is cheating you."

"That weasely little son of shit," the bartender cursed. "I'm going to wring his neck next time I see him. You're sure about this?"

Grumph nodded. "Had one try to pull same trick on me. Got good guy now, I'll give you his name. Bartenders have to look out for one another."

"Oh, you're a bartender, too?" The man stuck his hand out to Grumph. "Bertrand, pleasure to meet you."

"Grumph." The handshake was delicate, since both were clearly strong men, and neither wished to hurt their new friend.

Thistle took the opportunity to slip quietly off his stool and make for the door, mumbling something about using the outhouse. Grumph was clearly working his own angle; Thistle's presence would merely get in the way. Besides, he had to think of a new place for them to regroup. The last thing they needed right now was for someone to see all four of them together and realize that there were really eight parties here. Better to gather away from prying eyes.

Hopefully, in the meantime, Grumph would be able to get them some less exorbitant rates on a place to stay.

*   *   *

An hour later, Eric and Gabrielle were shown into the tavern's backroom by one of the many waitresses. Grumph and Thistle were already there, working their way through bowls of stew that, after days of nothing but trail rations, may as well as have been made by the gods themselves.

Gabrielle let out a low whistle. "Hope you didn't splurge too much on a private dining room. Those pelts didn't fetch as much as we were hoping."

"One gold," Eric added, before anyone could ask. He set the single coin on the table to show the meager haul. "And that was with half an hour of haggling."

"Merchant said they're swamped with stuff. Evidently, there are a bunch of adventurers here, and they've been killing every wild beast for miles in their downtime. I thought he was blowing smoke until I saw the tavern," Gabrielle explained. "By the way, why did that girl greet me as 'the new applicant'?"

"I didn't want to draw suspicion about you two following us to the back room," Thistle explained. "Ostensibly, we're back here so Grumph can pass on a few trade secrets to Bertrand, the bartender. In reality, their shared occupation and a few actual trade secrets got him to lease us one of the servant's quarters for far less than the rooms upstairs."

"How much did he want for an upstairs room?" Eric asked, looking around with a keen eye, noticing the sparse décor and old straw bundles.

"Twenty gold," Grumph rumbled.

"Dragonshit," Gabrielle snapped.

"Sit down, eat, and I'll explain," Thistle said, motioning to the table. The humans took the cue and sat, filling their bowls quickly. Once that was done, Thistle continued. "Evidently, the governor of Appleram noticed the high flow of adventurers heading to Solium over the last few weeks and decided to get his hands on a bit of their coin. He's holding a tournament in two days, one with fairly respectable caches of gold as prizes. All these adventurers are here to compete, and, in the meantime, the town is bleeding them dry for every meal, night of sleep, and tool they purchase. I presume that's why the tannery was overstocked; they're trying to make enough coin to last until the tournament."

"Smart," Eric commented, tearing into a piece of overcooked chicken he spooned up from the stew. "Both he and you. Good way to make money, and since you managed to negotiate a decent rate, we can just hit the road again tomorrow."

"Yes, about that. I said Grumph got us a better rate, not a good one," Thistle clarified.

"How much do we have left?" Gabrielle asked.

"Well, as of right now," Thistle said, picking up the coin from the table, "one gold."

"WHAT!" The ferocity of Gabrielle's yell was only matched by the strength in her grip as her hand grasped her axe. "That's insane!"

"Calm down," Grumph told her. "It's a good deal."

"How is that a good deal?"

"Because he easily could have made twenty times that and fully intended to," Thistle told her. "He's not likely to see a chance to make this kind of money again for years, if ever. Bertrand has done us a tremendous kindness by allowing us to stay here at such a paltry rate."

"We could have slept outside," Eric pointed out. "We've been doing it for days now."

"There is a sizable flaw in that plan," Thistle told him. "Right now, we have an exceptionally high concentration of adventurers. I don't have to tell you how dangerous that makes being outside of town. We're lucky we arrived in the day, and that they've been going out to hunt, otherwise, we'd likely be dead already."

Eric nodded. No one understood why, but the more adventurers were around, the greater the number of monsters that were drawn. It was like they grouped up in scale to the number of adventurers present to give a proper challenge.

"That's it? You traded all our money for one night of lodging and a pot of stew?" Gabrielle asked, sitting back down. The flash of anger that had bubbled up had subsided, though she was surprised to have even felt it in the first place. She'd been raised to keep an even temper, as a proper lady should. These bursts of fury were a new, and not entirely welcome, occurrence.

"Don't be silly. I traded it for three nights of lodging and three meals each day," Thistle said.

"We're not even going to be here three nights," Eric pointed out.

"Actually, we are," Thistle corrected him. "We can't very well walk into Solium like this. No one would believe we beat a wild badger, let alone a kobold invasion. We require equipment that makes us look at least reasonably respectable, and for that, we'll need money."

"Money that you spent," Gabrielle muttered.

"Money I invested. What we had wouldn't have gotten us a decent buckler, let alone outfitted us all," Thistle said. "No, we need to make some real coin, and fast. Which leaves us with only one viable option."

"You have got to be joking," Eric said, filling in the gaps before Thistle could say it.

"I am completely serious," Thistle replied. "The four of us are entering Appleram's tournament."

10.

Thistle slurped down some stew while he waited for Eric and Gabrielle's flurry of objections to die down. Even if he'd wanted to address them, there was no way he'd be able to with the speed at which they were speaking. Instead, he filled his belly and sat in silence until they realized he wasn't going to speak until they ceased yelling. It took longer than he expected, which worked out well. He was still quite hungry, and it was impolite to eat when talking.

When silence finally reigned over the table once more, Thistle continued. "We don't have an option. I know I said we should lay low here, but that was before I realized the situation. This is actually better. If we can put on a good showing at the tournament, it will lend our story credence, and if anyone from the kingdom does any investigating, they'll hear about our party's deeds in Appleram."

"The keyword was *if* we put on a good showing," Eric said. "Did you forget that we don't have any idea what we're doing?"

"No, I didn't," Thistle said. "But we do have some skills and two days to train. Plus, there are six events, and admission is free for one event per adventurer; no doubt a ploy by the mayor to keep people from thinking about how much their food and lodging is costing."

"What are the events?" Gabrielle asked. This plan was crazy, but Thistle rarely did things without thinking them through.

Besides, their whole idea had been crazy from the get-go. Why should this part be any different?

"Glad you asked," Thistle said. "Six events are being held: Sword Fighting, Archery, Dagger Throwing, Feats of Strength, General Melee, and Magical Duels."

"I would have expected a joust," Eric commented.

"Not outside of a royal tournament. Most real adventurers aren't that skilled in mounted combat."

"You seem to know quite a bit about adventurers, Thistle," Gabrielle said. There was no malice in her tone, no wheedling waves in her words, yet they still halted the conversation effectively.

Eric and Gabrielle, heck, all of Maplebark had known that Thistle's past was more interesting than he let on. No one commented; no one probed. It was just one of those things. Strangely, the longer they wore the mantle of adventurers, the less normal "one of those things" seemed. The world didn't make much sense, and like a lost man stumbling out of the fog, they were beginning to notice the details around them.

"Aye, that I do," Thistle agreed. "And maybe I'll tell you that story, one day, but it won't be here, and it won't be now. We've got more important things on our plate."

"I apologize," Gabrielle said, although this time, her tone made it clear that her words were only that: words.

"No need. It's natural to be curious, but there is a time and place for such things."

"Anyway, you were saying about the events?" Eric probed, eager to change the subject and ameliorate some of the tension in the room.

"Aye, the events. I've got a decent hand at throwing daggers, so I'll enter that one. Eric, are you better with a sword, or a bow?"

"Sword," Grumph grunted.

"He's right," Eric admitted. "Sword. When I was trying to learn the bow, I broke three of the windows on Grumph's tavern."

"That's pretty impressive," Thistle noted.

"Not really. I was aiming for a target in the grove of trees off to the side."

Thistle knew the forest Eric was speaking of. It was nowhere near Grumph's windows.

"Sword it is," Thistle announced.

"I don't have my armor."

"Don't worry, you'll be using wooden tourney swords," Thistle assured him. "Besides, I think you're better off without it."

Eric couldn't argue with that logic, so instead, he merely gave a nod and turned his attention toward his meal.

"Next up: Grumph. I daresay you've got a real shot at winning the Feats of Strength event, old friend."

"True," Grumph agreed. "But I'm in Magical Duels."

"Come on, Grumph, do the one you can win. We need the money," Gabrielle wheedled.

"We *need* practice," Grumph countered, his thick, rumbling voice moving far more fluidly than it did around those he didn't trust. "Experience is worth more than gold."

"Very well, then. Grumph is doing the Magical Duels," Thistle said. He personally agreed with Gabrielle, however, he knew Grumph well enough to understand that when the half-orc was set on something, it would take an act of the gods to deter him. "Gabby, that just leaves you."

"I might be able to do okay at archery," she replied. "I was decent at it. Not great, but decent."

"General Melee," Grumph said.

"I hate to say it, but I agree with Grumph," Eric added, before Gabrielle's mouth could voice the objection she clearly felt. "He's right, we do need the practice. When are you going to get the chance to fight seasoned warriors without risking getting killed? Plus, I've seen you shoot a bow. You're better than I am, but that's not saying much. Do the event where you'll at least learn something."

"Gabby, to be clear, General Melee will use wooden weaponry as well; however, they will still be swung hard, and broken bones are not unheard of," Thistle told her. "I won't ask you to register in an event you're uncomfortable with. If you say Archery, then it's Archery. The choice is yours."

Though Gabrielle was surrounded by silence once the question was asked, she could still clearly hear voices. They were the corrective tones of her father, the mayor, and her mother, the socialite. The voices were firm, admonishing her for even considering such a course of action. Proper ladies did not enter brawls. Proper ladies did not swing axes about their heads. Proper ladies did not adventure. How did she ever hope to catch the eye of one of the royals from Solium if she continued pursuing these stupid endeavors?

Her mouth opened a fraction of an inch, ready to say the word "Archery" when another chorus of voices echoed through her mind. These spoke Gobleck and told her that she was a good tracker, which she'd shown herself to be. She was good at gutting the captured animals and skinning their hides, a task the goblins had taught her and that she'd picked up quickly. And — this voice was the quietest, yet someone she heard with the most force — she was a brave warrior who had saved many goblins with her blade.

No, General Melee was not a sport for proper ladies, but she'd been engaging in those sorts of activities for years already. She'd straddled the line, living publicly as the mayor's daughter, and living in the forest as an honorary goblin. The line was growing wider now, the division between the two, greater. She was going to have to choose which Gabrielle was the one she truly wanted to be, and while this might not be the point of no return, it would mark the first conscious step in that journey.

"General Melee," Gabrielle announced, her voice filled with more conviction than she actually felt.

"Are you certain?" Thistle asked.

"Yes, I am," she told him. And with that, she was. Her parents weren't here to make happy, her friends didn't care which she chose. For once, the only one she had to please with her decision was herself, and the truth was, Gabrielle had been far happier as a pretend goblin, than a pretend proper lady. Maybe it was time to stop pretending.

"Very well, then. First thing tomorrow, I'll get us registered. Grumph is going to see if Bertrand can get the other vendors in town to sell us equipment at somewhat decent rates and you two are free to do what you wish. We'll all meet at the training grounds for practice," Thistle instructed.

"Won't the other parties be there?" Eric asked.

"Almost certainly," Thistle confirmed. "Don't worry about them. Just work your hardest to improve in the time before the tournament. They'll be more concerned with their own skill-sharpening, than sizing us up."

Despite knowing his policy on truth versus falsehood, Eric couldn't shake the feeling that Thistle had just told them all one hell of a lie.

*   *   *

The training area was set up where the tournament would actually be held, since putting together two structures to serve the same purpose would be at the level of idiotic redundancy reserved for the highest halls of government. True, many of the banners were still furled, and the decorations had yet to be unveiled, but the bare bones of the tournament grounds were there: wooden weapons, targets, and fenced-off areas for sparring. There were no arrows or magical tools because those were prone to breaking or being used up and were therefore sold by the shops in town.

Thistle was the first to arrive; registration had taken less time than he expected. All he'd needed to do was provide names, and which events each person was entering. The clerk had been profoundly disappointed that none of them would be paying for the privilege to compete in additional events, an attitude made clear by his constant reminders that the more one competed, the more they could win. The gnome didn't begrudge the clerk his attempts to gain a little extra coin, but it became quickly tiresome. He made his exit and headed over to the training area to survey it himself.

On the whole, he was impressed. Appleram didn't have much tradition of sported combat, but they'd put together a respectable arena. It wasn't as fancy as one might see in Solium; however, in a way, that appealed to Thistle more. He preferred the simple, genuine attempts, rather than gilded fluff. It was why he'd settled in Maplebark, after all. Since there were no other competitors present yet, Thistle decided to squeeze in some extra practice.

Having only two daggers made the throwing process a bit tiresome. He would hurl both, then shuffle across the dusty ground to the target, yank the daggers out, and drag himself all the way back. By the fourth round, he was expecting his body to protest, years of experience telling him this was as much motion as he could complete without pain. Strangely, the soreness didn't come. Rounds five, six, and seven passed, all without so much as a twinge. It was not until round eight, when he accidently threw one of his daggers with too much force and wedged it halfway into the thick wood of the target, that Thistle remembered his new job was supposed to give him greater strength and endurance.

With a concentrated effort, he chunked his second dagger into the target, this time actually causing a small part of it to crack. Thistle wore a subdued smile as he made his way across the arena to retrieve them. The title of paladin might not come with a long job-expectancy, or much of a social life, but he had to admit that he didn't mind the fringe benefits.

Gabrielle and Eric arrived next. After a few moments' discussion, they each picked up wooden versions of their usual weapons and headed off to one of the sparring rings. Since both would be engaged in martial combat, it made sense for them to train against one another. The first few rounds were more of a dance than a fight, light tapping that only ended when someone called the other as "out" or one admitted defeat. Each was getting accustomed to the new weight and shape of their wooden weapons. The trees around Appleram were notorious for the dense, sturdy wood they produced. While not as heavy as a normal sword or axe, these definitely had more heft than if they'd been made out of the same materials as the targets.

As they settled into the flow of combat and grew more comfortable striking each other, the fights quickly became an exercise in frustration for Gabrielle. Eric — slow, clumsy, ineffective Eric — became increasingly more difficult to hit. Freed from the weight of armor he'd never been strong enough to bear, Eric's grace was a thing of strange beauty. He moved effortlessly around her faux blade, slipping to the side of each strike with inches of space to spare then slashing her across the arms or stomach. True, his lack of strength meant the blows weren't terribly forceful, but that wouldn't have stopped a real sword from opening up some serious wounds on her.

With each round Eric won, Gabrielle's frustrations grew. How was he so good? She managed to forget that he'd been forced to train regularly with the other guards for the past several years, instead, focusing on how unfair it was that he vanished like a whisper in a crowd every time she swung toward him.

The breaking point came after she saw his heel catch on the ground and seized the chance to attack. Gabrielle swung high and wide, giving it all she had, sure this was the time she'd win. Somehow, Eric recovered his footing and dodged the blow, circling around in the same fluid motion and pressing his wooden short sword against the back of her neck.

"Got you," Eric said, his voice perfectly calm. It was the way he said it that got her. If he'd been glib or taunting, she could have dealt with it. But no, Eric said it as though he were stating the weather, as though it were an obvious fact. Of course he won, because he was just so damned much better than her.

Gabrielle knew he said something after that, but she couldn't make out the words over the sudden pounding in her ears. Her grip on the fake axe's shaft grew so strong that the sturdy wood creaked. Without thought or warning, she spun around, weapon pulled back. Though, in the moment, she ignored it, she would never forget the look of sudden terror in Eric's eyes as she faced him. It would plague her for years to come.

She released a guttural yell and struck with all her suddenly considerable might. The blow nearly landed true, a blow that would have shattered Eric's arm and shoulder at the very least. At the last moment, however, she felt her entire body be jerked back, throwing the blow wild and smashing the wooden axe into the dusty ground. Gabrielle was lifted off her feet, arms pinned to her sides as she thrashed about wildly.

It took a few minutes, but eventually, her anger subsided enough for coherent thought to return. For the first time, she realized that the arms holding her belonged to a half-orc, and from there, it didn't take much thought to put things together.

"I'm... I'm okay now, Grumph," Gabrielle said shakily.

"What in the seven hells was that?" Eric asked.

"Side effect," Grumph said before Gabrielle could answer. "Go practice alone. We need to talk."

Eric nodded his understanding and jogged off toward one of the human-sized dummies set up near one end of the arena. Once he was gone, Grumph's grip loosened, and he set his friend carefully down on the ground.

"I don't know what happened," she said, shocked by how hard it was to get her legs to bear her weight.

"I do," Grumph replied. "Follow me." With that, he headed off, away from the arena, past a few of the other adventurers who had wandered in to train, and toward an outcropping of trees not quite dense enough to be considered part of the forest.

Part of Gabrielle wondered why he was leaving the arena; however, a much larger part wondered what was going on inside her. That was the question that begged answering, and soon. Taking a few deep breaths and making sure she could move under her own power, Gabrielle followed her half-orc friend to the woods.

*   *   *

The arrival of other adventurers had forced Thistle to switch up his training tactics. He was still throwing his daggers, still trundling across the wide expanse of land to retrieve them, and still walking all the way back to throw again. What was different, now that others were also there, was that Thistle was missing.

It was a simple strategy, really. Instead of aiming for the center of the target, Thistle would aim for a spot closer to the outer edge. He'd change spots each time, throwing one in the center on occasion, too, just to keep it interesting. In this way, he was still working on putting the dagger exactly where he wanted it, but to an observer, it would appear his throws were all over the place. Despite knowing he'd be putting on a show for these people in a few days' time, laying low was too ingrained in Thistle's nature to buck against it.

"Nice throw," said a female voice from behind him. Thistle turned to see a half-elf woman walking forward until she was parallel with him, perfectly situated to throw at the nearest adjacent target. She was quite pretty, if you went in for that sort of thing, with lavender eyes and golden hair, not to mention a body accentuated nicely by the tight leather armor wrapped around her.

"One of the better ones of the day," Thistle replied, hobbling to the target to retrieve his daggers. This one had landed close to the center, so he made a note to ensure the next several were thrown at the edge.

"Hope you get more of them," the woman replied. She pulled a pair of her own daggers from sheaths at her side — long, silver beauties with intricate carvings across their mirror-like surfaces. A quick motion from each arm and the blades were buried on either side of the target's bull's-eye.

"Not too shabby yourself," Thistle complimented.

"I try." The woman let out a low whistle and both daggers glowed lightly, vanished, and then reappeared in their sheaths at her side.

"Handy trick." Thistle sent his own blades into the high and low edges of the target.

"Daggers with a calling spell are the only way to go. I'm Sierva, by the way."

"Thistle," Thistle replied, once his journey to and from the target was complete.

"Pleasure to meet you. Looks like we'll be competing against one another," Sierva noted.

"Aye, so it does." This time, Thistle watched her as she whipped the daggers through the air and sent them quivering into the target. Both landed close to the bull's-eye, but neither actually hit it. This would have been a more comforting observation if not for the fact that Sierva's eyes had never focused on the bull's-eye in the first place. She was using his same strategy: purposely "missing" in order to appear more inept. What was more, given how many empty targets were around, she'd likely caught on to the fact that he was doing it, too. That was why she'd greeted him and gotten close enough to be observed. She wanted him to know she'd caught onto his trickery.

Thistle smiled as he took aim and let the first of his own daggers fly. He'd been worried things would get boring, but it seemed he might have a little fun at this tournament, after all.

*   *   *

Unlike Thistle, Eric wasn't particularly interesting to the other adventurers who wandered into his area of the training arena. Most of them seemed to stick together, whispering when others came by. A few of them shot Eric looks, suspiciously gauging whether he was a danger, but after watching him smack the dummy around, they lost interest.

He couldn't really blame them; he knew he didn't look the part of a fellow adventurer. They were all decked out in well-made clothes and fitted armor, while Eric was wearing a homemade tunic and pants, along with shoes that were barely holding together. His mother had taught him to patch his clothing, though in the rush to get out of town, he hadn't thought to bring along any sewing implements.

Hopefully, his footwear would hold out until at least after the tournament. If even one of them won, it would provide enough to equip themselves with the necessities. Eric took a break to catch his breath and watched a few of the other groups sparring. Most of them were good, but not spectacular. A few, he felt sure he could actually win against. There was the occasional rarity, though: warriors in armor that nearly hummed with magic, and who struck each other with such power that the dust behind them was blown away. One was a dwarf swinging a club nearly the size of him. Another was human, longsword dancing lightly in his hands. When Eric looked at these competitors, he felt a hot stone of certainty in his gut that, if one in his group did win, it wasn't going to be him or Gabrielle. Even if they had even odds against the bulk of the others, one of those two he was watching spar would likely be walking away with the win.

Eric took up his wooden sword once more and began training, determination renewed. Maybe the impressive contenders would both go to General Melee, in which case, his party would be counting on him to win some prize money from Sword Fighting. It was like the leader of the guards had always said: "In a real battle, anything can happen."

He'd meant it as a caution to be prepared for whatever their opponent might throw at them, but Eric had gleaned a different meaning from those words. To him, it meant that, no matter how difficult an opponent might be, there was always a chance.

Eric intended to make the most that chance, if it was presented to him.

* * *

The grove Grumph brought Gabrielle into wasn't particularly peaceful: nearby sounds of battle still echoed from the training area, bouncing off the trees. Still, the shade, greenery, and distance from others did help Gabrielle calm down. For the life of her, she couldn't imagine why she'd snapped at Eric like that. Gabrielle was on the verge of telling Grumph to forget everything, that it had been a fluke when he spoke.

"You've had anger for a long time," he said simply, rough voice brought down softer than she'd expected.

"No, just since the goblin camp," she replied.

Grumph shook his head. "Years. Always angry. Unhappy with your life. Unhappy with your place in the world. Anger boils, constantly. Builds pressure as time goes by. Anger didn't begin at goblin camp; that was when Anger broke free."

It was more than Gabrielle had ever heard him speak at once. Grumph always kept things short, simple, and concise. That fact alone impressed upon her the importance of what he was trying to convey to her. Besides, hadn't she just admitted to herself that she'd been trying to live two lives, being forced to compromise pieces of herself nearly every day? Maybe that sort of thing had worn on her more than she'd let herself realize.

"But I've never had a temper before," Gabrielle pointed out.

"Sarcasm, biting words, fierce tones. You kept it sealed, released only in small spurts."

"That still doesn't explain why I've got one now, though."

"If I have barrel of mead with a spout, I control how much mead comes out," Grumph told her. "If I kick open a hole, mead comes out as it sees fit. Spout is no help anymore. You broke open your sealed Anger when you saw the goblins dying. Now, it is flowing out when it chooses."

"Fine; if — and this is definitely an 'if' — but if I accept that idea, how do I fix it?"

"A broken barrel cannot be fixed unless mead is emptied. I don't know how to empty a person of Anger," Grumph admitted. "Fixing is off the table for now, so we have to work with next best thing."

"What's that?"

"Learning to aim," Grumph told her, a slight smile creeping across his wide, hairy face.

11.

The day of the tournament was a gorgeous one: sun shining brightly overhead and not a single cloud in the sky. Of course, this was the worst possible weather for the competitors; it meant glares of light in the eye from every reflective surface and stifling heat for those equipped with armor. Despite this, spirits were high as the various parties wandered into the arena.

Unlike on the days of training, all the decorations had been set up and unfurled the previous evening. Large banners, sizable signs, and endless knick-knacks were positioned all over the arena. While at a royal tournament these would have shown the standards of great houses, or of the warriors for whom various groups were cheering for; here, nearly all of them were advertisements for various stalls and vendors in town. One for the local herbalist, showing a wounded knight being magically healed, would prove to be particularly well-targeted advertising by the day's end.

Another notable difference from the days before was the people in attendance. A peasant or two had wandered by the training grounds on days prior, though the vast majority of them were working, or manning shops in order to squeeze every coin they could from the adventurers. Now that their cash cows were otherwise occupied, it made all the sense in the world to come watch a free show. After all, they'd put in a lot of work over the last week. They deserved a day off.

The mood in the stands was festive, buoyant even, as locals with more gold under their mattresses than they'd ever had before kicked back to be entertained. A few die-hard entrepreneurs were walking through the stands, selling mead and meat, though pointedly not calling out prices. They wouldn't want an adventurer to overhear how much things really cost.

Near the center, in a part of the stands slightly sectioned off, was the mayor of Appleram and his two children. Despite his high office Mayor Branders still worked his farm daily, leaving him a muscular man with a sun-beaten face. The young boy and girl scrambling about energetically had similar features to his, but theirs were turned up in smiles and glowing with excitement. They raced alongside the railings, pointing to each new adventurer who entered the arena, frantically speculating about what their events were and how they would do.

The mayor's children were far from the only ones doing some speculating. A buzz swept through the crowds any time an adventurer did so much as stretch their back. Bets on who would win what events were made and taken in covert gestures and secret hand-offs. Many made their guesses based on the interactions they'd had with the adventurers during the week while others used physical stature as their betting benchmarks, and still a third camp made their speculations based entirely on the quality of the armor an individual was wearing. Due to this third camp, there was already heavy money riding on the party Eric had watched during his training and more would certainly be added to that sum as the day wore on.

One group, on whom no one had placed even a single copper coin, was the party containing a human female wearing a large axe, a half-orc clutching a spellbook, a crooked gnome fiddling with a pair of goblin-made daggers, and a human male with a hole in the left heel of his shoes. Truthfully, their drab equipment didn't stand out as much as their motley assortment of races, and even that wasn't terribly divergent from the other groups. Many of the other parties had a similar quality of gear and more than one race of warrior in their arsenal. What set this group apart was the simple truth that they appeared to have no idea what they were doing. As they wandered around the arena, muttering to themselves, the other parties were warming up, doing some mock sparring, or just posing for the crowd. These four merely kept to themselves, tried to stay out of everyone else's way, and waited for the events to begin.

They did not have to wait long. The mayor soon rose from his seat and walked to the edge of the railing. The crowd immediately grew still; even his children subdued themselves. Mayor Branders was not a violent man, nor did he have a proclivity to raise his voice, but there was something about the way he moved, and how his eyes gauged everyone he met, that spoke of more power than he let on. He was like a pot of simmering silver: simple and serene to look at, but with a scalding danger waiting beneath the surface.

"Citizens of Appleram, travelers, and brave adventurers, I thank you for joining in our humble festival." Even without magical aid, his words carried across the arena effortlessly. Mayor Branders was a man who was seldom, if ever, asked to repeat himself. "I'm not a bard, so I'll be quick. Good luck to all the competitors; battle with honor and dignity, and no cheating." Though the last two words were pronounced the same tone as the others, they rang powerfully in the ears of each person present. "We shall begin with Dagger Throwing. All those signed up to compete, to the targets at the west of the arena. Everyone else, stay clear."

Words spent, Mayor Branders walked back to his chair and sat, while in the arena, adventurers scurried toward, or away from, the arena's western side. Within moments, it had filled with competitors of various shapes and sizes, each holding their daggers at the ready.

The tournament had begun.

*   *   *

"The rules for the Dagger Throwing event are simple," yelled the portly man standing between the gathered contestants and the targets. "We will have five rounds; each competitor will throw one dagger each round. The closer you get to the bull's-eye, the better you score that round. I'll watch and keep tally, and the highest score at the end of the final round wins. Oh, and there's one more thing. If, during any round, you miss the target entirely, you are immediately disqualified from the competition, regardless of score." His wide face broke into an unashamed grin. "We thought that would keep it interesting." With that, he walked toward a wide table and a flurry of other peasants rushed to set up the first targets.

"Seems we're neighbors again, Thistle." Sierva stepped forward from the still-milling crowd, taking the spot to his right. Most of the competitors had waited to see who went where, wanting a place where they wouldn't feel crowded, or overshadowed by the grandeur of their competitor. Thistle, on the other hand, had staked his spot immediately upon arrival. It would be too easy to get knocked about if he tried to jostle through the crowd.

"Quite a coincidence, though a pleasant one," Thistle replied politely. Of course, since she'd chosen that spot, it was really anything but coincidence, but propriety was propriety.

"Tell me, what do you think of that last rule? The immediate disqualification if one misses."

"I'd say the reasonable assumption is that anyone who misses completely is likely too far behind in points to have a chance at placing, so pulling them out saves everyone's time," Thistle proposed.

"Perhaps, though it seems a shame to rob them of a chance to regain ground," Sierva commented.

"You have another thought?"

"More a tickle of suspicion than a full thought," Sierva admitted. "It just strikes me as off, but I can't think of why it bothers me."

"Well, if I were a less trusting and far more paranoid individual, I might have an inkling to offer," Thistle said, both volume and tone carefully controlled. Whether it was his years of henching, his amount of exposure to heroes, or some secret paladin sense, Thistle had a hunch that Sierva was a good person. Certainly, she might beat him, but that was the nature of competition. A little information now could equal a favor later, and Thistle was fond of having useful people in his debt.

"And what might that be, if you were indeed cursed with a suspicious heart?" Her eyes didn't linger on him; instead, they watched the targets being set up. To a casual observer, they appeared to be nothing more than competitors making chit-chat before the battle began.

"Were I indeed so wretched, it might have seemed strange to me that, while the town was bleeding its new inhabitants dry, the mayor allowed a free event's entry to any person who wished it. That, coupled with the generous chunk of prize money for each, seems as though Appleram was losing out on a chance to make notably more coin. Adding a disqualification rule, though… that might just send the gold coursing back into the town's coffers since, after all, the only way to avoid paying out the prizes would be if there were no winners."

"Of course, that would be impossible," Sierva replied. "Unless every competitor was to be disqualified under some rule."

"Aye, it would take nothing less," Thistle agreed, polishing a goblin dagger on his shirt as he spoke. The targets were nearly all set up. Soon, the time for talk would be at an end.

"Well, let us be thankful you are not such an awful person as to have doubts of our gracious hosts," Sierva commented.

"I say a prayer of gratitude every morning to just that effect."

Sierva looked over at the gnome, her lavender eyes nearly shining in the light of the day's fierce sun. "Good luck to you, Thistle. I intend to win; however, if I do lose, I hope it will be to you."

"Consider the sentiment echoed."

"Throwers, prepare yourselves," yelled the portly man from the table. "Strike your target on my mark!"

Thistle pulled back his arm, felt the cold metal of the goblin dagger resting between the tips of his fingers, and let everything in his world outside the target fall away into nothingness.

"Fire!"

*   *   *

The adventurers not competing in the current event had been directed to what was, essentially, a giant pen. Railing ran along the sides, butting up to the edge of the arena and extending back towards the town, then wrapping around in the direction of the tournament. There were a few mock weapons scattered here and there for anyone who wanted to squeeze in some last-minute training, but the intent of this space was made clear by its sparseness: they were to sit still, wait their turn, and not distract from the current show.

Evidently, many of the other parties didn't have a wolf in the fight for Dagger Throwing, because rather than paying attention to the competition, they were doing their own warm-ups. The upside was that this meant the competitors who did want to watch the competition were able to do so without having to jostle for a good viewing spot.

Eric, Grumph, and Gabrielle all let out cheers after the first round, when Thistle managed to sink his dagger right into the bull's-eye. A quick glance told them that only a few others had completed the feat and that some had actually missed entirely and gotten themselves disqualified. The loudest cheer went up from their left. Eric looked over, surprised to see the well-armored team he'd watched yesterday lined up along the railing and hooting for all they were worth. They must have had another member on their team who was competing.

It was because Eric's eyes lingered that he saw the cart being hauled along a dusty trail behind the pen. It was largely covered with a tarp; however, the mild breeze rustled the covering as the cart moved, affording his eyes a momentary peek inside. There was a flash, so quick and brief he'd have thought he imagined it, except that it was familiar. A creeping worry ran down his neck like frozen leaves falling off a winter tree.

"I'll be back in a moment," he told his friends, never letting the cart leave his field of vision.

"You're going to miss Thistle's event?" Gabrielle asked. "Don't tell me your nerves are upsetting your stomach again."

"No, I'm... it's probably nothing. I just need to go check something quickly." Without another word, Eric was off, moving through the pen as inconspicuously as possible while still keeping up a steady pace. He flowed through the crowd without thought, which was good, because he'd never have pulled off such grace had he been conscious of his movements.

"Odd," Grumph said, then turned his attention back to the contest. Thistle hadn't bull's-eyed his second target, but he'd come close. The mighty half-orc's hand still thundered with applause as the targets were changed and daggers retrieved.

*   *   *

Thistle thanked the attendant who returned his dagger to him, noticing Sierva at his side, doing the same. Once the attendants had moved on to other competitors, he voiced his curiosity.

"Couldn't help thinking you could save the folks some trouble and bring your own daggers back like yesterday."

"Perhaps, but in light of the extra disqualification rules, I've decided to handle things the old-fashioned way," Sierva replied. "The calling magic on them doesn't give me any advantage, but people can be touchy about magic in a martial competition. Technically, the only events allowed to use it are Magical Duel and General Melee."

"Best to play it safe then," Thistle agreed. His vision turned forward, toward the new targets being put in place. "This seems even smaller than last round."

"I noticed. About half the size of the originals," Sierva added. "Makes a bull's-eye nearly impossible."

"And missing far more likely."

"So it would appear," Sierva agreed.

"Makes you wonder how small the ones in the final round will be," Thistle said.

"Let's just focus on staying in long enough to make it there," Sierva suggested.

"Aye, good thinking."

They let the words fall away as their attention became focused on the targets in front of them, each no bigger than the lid of a small vat. This one, Thistle was confident he could hit. Any smaller, though, and he'd be tossing a prayer to Grumble. He wondered if that counted as cheating, given his new position in the god's employ. Oh well; even if it did, it likely wouldn't make much of a difference. Grumble was a fair god, but not well-known for his attentiveness.

* * *

The cart had woven around the arena, moving all the way to a building on the other side. Though the building connected to the arena in the stands, near the mayor's position, it was technically outside the fence marking the area. Outer doors, manned by four guards, halted the cart's haulers. Words were exchanged — words too soft for Eric to hear at the distance he was keeping — and two of the guards went to check out the contents of the delivery. Doing this required lifting up the tarp, and should have provided Eric with a glimpse inside. Unfortunately, the angle they lifted at only made more material flow over the part Eric wanted to see. Whatever they observed satisfied the guards, because they pulled the tarp back into position and motioned for the others to open the doors.

Then, when they were tugging the material back to the edge to secure it, Eric caught another flash. Perhaps the first glimpse he could have written off as imagination, given enough time, but this one he'd been watching for: a dull red pulse of light from a barely-exposed crystalline surface. Four days ago, it would have meant nothing to him. Four days ago had been before he saw the gleaming red gem in the goblins' camp, mere hours before denizens of hell sprang forth. It could be a coincidence, true; the goblins had hoarded many magical items in their storage hut. But the similarity between the gem's color and the blood-red tinge of the demons' skin was undeniable.

Eric still heard the clacking of their claws at night during the worst dreams, and sometimes, for a few heart-stopping seconds after waking. It could be a coincidence, but a twisting splinter of worry in his gut refused to let him accept that possibility and move on. He had to be sure that the gem was innocuous, or that it wasn't the same kind the goblins had found.

That meant he had only one option. Eric, the former guard, was going to have to break into that building.

*   *   *

"What do you think, about the size of a coin?"

"I'd say that would be a fair approximation," Thistle agreed.

Of the six remaining competitors, they were taking the size of the fourth round targets with the most calm. The other four were raising a ruckus, while the crowd was cheering and tittering at the new challenge. Likely, they didn't realize the implications of such tactics: to them, this just made for a better show.

The weight of his dagger shifted as Thistle readjusted his grip. What he wouldn't have traded for a better set of blades. These were functional, and he'd overcome their rudimentary design and lack of balance so far, but the margin for error was narrowing by the round. At this point, there was no longer any need to keep score. Whatever one got in the first three rounds would be the deciding factor; now it was just a matter of making it to the end.

Eventually, the other four competitors realized what Thistle and Sierva already knew: no one was listening to their complaints because no one cared. The money had been collected; all that remained was to take out as many competitors as possible. Good service for adventurers was for the tavern, not the tournament. Once this sank in, they moved back to their throwing positions, and tried not to let the anger cloud their focus.

"I wonder how they'll handle the other contests," Sierva speculated.

"They've got something, I've no question on that," Thistle told her. "I'm glad this is my only one."

"Perhaps that would have been a better strategy. I still have Magical Duel remaining."

Thistle's eyebrow rose slightly. "You do magic?"

"Of course. I am a wizard, after all. Throwing daggers is just a favorite hobby."

Thistle looked her over once more, taking note of the flexible, sturdy armor. She didn't look like any wizard he'd encountered, but then, neither did Grumph, so perhaps he should stay such judgements.

"You're quite good, for it being a hobby."

"I suppose we'll see if that's good enough."

*   *   *

Eric had never been a very adept guard, but that hadn't come from lack of trying. Quite the opposite: knowing how unskilled he was, Eric had studied harder than any of the others to improve. He'd gone over the floor plans of the mayor's house, constantly searching for undefended points that needed more attention. In his free time, Eric read books on trap-making and methods for breaking and entering so that he could be steps ahead of any intruders. He'd even tried a bit of lock-picking, to see if he could find a way to improve the models' designs. That ambition failed, but it still left him with a working knowledge of most common locks. No one in Maplebark knew more about guarding than Eric, which made it all the more frustrating when he'd consistently failed to keep Gabrielle from getting kidnapped.

Now, stepping carefully into the guarded building, he was grateful for all that research. Learning how to stop thieves had inadvertently also given him a good background on how to be one. He'd realized that the outer doors would prove impossible to assail without drawing a ruckus and sneaking in on a cart was unlikely, since those were searched. No, the weak point of the structure was the outcropping that connected to the stands. There was a tunnel leading from it to a spot deeper in, a place where Eric assumed it opened up in the mayor's area. The beams and columns surrounding it were dense, too dense for anyone to move freely through them. For that reason, the guards only walked around to check it infrequently, and then, it was more a glance than a thorough scan. Eric understood: guarding meant it was impossible to see everywhere at once, so you had to allocate your time to the places where the chance of intrusion was the highest. In this case, it meant the outer doors.

Of course, that also meant a lean, nimble man had enough time to work through those beams, making his way to where two of the tunnel sections joined. It was still slow going, but the inattentiveness of the guards gave him the freedom needed to accomplish the task. The shoddy construction of the hastily built arena also assisted him, as it meant the sections were joined loosely, making it easy to wedge open a gap and wiggle inside. Had Appleram spent any real time or money on their impromptu tournament, such tactics would have failed catastrophically. Thankfully, the emphasis had been on getting the structure built quickly, before the adventurers lost interest.

The actual contents of the building were approximately twenty boxes, six small chests, and three carts. A quick inspection of the chests revealed they were filled with coins, so presumably this was where the prizes for those who won were stored. The boxes held various bric-a-brac: tunics and scrolls and banners all emblazoned with an "Appleram Tournament!" logo — probably souvenirs they were planning to sell sometime during or after the contests.

The carts held other prizes: a gilded buckler that Eric suspected was more paint than gold, a silver statue of a dragon with blue gems for eyes, and a very ornate hat with an odd, mismatched design. Eric picked up the hat and turned it around in his hands. He was amazed by how truly hideous it was. Perhaps this was the fashion in the kingdom, but he'd take a good wide-brimmed hat to keep the sun at bay. With that thought, the gaudy hat shifted and was replaced by a simple one with a wide brim, just as he'd envisioned. Eric set it back down and it took back its original form when it left his hand. The magical, style-changing hat was interesting, but he was already worried about one magical item; he didn't need to mess around with a second.

Then, a few feet over, Eric saw it. There was no question; it was almost exactly the same as the gem he'd seen at the goblin camps. Same dull red glow, same egg-like shape, and same shifting patterns if one stared long enough. There were, however, two differences from the gem Eric had seen previously. This gem's glow wasn't constant; it brightened and dulled rhythmically at regular intervals. As he stared at it, Eric thought he caught the slightest increase in the tempo. That, he imagined, couldn't be a good thing.

Because the other difference between this gem and the one from the goblin camp was that the gem currently in front of Eric was bigger. Roughly three times bigger.

* * *

Thistle stared in amazement at the protruding dagger, barely imbedded in the wooden target, yet holding firm all the same. He was sure he'd felt it slip slightly on his throw, a minor error that should have eliminated him from the game. His saving grace had been an unexpected wind gust that moved his dagger's course. Only by half an inch, but it was enough. Of course, one gnome's good fortune was several other competitors' oblivion. Only a single other dagger had found its target besides his own, one that belonged to a long-haired human several spaces down from him.

"Damn wind," Sierva cursed, accepting her dagger as the attendant rushed it over to her.

"Sorry," Thistle said.

"Don't worry, it wasn't your fault," she assured him. Thistle felt a kernel of doubt, though. Perhaps the wind had been chance, or perhaps Grumble was showing favoritism to his newest recruit. The gnome shook off such thoughts forcefully. If one looked for the will of the gods in every turn of fate, it would soon overwhelm them. Better to take things as they were unless the deity physically showed themselves.

"Good throw," Sierva complimented a moment later.

"Not really. It would have gone wide if not for the wind."

"Your form was fine; I think the issue is, without meaning offense, that you're using daggers ill-suited for throwing."

"Aye, no argument here, but we work with what we have," Thistle agreed, accepting his own blade from the attendant. He heard a rustling sound to his left and glanced over to find a leather belt dangling in front of his eyes.

"A loan," Sierva explained. Her daggers were sheathed on opposite sides of the belt, silver handles gleaming in the light of the relentless sun. "Whatever the next phase is, you need a better blade."

"Are you certain?" A weapon, especially one with that much worth, was a precious and personal thing. To hand it off to a stranger was quite odd indeed.

"I'd like to see one of us win; didn't we agree on that? Besides, I detest this town's greedy trickery. Separate them from at least some of the gold that's been spent in the last week."

"With all the skill I possess," Thistle promised, accepting her gift. He wrapped the belt around himself twice in order to get it to fasten, then pulled the blades from their sheaths. They were light, delicate things that belied the danger in their sharp edges. Up close, they were even more beautiful than before, the intricate etchings weaving across the surface in a pattern that shifted as the eye moved. Though slightly bigger than his goblin daggers, they were easier to hold, and their balance was immaculate.

"Good luck," Sierva told him, walking back toward the pen with other, now-disqualified competitors.

That was when Thistle looked forward and saw the final round's trial. The good news was they hadn't shrunk the targets. Each was still about the same size as a coin. The bad news was they had tied those coin-sized targets onto the foot of two crows, each of which were squirming for freedom in the attendants' hands. A cheer went up from the crowd as they pieced together this next challenge, still unaware or uncaring about the ramifications it had on the competitors.

Thistle chanced a glance to the mayor, who sat stalwart as he watched the proceedings. He, at least, wasn't celebrating. So, he was likely a man who was doing this because he saw it as necessary, rather than to be overtly stingy. Thistle filed this mental note away, then stopped looking at the crowd and focused on the near-impossible task in front of him.

If the wind had been Grumble, Thistle hoped that wasn't all the god was ready to contribute. The chances of winning without some divine aid were about as good as if he went one on one with a great dragon. Still, miracles happened, so there was no reason not to at least give it a throw.

"Competitors," the portly man called from the sidelines. "At my signal, the attendants shall release the crows. You may throw one dagger whenever you choose after that."

Both Thistle and the human nodded, unwilling to look away from the shrieking birds with targets attached.

"Prepare yourselves," he yelled, clearly readying himself to give the signal.

"RUUUUUN!" The voice came with such speed and ferocity that both attendants jumped, releasing their birds inadvertently. The human let his dagger fly, shearing a few feathers from his crow's wing but otherwise missing entirely. Thistle, on the other hand, turned to the source of the noise, only mildly surprised to see it was Eric, dashing through the center of the arena, red-faced and panting.

"Everyone needs to get out! NOW!" Eric's voice carried more weight in those words than any of his friends had ever heard him conjure.

"What is the meaning of this?" the mayor asked, stepping forward and addressing the intruder from his position on the balcony. "Why have you disturbed our tournament?"

"Because we're about to be attacked and we have to evacuate," Eric explained.

"Appleram keeps watch over these roads, and has a fine militia. There have been no raiders or outlaws spotted anywhere near here. So what, pray tell, is going to attack us?"

Thistle winced inwardly at the words; he'd heard such phrases enough to know they had a strange magic. Words like that presented a theatrical opportunity that neither the gods, fate, nor whatever uncaring being oversaw the world was able to resist. Sure enough, the mayor had barely spoken when a huge explosion from the northeast corner rocked the arena.

"Demons," Eric replied, his voice hollowed by the realization that he was too late. Very few heard him over the screams of the audience members now fighting back a fire.

"There are demons coming."

12.

It had been such a simple plan. Exit the building, find Grumph and Gabrielle, consult Thistle, work out what to do next. After watching for a few minutes, Eric had determined that the pulse of the gem was indeed, speeding up, but it was doing so at a steady rate. He didn't even know for sure if this gem had anything to do with the demons; right now, it was just a coincidence and a hunch. Besides, if it was building toward a detonation, then it seemed a reasonable guess that he had at least enough time left to formulate a well thought-out plan of action.

That was when he heard the scratching. It was from a cart over, the one in which the odd hat rested. Eric searched quietly, pausing as needed to see if the sound was still coming. It took some doing, but eventually, he found the source in a large crate near the back of the cart. Inside were two more gems. One was pulsing a bit slower than the first Eric had spotted.

The other was going so fast, it seemed almost like a constant shine. This second gem also appeared to be the source of the scratching. As Eric peered into its depths, he realized the swirling patterns on the gem's surface were far clearer in this one — so clear, he could make out an image. That image was, unfortunately one of all-too-familiar claws scraping against the other side of rapidly pulsing gem.

All hope of a plan evaporated, and Eric rushed back to the makeshift entryway he'd made in the tunnel. He exited the beams faster than he would have thought possible, mind too preoccupied on what was happening. This was no longer a hunch; what he'd seen in the third gem had removed all doubt. Now, he needed to warn people; as many as possible, as quickly as he could. These gems were bigger, and he didn't know what that meant, but he could make a damned good guess at what three of them would entail.

Eric's speed was so great that, though the guards noticed him emerging from the rafters, they were only able to shout at him as he tore off in the direction of the arena. His newly-discovered speed after years of wearing bulky armor assured him they had no chance of catching up. Even then, the thought of being pursued might have quickened his step, were it not already being hastened by the memory of the claws scraping against the inside of the gem. That was more than enough motivation to give him speed.

He broke into the main part of the arena just as a portly man was barking orders, but Eric paid him no heed. There was only one target for the former guard: Mayor Branders. He was the man who could move people along, the man who might get them to safety before things went to hell. Or, rather, before hell came to them. With a deep gulp of air, Eric bellowed with all his might.

"RUUUUUN!"

*   *   *

The high-pitched ringing filling the ears of all present, a side effect from the explosion, had scarcely begun to subside when a second boom filled the air. This time, there was no delay, a third followed immediately on the second's heels. This final blast proved more than the hastily-built stands could handle, and a section near the mayor's position began to collapse. Many were able to scramble away, but a few went tumbling to the ground below. Scary as it was to see people falling away, it was nothing compared to the terror of what came next.

Once they landed, the screaming started.

Grumph and Gabrielle raced forward from the pen, joining up with Thistle along the way, and making it to Eric's side in expedient time.

"What's happening?" Thistle demanded, his voice firm, but calm, despite the growing pandemonium.

"Demons," Eric said. "I saw one of the gems like at the goblin camp, followed it on a hunch, and saw inside it. There were more demons, and it sounds like all three gems have let them out."

Thistle took a breath and let the absurdity wash over him. Dealing with magic was tiresome for a logical person because it often refused to make sense. Nevertheless, time spent debating the rationale of demons popping out of gems would be precious moments wasted. It was better to accept this strangeness as fact until it could be thought through later. Right now, all that mattered was that the demons were coming. Even if Thistle had doubted Eric's deduction, the explosions and screams were more than enough to sell him on the demon theory.

"We won't have long, but this time, we've at least got a few advantages," Thistle said. "Eric, go rally the garrison and the guards. Let them know what they'll be facing so they don't go in blind. Gabrielle and Grumph, go let the adventurers know what's happening. We've got enough swords and magical muscles to beat these beasts back before they get established. I'll talk to the mayor and try to get him to evacuate the citizens."

Thistle's directions were interrupted by the sound of splintering wood. A demon, nearly identical to the ones they'd faced only days ago save for the fact that it was over twice as large, smashed its way out of the stands and into the side of the arena. The clacking of its claws filled the air, broken splinters of wood tumbling away as it crushed them effortlessly. Among the debris, a keen eye could pick out bloodstains on the wood, answering the question of why the screaming had grown noticeably quieter.

"Well then, I guess we don't need to alert people, after all," Gabrielle sighed, unsheathing her axe with some effort.

"You're very wrong," Thistle informed her. "Remember, these aren't just demons. They're smart, at least, smart enough to work together. If we don't spread that information, lives will be lost."

Grumph snorted in agreement as he sprinted off toward the pens. Gabrielle hesitated, then followed a few moments later.

"I think I know where the guards will gather in an emergency," Eric said, taking off in another direction.

Thistle turned his attention up to the stands, where panic had already engulfed the sea of people scrambling to get away. He was a bit surprised they'd bought that part about alerting the mayor. What could one man do to direct so many people rightfully drowning in fear? No, Thistle had given them that falsehood because he knew they wouldn't follow orders if he told them the truth.

A few creaking steps brought him forward as he let out a low whistle then yelled toward the towering demon with all the volume he could muster:

"Hey, ugly, I killed one of you just a few nights past. Friend of yours? If so, I'd be happy to reunite you."

The demon turned its rat-like head and looked directly at him. From the hole it had left, three more equally-sized monsters emerged, their eyes also glaring in his direction. Well, he'd wanted to grab attention, and he'd certainly succeeded. His nimble fingers danced to his sheaths, surprised at the quality of daggers he'd found there. Right; he'd borrowed Sierva's blades before things went crazy. He hoped she had magic to find them, because he doubted he'd get to hand them back.

One demon, perhaps, he might have been able to slay, with his new magic and Grumble's blessings. Two would have certainly killed him. Four made what he planned seem so staggeringly stupid that part of him wondered why he was standing there. That part was quickly silenced. Thistle knew the terms of the bargain he'd struck; it was why he'd been so hesitant to take it. For all the perks and gifts that came with being a paladin, there was also an unshirkable duty attached. Paladins didn't run. Paladins didn't hide. Paladins were the shield of flesh between the forces of darkness and those without strength to defend themselves.

Paladins held the line, no matter what. Thistle's eyes narrowed as he whispered a prayer of blessing, causing each dagger to glow briefly. Maybe he could at least take one. He hoped it would be enough.

* * *

Grumph and Gabrielle had left a pen full of adventurers idling in a state somewhere between curiosity, confusion, and boredom. They arrived to a chorus of metal scraping against leather as weapons were drawn, armor refastened, and arrows nocked.

Adventurers were, on the whole, loud, disruptive, and often boisterous to a point of spectacle, but no one could deny that, when shit hit the fire, they were always ready to charge in head-first. None of the normal folk truly understood this brazen attitude, to dive into dungeons and unexplored depths as though their lives weren't on the line if things went poorly. Whether or not they understood it was irrelevant at the moment, though. All that mattered was focusing it.

"The demons are smart!" Gabrielle blurted, mouth moving before any sense of eloquence could make its way into her words. Most of the adventurers ignored her, but a few of the nearby ones turned their heads. After a dismissive glance, those heads went right back to whatever they'd been previously occupied with. A familiar bubble of anger tried to rise inside her; however, she was able to push it away. Now was not the time to let her fury bubble forth. That would come all too soon as it was.

"Listen to me!" Gabrielle called again, forcing herself to project her voice while maintaining a calm tone. "My friends and I fought some of these monsters three days ago. They were organized, cutting off escape routes, and splitting our forces. If you go in expecting them to be dumb beasts, you risk being taken by surprise."

"So, you say you fought these things before, yes?" The voice came from a dwarf encased in a dented set of old armor. A thick axe was clutched in his right hand while his left held an aged mace.

"We did," Gabrielle confirmed.

"And how many of you did they kill?"

"My party all made it out, but dozens of nearby goblins were slain before the demons were stopped."

"I see," the dwarf replied. "Given the way you grip that axe, I don't take you for much of a fighter, so if all your people made it out safe, then I doubt we have much to worry about. If the only things these beasts are a threat to are goblins, then I say we let them run wild."

Grumph started to step forward, but Gabrielle was faster. In a whirl of motion, she jammed the butt of her axe's shaft between the dwarf's legs, shifted her weight, and spun the weapon around and upward. This knocked the dwarf's legs out from under him and sent him tumbling the, admittedly short, distance to the ground.

"These demons have claws that can cut through thick leather armor like it's a gossamer web, they can leap clear across a camp in one jump, and their flesh is as thick as a dwarf's skull," Gabrielle said, her voice only a few shades above a whisper, yet clearly audible to the many people who were now paying her very close attention. "The ones we fought were half this size, and still soaked the ground in blood before they were done. If you want to take this lightly, then so be it, but I'd see every warrior here forearmed with knowledge before the killing starts."

"You certainly know how to draw attention," said a copper-haired man adorned in silver armor that shone in the midday sun. The ornate handle of a longsword jutted out from his scabbard. Gabrielle was sure he'd been much further away when the dwarf made his wisecracks. To cover such ground quickly was quite impressive. "I, for one, would like to hear what you know."

"Might as well listen," the dwarf agreed from the ground. "It'll take me a few minutes to pull myself back up, anyway."

Gabrielle nodded, waited for as many others as could fit to gather around, and then began to speak.

* * *

The trick to getting guards to listen was to put yourself outside of a situation where protocol could be followed. There were rules for messengers, procedures for other guards, and general bureaucratic bugbearshit designed to make sure that any information accepted came from a reliable source. Of course, that was only viable if the person giving the information knew anything beyond the initial intelligence.

Eric found the circle of armored guards speaking in fast tones just where he'd expected they would be and immediately sized them up. The captain was clearly the man farthest away, with a few scars visible under his helm and an aura of command. Instead of approaching him, Eric dashed toward a guard close by whose helmet had a plume on top.

"Captain," he gasped, this part somewhat genuine due to all the running. "I was sent with information for you."

The plumed guard looked surprised, then uncertain, and then scared once the real captain began walking over.

"What's the meaning of this?" His voice was rough like his face and the scowl across his brow did nothing to make either less severe.

"I was told to come find the captain of the Appleram guards, and to pass on a message," Eric replied, eyes darting between the actual captain and the guard with the plume.

"Who sent you?"

"I don't know," Eric replied. "Tall man, dark hair, simple clothes. Grabbed me, gave me the message, told me it was a matter of life and death." Based on those he'd seen walking around

Appleram, that description fit around thirty percent of the men, more, if one had loose opinions on what constituted being tall.

The captain stared at him, scowl deepening. His training made him want to ask verification questions, but his choices were limited when Eric was stating outright how little he knew. "Why didn't this man come himself?"

"I don't know."

"What made you so willing to do it, then?"

"Because the monsters were in the other direction," Eric replied.

This was enough to satisfy the captain. If he'd claimed noble intent, Eric would still seem suspicious, but the captain knew that when danger came from nowhere, most folks were hell-bent on getting away.

"What's this message, then?"

"He said these things were demons, that they were smart, and that they would work together. Said their claws can cut through armor with ease and that blessed weapons are your best bet."

The captain nodded, no expression besides the scowl, which Eric was beginning to suspect was a permanent fixture on his face. "Anything else?"

Eric shook his head. "That was it."

"Fine. Thank you for your service. Now get clear of this arena, quickly," the captain ordered.

Eric nodded, slipped out of the circle, and ran toward the exit. Once there was enough room between him and the guards, Eric doubled back and made for an entrance to the main part of the arena. He'd nearly run away the first time and that knowledge still haunted him. This time, he wasn't leaving without his friends.

*   *   *

The first dagger had taken a demon in the shoulder. There was a howl of pain, and the demon reeled on impact, revealing a blade sunk all the way to the hilt in its flesh. Definitely an effective blow, though it was not the explosion of bone and muscle that had come from the last time Thistle had thrown a dagger at one of these things. Well, Grumble had said the first one was a bit special.

Careful steps brought the demon closer to Thistle, the other three directly behind. Its red eyes stared at the other blade in Thistle's hand, wary, but also able to do enough math to understand that one blade wouldn't stop all of them. Logic told Thistle that as soon as he let the second fly, the demons would rush him. He really, *really* needed to start keeping more of these damned daggers on him. It was a mistake he was unlikely to get a chance to learn from.

The second dagger struck the demon just below its red throat, prompting a wet gurgle of pain. Left unremoved, Thistle was certain that dagger would force the demon to bleed out. He wished the kill had been cleaner, but hopefully, this would make a difference.

The group of monsters lurched forward now that he was unarmed, massive claws clacking in anticipation. Not that they'd need them; with their size they'd likely crush Thistle before he landed a strike.

An explosion of blue light erupted from the center of the group, engulfing all of them and washing a wall of cold over

Thistle. When it cleared, each demon was coated in bits of ice, and none of them seemed as mobile or enthusiastic as before. It had been a cold spell, that was obvious, but it made Grumph's seem like a brush with an ice block.

"Call the daggers," said a familiar voice to his left. Sierva had appeared, though he had no idea when, and trace amounts of magical light still lingered about her.

"What?"

"Call the daggers. They're enchanted to return to their sheaths," she reminded him.

"I don't know that I can do the whistle from memory," Thistle admitted.

"The whistle was my signal. Just call them how you please. The magic will understand."

A sharp sound rang out as the ice began cracking away, and the demons resumed their movements. Not having the luxury of time to doubt, Thistle did as he was told.

"Here, boys!"

Sure enough, the blades vanished from the demon's hide and reappeared instantly in the sheaths at his side. This was a feature he could grow accustomed to. Thistle glanced back at his fellow competitor and noticed she was breathing hard.

"Don't suppose you've got a plan?"

"Hold them off until I can cast again," she answered. "Spells like that still take a good bit out of me."

"Aye," Thistle replied. There was nothing more to be said. This was his duty, after all.

His dagger flew with unexpected precision, this time, taking the demon right in the center of its horrid throat. There was no death gurgle, for the blade had severed all the bits used to make sound. Instead, the beast merely flopped to the ground and shuddered uselessly as its blood muddied the dust around them.

Thistle whispered a few words under his breath and the first dagger was back in its sheath by the time the second took another demon in the stomach. Between the effects of the cold spell and the corpse of their friend, the remaining creatures were showing caution toward the gnome and the elf. It wouldn't last forever, but at that moment, it was enough.

13.

The counterattack began with the adventurers, to the surprise of exactly no one who knew anything about them. The guards would have to make choices with the knowledge that their first job was defending the citizens of Appleram. Adventurers, however, were under no such moral obligations, and rushed into battle with the sort of enthusiasm one only finds in idiots, champions, and the unapologetically suicidal.

With a roar of excitement, they crossed the arena, arriving in time to lend Thistle and Sierva some much-needed support. Now, faced with targets that had to move in close to attack, the demons shifted their attention to this new prey, chopping and slicing with hellish glee. For a bit, it seemed like the beasts were hopelessly outnumbered and outmatched, the adventurers felling a second of the four in mere moments.

That was when the others arrived. From the stands burst four more of the large-clawed demons and nearly countless unfamiliar monsters scuttling along the ground. These low-slung, red-shelled creatures had eight legs, a nasty set of mandibles near the mouth, and three-foot-long tails with spear-like tips that nearly doubled their length. Unlike the clawed demons, these scuttlers drew less initial attention, moving beneath the feet of the adventurers and striking intermittently. Less than five minutes after the wave of scuttler demons emerged, the adventurers' coordinated attack dissolved into a chaos of hacking, slashing, and stabbing amidst attacks from the ground coupled with the giant demons tearing through flesh. They continued to press on, injuring and eventually bringing down another clawed demon.

Without warning, four of the remaining large demons leapt into the air, landing on various sides of the mob and splitting the focus from a single melee to a multi-pronged attack. Had they not been ready for it, the adventurers might have taken too long to regroup, eventually costing them their lives. Thanks to Gabrielle and Grumph, though, they whirled on their attackers' new positions, circling around the demons to split their attention. Bodies still fell at a faster rate than anyone wanted to see, but those left standing were bloodying the beasts right back.

A slight rumble was the only warning anyone received before the ground exploded upward, showering the arena in dirt, and hurling people and demons alike in various directions. From the gaping hole now at the center of the battle emerged a massive head that looked as though someone had merged a snake and a Minotaur, resulting in a reptilian, horned monstrosity. Dozens of thick, insect-like arms waved in the air from all sides of its armored body, each long enough to spear a human from twenty feet away and fling them to its waiting maw. This was a fact everyone learned firsthand as one unfortunate soul landed too close to it.

With that, all hope of strategy was gone, and the world dissolved into blood and chaos.

* * *

Grumph landed in a pile with four other humans. Two of the large demons came clattering down moments later, mere steps away from the adventurers. Few things will drive a man up from the ground faster than the prospect of certain death, and soon everyone was on their feet and as alert as if they were waiting for a nymph to walk by. Two of the humans, one wielding a set of small swords and one with a rapier, pressed a demon, while the other two, a pair so similar they might be brothers, attacked the other with axes in their hands. This left Grumph, the odd half-orc out, to determine which group to help.

The axe brothers were engaging their quarry directly, one drawing its attention while the other struck from behind. The rapier and dual-blade wielder were trying a different tactic, dancing out of the demon's range, and only darting in for quick, shallow strikes. Both styles might keep them alive for a bit, but it would be hard to win with either.

So far, Grumph had cast four of the five spells. He'd learned that they conjured a blast of cold and ice, a small fireball, a glowing weapon that appeared in his hand and reshaped itself as he wished, and a pail of water. The ice would distract and annoy the demons, he'd seen that at the goblin camp, but fire was altogether worthless against anything from a fire-based realm. The weapon he could work with, but that spell took a lot out of him. He probably wouldn't be able to cast much more if he tried that one.

Then, with a reflexive thrust, one of the demons managed to slash the rapier wielder across the gut, sending the thin man stumbling backwards. With a few whispered words and a quick gesture, Grumph cast his spell.

The pail of water materialized a few feet above the demon's head, falling immediately and spilling its contents all over the monster. This distracted the demon so much that it was utterly unprepared when the metal pail landed upside down on its head, momentum wedging it in place. Its claws, horrible and deadly though they were, proved little help in yanking the pail free.

Granted, with enough time, it surely would have pulled something off, but before it had a chance, Grumph finished casting his second spell.

A mighty *clang* filled the air as the glowing mallet clutched in Grumph's meaty palms smashed into the pail and the head contained within. Metal bent inward with the blow, denting the pail and securing it to the monster's head. With a few more blows and help from the dual-wielder, the demon was soon finished off, a slick slurry of blood dripping down from the still-stuck pail on what had once been a whole head.

Grumph adjusted his grip and turned to the next one. Magic was well and good, but only a fool ignored all the assets at their disposal. Besides, it was a magic weapon, so this counted as wizard's work.

*   *   *

Gabrielle's trajectory sent her into a large cluster of other adventurers, along with a sizable number of the clawed and scuttling demons. With no time to wonder just what she intended to do, Gabrielle whirled her axe around and charged a group of the smaller demons. Their long tail-blades clinked off her axe with a dull, tinkling sound, and they skittered away when she drew close. One was a bit too slow and she swung long, driving her own weapon's blade through the thin carapace on its back. She heard a sickening splatter as the small demon was rent in two. With that, its legs ceased to scuttle.

"They're weak," Gabrielle called to her fellow warriors. "Fast but weak. They go down easy."

The others nodded comprehension, some moving to assist her, while more dealt with what they perceived to be the greater threat:

the clawed demons. One of her nearby assistants, an archer, judging from the confident way she held her bow, unleashed a flurry of arrows on the moving horde. Not every demon hit was killed, but they were at least slowed. Another at her aid was a dagger thrower, the man who'd made it to the final round with Thistle. Each blade he launched through the air pinned a scuttle demon to the ground. Their struggles stopped almost before the hilt finished quivering.

A different pair of adventurers joined Gabrielle in the melee, one wielding a halberd and the other, a staff. Halberd did ample damage, clearing the vermin away with pinpoint accuracy, while Staff laid down small spells that didn't kill but certainly wounded. Gabrielle took up a defensive role, since her range was shorter. She kept the scuttle demons from swarming any of the others, often having to dash between spots in order to draw attention and keep the others safe.

The five of them worked seamlessly, teamwork fostered by the universal desire not to die. Within minutes, they'd cleared out over three-fourths of the scuttle demons and none of them had taken significant damage. That changed, not because of any failing on their part, but because of an ill-timed death on the other team.

A swordsman who had been part of flanking and containing the clawed demon missed his step, causing him to stumble. The demon pounced on this opportunity, cutting the man in half with a single motion, then racing forward to assist the Scuttles. Even if what was left got free, they would surely distract the adventurers fighting the Claws, allowing the demons to overtake the group.

This Claw was particularly smart: instead of attacking one of the people on the offensive, it opted to go for their only defensive member. Gabrielle, back turned as she swung her axe through another Scuttle's body, never saw the monster coming. The only one who did was the dagger-thrower, momentarily turned around to grab more blades from his pack.

He moved on instinct, no time for consideration. With one hand, he whipped out a blade, aiming for the charging demon's eye while his feet carried him forward to cut off the path to Gabrielle. Only one of his attempts succeeded.

A choked scream drew Gabrielle's attention momentarily away and she swung around to see the dagger-thrower with a claw jutting out of his torso. The demon had impaled him and was now trying to shake the corpse loose. Its eyes glared at her as it swung its arm, flecks of blood flying all over the increasingly red ground.

Figuring out what had happened didn't take more than a little bit of mind and Gabrielle had far more than that. She understood that this man, whose name she'd never known, had put himself in the way of an attack meant for her. The bubbling of rage that was becoming so familiar surged as she watched his body finally slide free of his killer's arm.

So stupid. Why did he do that? Why did he feel the need to protect her? Gabrielle's anger wasn't at the man for his action, or even at the demon for capitalizing. Gabrielle was mad at herself, for still seeming like the kind of person who needed to be protected. She didn't want to be weak; she didn't want to be kidnapped. She didn't want to be a damsel, and the fact that she'd just become one again really pissed her off.

Fortunately, there was a clacking-clawed outlet for her aggression mere steps away.

*   *   *

"Back!" Thistle ordered, flinging one of Sierva's daggers forward and impaling a Scuttle that had popped out from under a seat. The children squealed in terror, nearly falling over as they scrambled away from it. Thankfully, Thistle's blessed blades sundered the smaller demons with any hit on the main body. Its twitching had nearly stopped by the time the dagger reappeared in the sheath at Thistle's side, and he motioned for the children to move forward once more.

While most people in the vicinity of the monster's exit had been sent flying off to the side of the arena, Thistle's central position and gnome stature meant the force was powerful enough to hurl him into the stands. How he'd emerged from the pile of splinters unharmed was thanks, most likely, to Grumble, either directly, or through the divine perks of servitude. Thistle's first instinct had been to leap back into the fray; however, the sounds of terrified tears had drawn his attention.

Under a nearby seat, clutching each other and crying softly, were Mayor Branders's children. It seemed a reasonable guess that they had been separated from their father in the confusion and opted to hide. With a weary sigh, Thistle called them forward and assured them everything would be all right. Whether it was his paladin's aura, or just sheer desperation, the children immediately latched onto him and agreed to come along.

Navigating their way out of the stands proved tougher than Thistle expected. Between damage from the explosions, groups of other people trampling about, and the roving Scuttles popping out all over the place, he'd nearly gotten everyone, himself included, killed twice before they made it out of their original section. Thistle noticed that the bulk of others he saw were moving west and that almost none were coming back in the other direction. That meant either there was a way out or certain death. Fifty-fifty was better than his chances if they stayed put, so the group pressed onward.

The one blessing of their journey was that the Scuttles they encountered moved singularly rather than en masse. A group of them easily could have overwhelmed Thistle and the children, yet they encountered no more than one at a time. Such behavior bothered Thistle, who had seen them moving as a unit earlier. Even without his blessed daggers, outside of their group these creatures were weak. It made no sense for them to spread out like this. Assuming they weren't as intelligent as the Claws, sheer instinct should still have kept them bunched together.

Thistle wished he could have seen how the fight below was going; unfortunately, between the debris, constant movement, and fact that his own height was barely greater than that of the children's, he had to resign himself to listening to the ordeal below. From the sounds, it seemed like things weren't entirely lost. The majority of the shouts he heard were ones of direction, not terror or surrender. Hopefully, that ground demon was built more for intimidation than practicality.

Another Scuttle popped up, this one letting out an odd, chittering screech before Thistle's dagger chopped it in two.

"I don't remember the others making a noise," he mumbled after calling back his blade, staring at the spot where the demon's remains were oozing onto the wood.

Before he could say anything else, the wooden chunks blocking his sight to the arena below fell away, and he immediately wished they hadn't. The wood, along with the entire section of stands where they were situated, had been smashed away by the giant ground demon that was now waiting below with an open, salivating mouth. The floor, no longer supported by anything other than habit, fell away, sending them falling toward the waiting mouth.

"Aaaaaaah!" the children screamed.

"Aaaaaaah!" Thistle screamed right along with them because this was a damned good moment to scream. In the back of his mind, where his logic lived, an epiphany struck as he finally realized why the Scuttles had spread out in such a manner.

They were a detection system to find the ground demon more prey.

* * *

Eric was moved the least of the four by the explosion, reflexively diving to the ground moments after having been launched in the air. As a result, he got an upfront seat for the horror that was the giant ground demon. After the first casualty, archers and knife-throwers let loose volleys of attacks, all of which bounced off the interlocking scales of the demon, leaving scarcely a scratch. The next volley was one of magic, a rainbow of different spells bouncing off its flesh. One or two seemed to wound it slightly, but the demon paid them almost no mind at all.

Instead, it focused on eating more people. It would smash into stands intermittently, tearing away sections of wood and gobbling the people who had been standing there moments prior. Occasionally, an adventurer using a melee weapon would draw too close to it and be speared by one of its endless legs, but these occasions scarcely grabbed more than a few seconds of its attention.

A dull ache in his hand drew Eric out of the trance he'd fallen into while watching this vast monster. It took him a moment to realize he'd been gripping the hilt of his sword so tightly it caused the metal to dig into his palm. He wanted to do more than grip his weapon; he wanted to hurt this demon that was killing so freely. Eric licked his lips and watched the waving legs swing through the air. Maybe, just maybe, he was fast enough. Maybe he could get in close enough to swing his sword and take off some of those legs. If he was lucky, he might even get a strike in on its side.

Eric took a tentative step forward and immediately felt a hand close on his arm.

"Give it a moment," said a thick voice to his side. It was one of the armored people he'd watched so attentively, the dwarf with the massive club. "When it goes to hit the stands, its legs slow up a bit. That's when our kind has the best chance of hitting." The dwarf hefted his melee weapon to his shoulder, leaving no doubt what he'd meant by the words "our kind."

"Thank you," Eric said.

"No need. This works better if more of us charge it," the dwarf told him.

Eric realized that all around the demon were adventurers with their weapons out, braced to charge, merely waiting for the right moment. Most of the parties he recognized were split, members forming triangular patterns around their massive target. Later on, Eric would realize that was so that if the demon attacked an area where one of them stood, the others would still have a chance at killing it. When he understood their brutal, selfless efficiency, he would be all the more impressed by these warriors.

They didn't have long to wait until their opportunity came. The demon, reacting to some unknown impulse, pulled more of its body out of the hole and smashed into a section of the stands with its head. As it did, the waving legs slowed and the adventurers rushed forward. Eric was with them, trying hard not to think about the lives of the people in the stands. It seemed cruel to have waited for it to kill more of them, but there really hadn't been any other way. He kept his eyes on the monster, not wishing to see the deaths of more innocent people. His ears, unfortunately, were not so easy to turn away.

"Aaaaaaah!"

Eric looked, unwillingly, as the sound of frightened children reached his ears, which is why he was watching when Thistle let out his own, gnomish scream. The three figures tumbled through the air, right toward the waiting jaws of the demon.

"Thistle!" Eric had no idea what he hoped to accomplish by yelling. It wouldn't stop what was about to happen, it wouldn't bring back his friend, and it wouldn't make him feel any less useless as he watched the gnome die.

Still, Eric yelled just the same.

14.

Kicking children was, by and large, not an activity associated with paladins, at least, not with paladins of any god one could pray to in a respectable temple. So Thistle felt a touch awkward about the fact that his final action in this life would be sinking his small gnome feet into the torsos of the mayor's children, and pushing with all his might. Before the job change, it likely wouldn't have been enough, but his paladin strength gave him the extra boost to send both children hurtling in a new direction, one that would hopefully place them outside the ground demon's range. This also had the effect of moving him closer to the demon's open mouth. Such were the ramifications of mid-air readjustments.

As he tumbled through the air, Thistle pulled both of his daggers from their sheaths. It was a useless gesture. This monster would crush him in a single snap of its jaws, but he was determined to fulfill his duty to the end. Paladins always went down slashing; Thistle would not be the one to break that grand tradition.

In the span of seconds, he'd fallen into its mouth, a wide, red canyon filled with hundreds of razor-sharp teeth. The world grew dark as its jaw shut, sealing away the daylight. All that illuminated the space around Thistle was the set of daggers clutched desperately in his hands, which gave off a faint white glow. He wasn't sure if this was magic Sierva had put on them, or a side effect of the blessing; he just knew he was thankful for it.

Thistle flew past the first few rows of teeth, the kick-generated spurt of momentum carrying his small body through at high speeds. When he finally landed, he was partway down the demon's throat, just past its tongue. Immediately, the muscles of the throat constricted, coming together to force this delicious tidbit all the way down to the waiting stomach. Before it could fully surround him, Thistle dug both daggers into the soft flesh, plunging as hard and deep as he could manage.

"Hope you can't swallow right for a week," Thistle muttered, one last dash of spite against his killer before his inevitable death. With the damage done, he waited for the throat to crush him into pulp.

Instead, the entire arena got a very attention-grabbing surprise.

* * *

The demon's scream made nearly everyone present clutch their ears in pain. It rang out across the tournament field, causing a section of the stands to shake and collapse, then continued onward where it startled some unsuspecting birds roosting a mile away. As horrible as the sound was, it might as well have been the starting flag at a joust, because it signaled just what all the adventurers had been waiting for: an opportunity.

They poured into its lair like a spilled potion, surrounding the demon as it churned and bucked, battling some unseen foe. Eric was with them, hoping against hope that if he were fast enough, somehow, there would still be time to save Thistle. Maybe if they opened up its stomach, he'd still be alive and could be healed. It was a silly, delusional hope; Eric understood that quite keenly. That didn't stop it from fueling his focus as he slashed at the demon's arms with his blade, taking them off cleanly with every strike.

Around him, others were having varied success. Those with more physical strength, or magically-enchanted weapons, were able to duplicate Eric's feat of taking every limb they swung at. Others, unfortunately required three or four hacks before severing an arm from the demon's body. Even with the beast's attention elsewhere, this left them vulnerable for too long and often resulted in them getting stabbed, if not outright skewered. Still, as they continued their work, more limbs fell away, and fewer adventurers found themselves injured. Whatever was distracting this demon was doing an incredible job. All they could hope was that it would continue long enough for them to start on the body.

As Eric finished off the last of the tentacle-like arms in his area, he slashed at the demon's hide with his sword, cutting easily through the hard scales as blessed metal tore infernal flesh. Thick, gooey blood oozed out from the wound, and Eric redoubled his efforts. His friend was in there, alive or dead, and he'd be damned if he allowed Thistle's final resting place to be inside some glorified demon worm.

* * *

Thistle was, at this point, doing very little resting. Point of fact, he'd never worked harder in his life. After the monster's scream, one that had left him with twin trails of blood trickling from his ears, and had very nearly forced him to release his blades, the constriction had finally begun in earnest as the demon tried to dislodge the discomfort in its throat. However, for once Thistle found his size to be a boon, rather than a burden. Big as the creature was, it had clearly been bred for large meals and its physiology reflected that. Had Thistle been a touch bigger or lacked the dagger handholds, he'd surely have been sent down the express route to its stomach and impending digestion. As it was, he was just barely able to hang on against the pressing muscles pushing him downward. While the constriction failed to dispose of Thistle, it did succeed in moving him and the daggers slightly downward, rending the demon's flesh as it went.

After a particularly hard thrust, the constriction relented. Thistle took this opportunity to pull out one of the daggers and slam it back into an unharmed bit of throat, slightly higher than the previous wound. While it didn't result in another ear-splitting shriek, Thistle felt the creature jerk and twitch, shuddering in pain.

He had no idea what he was trying to accomplish. Perhaps a dim hope of climbing back up and out of the demon's mouth flitted about his head, but the logistics of getting past the teeth would have crushed that delusion as easily as the jaws would crush Thistle. No, this was not an attempt to survive, a break at freedom, or even some stupid belief that he could kill the demon from the inside. This was merely Thistle showing the quality that had defined him most in his youth: relentless stubbornness.

It was what had gotten him tossed from his church, what had forced him to travel with a band of adventurers, and what had ultimately led to winning his wife. Pliable as Thistle's mind could be, there were just some things he absolutely could not do, and dying quietly was one of them. Had he passed away at this particular moment, Grumble would have pointed out that this trait was what made him a candidate for paladin-hood in the first place. But Thistle did not pass away, nor did he relinquish his grip on the daggers when the next round of constriction began. Instead, he held on tight and stabbed again each time the opportunity came.

There was no end goal or strategy at work; Thistle just intended to give as good as he got before the inevitable occurred. Of course, had he been able to hear the sounds from outside the demon, he might have entertained a very different idea of what constituted "the inevitable."

*　　*　　*

There was no style to Gabrielle's technique as she swung her axe, no sublime grace that others would watch and find beautiful. She was, in fact, quite ugly. Her hair was matted in blood; hot, sticky stuff that also coated a large portion of her face, a face that wore the sort of scowl one sees just before a knife enters their belly. No, she was far from beautiful as she swung downward, rending another Claw's head from its shoulders and sending a hot spray of fresh blood into the air. Gabrielle didn't need to be beautiful. She was effective, and that meant worlds more than beauty in her current situation.

With a heavy grunt, she pulled her axe free and spun around, searching for fresh targets. The last few minutes had been a blur. After the dagger-thrower's sacrifice, her rage had broken free, sending her on a collision course with the Claw who had killed him. Alone, anger or no, she'd never have stood a chance against such a monster. But she wasn't alone. At her charge, other adventurers had taken the cue, swarming the demon with her and splitting its attention. They'd tried this tactic before; however, this time, they had Gabrielle, who demanded the monster focus on her with every snarl, grunt, and swing she sent its way. The demon was dead in minutes and her newly-formed party hurled themselves at the next one, and the next one, and so on, until she looked around and realized she might be out of Claws to kill.

At that realization, the anger ebbed, and Gabrielle was able to think clearly once more. She surveyed her surroundings carefully, on watch for any threats that might leap out at her. The Claws in her area were all dead, the last of them a headless corpse at her feet. Somewhere along the line, the Scuttles had been broken, their groups destroyed. A few rogue ones darted about, but without the advantage of numbers or the Claws, a single Scuttle proved little challenge for any adventurer. She could see other groups of adventurers and guards still fighting throughout the arena. From the way they were bunched together, it seemed likely they were cleaning up the last of their demons. Truly, the final challenge was the giant monster that had sprung from the ground. Gabrielle hefted her axe to her shoulder and began heading over.

"Be careful," said a familiar voice to her right. She turned to find Grumph, holding a glowing spear that seemed to be made of purple light, pinning a Scuttle to the ground. It was close to her, so close it could have struck had it made a few feet further. As she watched, he lifted his weapon up and it turned into a hammer, which he brought crashing down on the insect-like demon with a loud crunch.

"Thanks," she said, noting that her words sounded slightly slurred.

"You need rest," Grumph advised her. "Anger tolls the body."

She saw no reason to object; Grumph was certainly right. Already, she could feel the stiffness in her muscles, the heaviness of her weapon. Hell, even taking a few steps had been an arduous task. Grumph was right; she should rest. And she would: when the battle was over.

"Soon," she promised him.

Grumph merely nodded. He understood that arguing would waste energy she didn't have. She would fight until either the battle was done, or she was. That was the way of the barbarian, which Gabrielle most certainly was. He would do the job of a friend and keep her safe as best he could.

"One left," he said, pointing at the ground demon, which was thrashing wildly about.

"Big one, though," Gabrielle noted.

"Big still bleeds."

"Couldn't have said it better myself."

*   *   *

It was only Eric's natural grace that kept him from slipping on the massive pool of blood at his feet. He and the other adventurers had taken out nearly all of the demon's legs and turned their wrath onto its body. The hide was thick and tough, but with time and determination, they'd hacked through it, slice by slice. Each blow opened up new wounds, spilling gooey blood onto the ground. Within minutes, they were all soaked in the stuff; a few minutes more and not even the thirsty dirt could soak up any more. The effects of their damage could be seen: the demon was growing slower, its few remaining limbs weak and ineffective. Sooner or later, they would bleed the beast out. Eric just didn't know if it would be soon enough.

"Make a path!" The voice rang out from behind Eric, its source a human with copper hair and shining armor, one from the group he'd seen yesterday. Next to him was the elf woman Thistle had been throwing next to, as well as a vast conglomeration of people wearing robes and holy symbols.

"Everyone get clear! We're going to hit it with a coordinated strike, so move!" the man yelled again, his words finally penetrating the battle-fog most of the remaining warriors had fallen into. Bodies gave up their front-line positions quickly; the one thing any good melee fighter knew was to get clear when magic was about.

Eric scrambled away, nearly losing his footing twice, thanks to a combination of haste and exhaustion. As he exited the demon's crater, he saw a growing light radiate from the group, as each person there began casting a spell. The light grew brighter, dozens upon dozens of symbols materializing in front of each adventurer, magical energy so thick it made Eric's hair stand on end, even at such a distance away. The energy grew, swelling slowly like a filling water-skin. Then, just when he was certain no more could be contained, the energy burst.

No one there could actually make out what the attack looked like; twenty-five spells detonating on a single area simultaneously was more than mortal eyes could bear to witness. What they could make out, however, was the after-effect. The top of the ground demon tumbled forward, striking the dirt with a powerful thud. There was no chance of it getting back up, as it had no muscles to work with. The coordinated magical attack had sundered it clean through, chopping it down like a hideous, red-skinned tree.

Moments after impact, a cheer went up. The arena was filled with the sound of joyful accomplishment and relief as the monster lay conquered at their feet. It was done. The attack was over, and they'd survived. Most of them, anyway.

As quickly as the cheer began, it halted even faster when the demon's mouth began to twitch. Swords readied, arrows drew, and the crackling of magic filled the air once more. Everyone was braced to attack as the twitching moved, first from the back of its mouth, then to the middle, and finally, to its lips. These same lips were pulled open slowly, not by a tongue as many expected, but by a pair of small, gnome-sized hands.

Thistle emerged from the demon's mouth, careful not to nick himself on the rows of blade-sharp teeth, and breathed a sigh of relief as his shoes touched the blood-soaked dirt. Looking around, he realized the eyes of everyone were on him, ogling the insane sight of a gnome emerging from the maw of a demon. Never one to waste an opportunity, Thistle cleared his throat and spoke as loudly as he could:

"Anyone object to a do-over on that last throw? I got a bit distracted by the demons, and I'd wager my target has flown half a kingdom away by now."

The cheer he received would have been deafening, had the demon's scream not already broken the eardrums of so many.

15.

Night fell before any semblance of peace returned to Appleram. The corpses of the demons were trimmed, skinned, and stripped of all useful parts, then buried on consecrated ground and blessed by any adventurers who had a bit of divine connection. The remaining inventory of the storage shed — what little remained — was scrupulously evaluated. No item with magical potential was left unassessed, and anything even slightly tinged red was suspect to exceptional scrutiny. Those who'd been injured in the fray were healed with divine magic, the healers curing the poisoning in the blood that the demons' strikes had inflicted. Those who were beyond healing, or already gone, were mourned, buried, and stripped of gear by their adventuring party. The latter act gave no one joy, but there was no sense in entombing a friend with his chainmail when that same armor might keep another alive.

By the time Thistle, Gabrielle, Grumph, and Eric returned to the inn, they were wiped beyond measuring, every bit of energy and magic expelled. They greeted the innkeeper and staff with polite nods, slurped down a few bites of stew and rolls of bread, and collapsed in exhaustion with nary a word said among them. There would be time for talk later. All that mattered for the night was the sweet release of sleep, carting them off to a land where their bones didn't ache, and their eyes weren't burned with images of fallen corpses. In a small blessing, perhaps metaphorical and perhaps literal, none were troubled by nightmares, or dreams of any sort. They slept the slumber of the dead, cut off from the world until morning came, all too soon in its arrival.

As the group stirred, they became aware of a presence in their room, aside from one another. Sitting at the table, helping himself to a dish of porridge from a still-steaming pot, was Mayor Branders. The four faux adventurers slowly pulled themselves out of their cots, wandered over to the table, and took their seats. To his credit, Mayor Branders waited until everyone had served themselves before speaking.

"I do not care for adventurers," he said, his voice thick, and rougher than the previous day. It certainly made sense; he'd been doing ample shouting of commands when he restored order after the attack. "I never have. I see them as flippant, uncaring folk. They ride into town, slay a few monsters, spend some gold, hit on our bar staff, then float on to the next encounter. They have no roots, no ties, no sense of obligation."

The other four focused on their porridge, holding back the words of agreement they wanted to speak. Mayor Branders had the same impression of adventurers as any of the regular folk, the same they'd had only a week ago.

"So, when an advisor came to me, suggesting the idea for a tournament to draw them in, bleed them dry, and then swindle them out of prizes, I'm ashamed to admit, I allowed myself to be won over. I resisted at first, but, because of my prejudice against your kind, I let my mind be clouded by greed. It seemed like a victimless scheme in that it would only annoy adventurers, not decent people like those who lived in my town."

The group's silence continued, broken only by the occasional sounds of porridge entering mouths.

"Yet today, I find myself impossibly indebted to the very folk I thought to fleece. Without the adventurers, this town would be nothing but blood and ash. Every one of my 'decent people' owes their lives to the efforts your kind put forth yesterday. This is the sort of debt I cannot ever hope to repay, even if I possessed all the gold in Solium."

It was Thistle who spoke next, Thistle who had to speak next. The others didn't trust themselves to play this right, neither their minds to understand the situation, nor their tongues to find the right words. Only the tiny gnome could speak for them; only he had the talent and the respect.

"I'm going to make a guess that you don't intend to have this talk with every adventuring party in town."

"No, I do not," Mayor Branders confirmed. "There will be an official release of thanks, and I will work behind the scenes to make good on what I owe. It will not come overnight, but I promise you, Appleram will one day be a haven to every adventurer looking for a place to rest their head. Fair prices, safe accommodations, everything we can do to make their lives easier. However, I came to speak with you all because you hold a different debt over me. Not as a mayor, but as a father. You saved my children's lives."

"It is literally part of the job," Thistle assured him. "A paladin who won't help defenseless children is unworthy to wear the title, and won't for long once his god gets wind of it."

"Knowing your motivations doesn't preclude me from repaying what you've done for me. First off, you've won the Dagger Throwing event and are entitled to the prize chest."

"I never—"

"We both know you had the skill to make it, and you're the only one who never technically missed the throw. This is my jurisdiction as tournament official, and I'll hear nothing more about it. As a paladin, you are obliged to respect the rules and laws of a city, correct?"

"It's a little less defined than that, but you've got the gist of it right," Thistle admitted.

"Then the matter is settled." Mayor Branders paused to take another scoop of porridge from the pot. A man his size could put away half the pot, were he so inclined. "Now, I asked around a bit and learned you lot came into town looking for supplies. Lost what you had in a goblin raid. Thistle and the woman with the axe need armor. Anyone else?"

"I could use something light," Eric spoke up. Much as he loved his newfound freedom, he wouldn't mind having a barrier between his flesh and enemy blades next time fighting started.

"Light, huh? I'll see what I can do. I've got people working on something special for your warrior and something appropriate for you, Thistle. Now, as for weapons, does anyone need anything?"

"I could use a set of decent daggers," Thistle said.

Mayor Branders eyed the set on his hips carefully. "Seems like what you've got is beyond anything I'd be able to provide."

"These belong to Sierva, another adventurer," Thistle explained. "She loaned them to me for the last round of the tournament, and in the chaos that followed I had to use them. As soon as I find her, they return to her possession."

"Quite respectable of you," Mayor Branders noted. "All right then, I'll find our best blacksmith and put him on it. Anyone else?"

"I need a weapon," Grumph said, his rough voice somewhat muted. He was loath to pick up a melee item, but he had to face the fact that he simply didn't have enough magic to handle every situation with spells. Yesterday's battle had illustrated his need for something to knock attackers back with. If he hadn't had to waste magic creating his energy weapon, he'd have had more power to use helping others.

"Right, you're the wizard." If Mayor Branders felt any curiosity about the request, or the fact that it came from a half-orc boasting magical skills, he kept it to himself. "Staff, dagger, or something else?"

"Blade," Grumph replied. "One-handed, sharp, and sturdy."

"I see no problem with that. In fact, I may be able to get you something quite nice. That's weapons and armor, then. Anything else you lot need, aside from the basic provisions and horses?"

"No," Thistle said, speaking immediately. "You have already been more than generous. I feel we will owe payment for what has been promised as it is."

"You try to pay me and I'll throw you in a cell," Mayor Branders informed them. He finished off his second bowl of porridge and rose from the table, extricating himself with great care so as not to jostle those near him. "I'll need two days to get everything in order for you. Can you spare the time?"

"We can," Thistle informed him. "Time to rest would be helpful, and I must locate Sierva to return her daggers."

Mayor Branders nodded. "Right, then. See you in the morning, two days from now. I might send people by to get measurements, so if you leave, let the innkeeper know where you're going."

"Certainly," Thistle promised.

With that assurance, the mayor of Appleram stepped out the door, leaving the party alone for the first time all morning.

"I didn't see that coming," Eric said.

"Me neither," Gabrielle agreed. "Good thing the mayor is a decent guy. After the tournament trickery, I thought he'd be a real rogue."

"Kind, maybe. Smart, certainly," Grumph told them.

"Grumph is spot on," Thistle concurred. "Make no mistake, we should be quite thankful for the mayor's generosity; however, do not take his actions as totally altruistic."

"What is he getting out of giving stuff away?" Eric asked.

"Favor from the adventurers. Yesterday, immediately after it became obvious he was trying to hoodwink everyone, he was given a firsthand glimpse of how dangerous adventurers can be when rallied together. Now, they're riding a battle high, short on coin, and easily could be swayed to believe he was a corrupt mayor in need of sword-dispensed justice. By making overtures of apology, he sets the tone before anyone else has a chance to, minimizing the odds of receiving several broke adventurers' wrath."

"But he said he was only meeting with us," Gabrielle pointed out.

"And surely he meant it, but he'll have some communication with the others, via proxies or messages. We will be the symbol he holds up in front of them: the paladin who saved his children, and his party, are the first to receive the mayor's apologies and some recompense. It's rather impressive, actually. The man is a skilled politician."

"So, are we going to do anything to stop him?" Eric asked.

Thistle raised a small eyebrow. "Why would we stop him?"

"Because he's lying to everyone."

"So?"

"What do you mean '*so*'?" This time, it was Eric's turn to make an expression of surprise, his eyes widened slightly.

"I mean, who cares if he's lying?" Thistle countered. "If a man claims to love children, builds orphanages to help them, saves them from trouble, gets them food when they are hungry, and all the while secretly hates the devil out of children, what does the lie matter? Actions are more important than motivations. Mayor Branders wants to give us what we need, what *our town* needs, for us to pull this off, and he inadvertently helps our cause by making examples out of us. We get gear, reputation, and credibility when we arrive in Solium. The other adventurers will get kind treatment as well, plus a few bits here and there. Mayor Branders gets a town not swarming with angry adventurers. Whether he does these things out of the goodness of his heart or not, they still lead to positive outcomes. That's what matters most."

"You are strangely pragmatic about this stuff, for a paladin," Gabrielle noted.

Thistle gave a slight shrug and dipped a spoon back into his porridge. "No one gave me a codex on how to do this job, so I'm just swinging my sword in the dark."

"Seeing as yesterday, you helped save some kids, risked your own life countless times, and aided in halting a demon attack, I think you're doing pretty good so far," Eric said.

"It's a start," Thistle said, then turned his attention to finishing breakfast while it was still warm.

*   *   *

The day wore on slowly, leaving the group to linger about the inn while resting. After lunch, Thistle left to lend aid at the makeshift medical tents that had been set up near the arena. Many had been kept from the grasp of death already; although they still needed ample healing before they would be whole once more. It was good practice, aside from being a good deed, and it was helping Thistle learn something important for any adventurer: his limits. The divine magic he drew from Grumble was far from infinite; in fact, he could exhaust it in minutes if he healed continuously.

Thistle was meditating on this as he walked back toward the inn, so lost in thought that he nearly missed the voice calling to him.

"Well, well, I used to have a pair of daggers just like that." The tall figure approaching him stood out on Appleram's dusty roads. It was taller than most of the crowd around it, for one, and the elongated ears were certainly an oddity amongst the humans scurrying about. The figure met with Thistle in front of a small wooden building, the shop of a fletcher, judging by the sign on its door.

The gnome glanced upward, and a smile lighted on his small face. "Sierva, you look well."

"As well as can be expected after a demon attack." She brushed her hand on her trousers; the leather armor had been left behind this day. Without it obscuring her form, it was evident how fetching she was by human standards. By an elven gauge, she carried too much muscle and breast, and of course, no dwarf would have looked twice at her, as dwarves were notorious for appreciating women low to the ground and powerfully strong. Thistle, being a well-traveled gnome, noted her beauty with a clinical interest then filed it away in his mind. His standard of beauty had been set by his wife, and no form this side of the heavens would ever take its place.

"I'm glad you found me; I've been wanting to return these." Thistle unfastened the belt clinging to his hunched waist and offered up the daggers. "Apologies for abusing your generosity. Things just got too hectic for me to find you afterwards."

"I never doubted you'd bring them back to me," Sierva assured him, accepting the pair of blades. "Though, I wouldn't have blamed you for trying. These are the best pair I've ever crafted."

Thistle's face tilted in surprise. "You made them?"

"I dabble in smithing, as well as a few other crafting trades," she explained. "In my experience, making enchanted items is far easier than finding someone who has what you want."

"Aye, I can see how that would be. Perhaps I'll encourage our wizard to take up such hobbies as well."

"Your wizard, he's a half-orc, right?"

Thistle nodded, keeping his emotions concealed in the shadows of his mind. He liked this woman, and hoped she was not about to say something to change that.

"That's rather unique. And you had others in your party as well, didn't you? An axe-wielder, and a swordsman, if I recall correctly." Sierva ran the belt across her waist as she spoke, fastening the buckles and adjusting the position of the sheathed daggers resting against her legs.

"You know quite a bit about my friends," Thistle noted.

"You and your friends know quite a bit about demons, from what I've heard," Sierva countered.

For a moment, silence stood between them, an unwelcome guest shuffling its feet on the dirty Appleram road. Thankfully, it was sent away quickly, as Thistle let a wide grin grace his face and decided to push the conversation onward.

"Shall we stop with the dancing and speak plainly? You want to know what we've learned about the demons."

"That, and I wouldn't mind hearing how you acquired the knowledge, either," Sierva added.

"I expected as much. What's in it for us?"

"A sharing of information," Sierva offered, her expression friendly, but her words careful. "You tell us what you know, we tell what we know. This wasn't the first demon attack, and I'd like to get to the bottom of it."

"It's a start," Thistle said. "Where and when shall we meet?"

"Let's have dinner. My party has booked a private room at one of Appleram's more pleasant restaurants, The Keening Wyvern. We can sit, eat, drink, and talk. Sundown work?"

"Sundown is fine," Thistle assured her.

*   *   *

Grumph and Gabrielle had gone to squeeze in a bit of training after Thistle left to help the wounded, so Eric spent his morning walking the streets of Appleram. He did this partly in an effort to stretch his tired muscles, but it was also to become more aware of his surroundings. Eric liked knowing where obstacles were, the locations of blind alleys, and places he might duck into should a need for hiding arise. In his guard days, he'd assessed these proactively, making sure he knew spots that might be used against him. Now, he wasn't entirely sure what motivated him to make these mental maps, only that he felt more secure after becoming familiar with a place. It was why he'd known the arena so well, and that had paid ample dividends.

As his feet carried him along the worn road that linked Appleram's various establishments, he became aware of a strange discrepancy from the days prior. Before he had been glanced at by the townsfolk in the same way one might view a barrel in the path. It was there, it shouldn't be bumped into, and there might be something worth taking from it, were one the thieving sort. Today, they were giving him a wide-berth, stealing glances, and spitting out words in hushed whispers. Eric was no longer a barrel to them, which he viewed as an improvement, but they weren't acting like he was a traveler either. If anything, they were treating Eric like he was… an adventurer.

He tried to shake off the idea, but as soon as it entered his mind, it took root, feeding off the fertile soil of Eric's own observations. Their behavior fit, not just based on what he'd seen others do when adventurers came through Maplebark, but also based on what he'd done. They were curious, hesitant, and more than a little on edge at his presence. But that was crazy! Eric wasn't an adventurer, not really. He was only a crappy guard playing a part. Sure, it was a positive sign that he was fooling them, but still…

Was he still playing a part? Eric stopped in his tracks, nearly causing an old woman behind him to crash into his back, a disaster only avoided thanks to the distance she'd kept from him. He'd been so frantic with fear and excitement the previous day that he'd never paused to evaluate his actions. In the span of less than an hour, he'd eluded guards, broken into a secure building, lied to more guards, and fought demons. That sure sounded like an adventurer's afternoon. Even if he'd paused for the merest of seconds to consider what the person he was pretending to be should do he could have written it all off as part of the act, but that pause had never come. His actions, from the best to the worst, had been all impulse. He'd done what he, Eric the guard, thought was best at every turn.

When he began walking again, it was with a renewed vigor. Eric needed to move, needed to feel his body bend to his will. It was the only way to get out of his head and right now, he needed that space. He wasn't quite ready to face the revelation looming over him. He wasn't sure how one even got ready for that sort of thing.

All he was certain of was that it felt good to move quickly, so that's what he did.

*   *   *

Gabrielle swung her axe rhythmically, focused on nothing but the timing. Not the strength of the blow, not the angle of the blade, none of it. This was about feeling comfortable with the heft of the weapon in her hands, about learning how each muscle through her back and shoulders worked during various parts of the swing.

Soon, she would add attention to form, making certain she knew how the grain of the wood should feel against her palm, and how the tug of the axe should pull on her arms. Soon, but not quite yet.

Grumph sat a few yards away, the book of spells resting open in his lap. The two of them were at what remained of the arena, which had fallen into debris and splinters not long after the last demon was beaten. The hurried, shoddy construction had barely held together for the fight; once time went to work on the weakened supports, all but the sturdiest bits collapsed. Despite this, the arena's location was remote from the town, and there weren't many people eager to linger about, so it made for a peaceful training facility. There were others sprinkled about, but they kept enough distance to allow Grumph and Gabrielle to focus.

Not that focus was helping all that much. Despite his best efforts and several hours' concentration, Grumph was no closer to making the final spell in his book work. He understood most of the components presented, but there was something he was missing, something that made it all fit together. At first, he thought it required more contemplation, but the longer he sat without progress, the more he suspected he had reached his limits as a pretend wizard. The real ones trained under other mages, learning magic from the very basics. He'd done exceptionally well to fake it through four spells; perhaps this was the gap that only training would be able to bridge. Four would be enough to sell his cover, he hoped. His only other option was to find a spell caster to teach him, and that was assuming he even had the potential to learn. Grumph had poured enough mugs of ale for drunken wizards to know that very few were able to master every level of magic. The vast majority of them hit a wall that was nearly impossible to break through. It was possible that this was his.

"You going to sit there and read all day or you going to actually cast a spell?"

Grumph glanced up to find Gabrielle staring down at him, skin shining in the sun thanks to the coat of sweat she'd worked up. The blade of her axe was on the ground and she was leaning against the shaft as she rested. From the heaviness of her breathing, Grumph estimated she'd be able to start swinging again in mere moments. The young woman's progress was remarkable.

"Sit," Grumph sighed, closing the book. "Last spell is beyond me."

"What about the others?"

"Them, I can cast."

"I know you *can* cast them, I'm asking why you *aren't* casting them," Gabrielle said. "Training is training, whether it's an axe, a bow, or mystical arts. Doing something over and over will make you better at it."

Grumph readied a retort then swallowed it. She made a sound point. He'd been looking at magic as somehow different from the other pursuits he'd undertaken in his life, but there was no reason it should be. If he applied hard work and constant drilling, he could improve at it. Perhaps this was even the method needed to overcome his lack of understanding on the final spell.

"Good point," Grumph admitted, pulling himself out of his sitting position and reopening his book. He marched over to a part of the demolished arena that had once held practice dummies. A few remained, battered and broken, but still somewhat recognizable as humanoid in shape.

With a few flicked gestures and a mumbled word, Grumph hurled a bolt of magical cold right into one dummy's center of mass, engulfing part of it in a sheet of ice. He then stepped to the side, took aim, and repeated the feat once more. Gabrielle was right: one improved through practice.

And Grumph had catching up to do.

16.

The Keening Wyvern was an actual restaurant, not an inn with a bar and kitchen attached. It stood three stories tall and offered private rooms for dining, drinking, or whatever else one might care to indulge in. It was crafted from thick, dark wood that seemed to glow in the light of the candles that illuminated the rooms. The tables were set with actual tablecloths, rough though they were, and silverware was laid out next to the plates in an orderly fashion, the way one might expect at a formal occasion.

A place such as this could have never survived in Maplebark. Only the mayor would be able to afford it regularly, and he had his own dining hall that was of comparable splendor. No, this was the sort of establishment that was only able to thrive in a town with lots of adventurers funneling through, dropping their gold as easily as they dropped the indigenous creatures they happened to encounter in the wild.

Grumph, Thistle, Gabrielle, and Eric all took in the sights of the restaurant as they entered, making note of various bits that interested them. It was quite impressive and served to make them wish they had clothing slightly more suited to its grandeur instead of the dusty traveling clothes they were adorned in.

If the woman working the front took issue with their garb, she kept it well hidden. She led them up the polished staircase to the third floor then down the sprawling hallway toward an open door. Already seated in the room were Sierva, a human male with copper-colored hair, and a dwarf with a large club strapped to his back. Though they'd shed their armor, Sierva's companions were easily recognizable from the tournament.

Sierva rose upon spotting her friend, offering a wide smile. "Thistle, glad to see you once more. Please, won't all of you join us?"

The group obliged, sitting in chairs across from the other three and getting comfortable. In the time it took them to get settled, the woman who had led them up slipped away, shutting the door softly behind her.

"Well then," Sierva said once everyone was seated. "I believe we should start with introductions. I am Sierva, as Thistle knows, and these are my companions: Galdrin and Chuff. Galdrin is the tall one, and Chuff has the beard."

"Pleased to meet you," Galdrin greeted. His voice was more measured than it had been the previous day, which was understandable since he was no longer rallying troops against a demon attack.

"Greetin's," Chuff said. He sounded much the same, but that was par for the course. Conventional dwarven behavior tended to present its broad emotional range in subtle, understated ways. To an untrained observer, dwarves might consistently sound the same, but to a fellow dwarf, there was a symphony of feelings hidden amongst the inflections of words and twitches of the eyes.

"Likewise," Thistle replied. "My companions are Grumph, Gabrielle, and Eric." As he spoke each person's name, they raised their hands in a half-wave, half-greeting gesture. "We're journeying to see King Liadon, since we have a summons from him." Thistle knew he was offering information they hadn't asked for, but he was determined to cement their story with as many people as he could, no matter how inconsequential they might be.

"Liadon is fond of tasking adventurers with dangerous work," Galdrin noted, giving his head a slight shake. "May I ask what you did to earn such an honor?"

"We killed a brood of kobolds that were harassing a town, saving a royal merchant in the process. The summons was his reward to us." This time, it was Eric who spoke. Before the meeting, it had been agreed that they would seem suspicious if only Thistle seemed to know about their story. Spreading out the details would help their facade.

"Kobolds? Do yerself a favor, when you gat to the kingdom, lead with the demon slayin'," Chuff advised. "If you go in wit a kobold summons, ye'll get nothin' but cellars full o' rats for the first month." Despite the dwarf's strange dialect, most of the table was able to put together his meaning.

"We thank you for your advice," Thistle replied. "And since you've broached the subject we're all here to discuss, shall we talk about demons?"

The mood of the room quickly shifted. Gone was the flippancy and polite humor; in its place hung a cloud of severity. Sierva leaned forward, setting her elbows on the table and resting her chin atop her knuckles.

"I want to know everything you've seen so far. Leave out no details concerning the demons, for even the smallest one could be the clue we seek."

"Pardon me, but I believe we came here for an information exchange, not a giveaway," Thistle pointed out.

"You have my word that we will tell you what we know after, but I want your memories pure. There is a chance my information could taint your recollections, so I beg you to trust my promise and speak first."

Thistle weighed his options. He liked Sierva and she'd shown him nothing but reasons to give her the benefit of the doubt. Still, his minion experience hollered in the back of his mind, urging him to remember that words are often forgotten, and promises easily broken. To trust was foolish, and worse, dangerous. But he needed what they knew. In the last two places they'd stopped, there had been demon attacks. Whether it was coincidence, or they were occurring all over the kingdom, it would be foolish to presume these beasts would be the last his party would meet. Better forearmed with all the knowledge they could muster. Besides, under it all, he got a feeling from Sierva that put him at ease. Whether it was intuition, or the legendary paladin capacity for sensing goodness, he didn't know; he just decided to take a gamble and trust it.

"Very well," Thistle said at last. "We will tell you everything we encountered at the goblin camp where we were captured, as well as what we each experienced at yesterday's tournament." He turned to Gabrielle, who sat next to him, and gave a subtle nod of his head. Gabrielle cleared her throat once, adjusted her position in the chair, and began to speak.

"After the goblins took us, we were stripped of our weapons and put into cages…"

*   *   *

By the time the story chain had passed through Gabrielle, Eric, Grumph, and looped back to Thistle, dinner had been served and largely consumed. Sierva's party had clearly spared no expense, ordering several platters of various grilled meats, ample bowls of vegetables, and even bottles of wine. It made the tale-telling go much more pleasantly, and as Thistle finished his story of being stuck in a demon's throat, the rest of the table listened with full bellies and open ears.

"Sounds like quite a harrowing experience," Sierva said. "I commend you for keeping your head. If not for the distraction you provided, we might have lost many more adventurers before that monster was slain."

"I pride myself on keeping a level head," Thistle replied. "Now then: you've heard all we know. The time has come for you to speak."

"Very well. What I have is more rumor than knowledge, but rumor that has persisted long enough that it has begun the ascension to the rank of legend," Sierva opened. "Over the past several millennia, the demon eggs have appeared only a handful of times. In each known occurrence, they hatch, release some variation of infernal monsters on our plane, and kill everyone within a defined area before vanishing."

"Wait, that's not right," Gabrielle said. "Demons kill until they're slain or banished. They don't just stop and go home."

"Normal demons, no, but, as we already know, these are a special breed," Sierva reminded her. "Usually, demons are summoned through gates or magic, not hatched from gem-eggs, and rarely do they show the sort of tactics and teamwork exhibited by the ones you have encountered so far. These demons are different, special, and their method of destruction is just one aspect of it."

"You said these types of demons had appeared before. When and where?" Thistle asked.

"The reports are scattered, chiefly because survivors of these incidents are so rare," Sierva explained. "It is my theory that the attacks have actually happened far more frequently than we realize, but because no survivors were left, it's been impossible to identify the demons as the killers."

"All right then, let's gloss past the wheres and whens, and jump right into the meat of it: why? What you've described is more like a wizard's blast than a demon attack. They appear in one area, kill all they see, and then retreat to some unknown location. That suggests a targeted strike, not demon slaughtering," Thistle said.

"He's a quick one," Galdrin said, pausing from enjoying the last of the giant-snake fritters.

"Quick, and correct," Sierva added. "Yes, Thistle, you and I arrived at the same conclusion. From the way the eggs appear, to how the demons attack, it all points to a single conclusion: these are effectively bombs, sent to wipe out specified targets. Even yesterday, we saw it at work: despite the plethora of demons released, not one of them ventured outside the tournament arena, despite all the townsfolk so close at hand. The people who fled past its borders reported seeing the small demons chase them to the edge, then turn around to find prey inside the grounds."

"Maybe I'm missing something, but what does this really tell us?" Eric asked.

"Nothing, unfortunately," Thistle said, letting out a small sigh. "We now have a better idea of the purpose of the demon eggs; however, we have no idea why the goblin camp, or the tournament, was targeted. One could argue that we're the thread connecting them. Then again, in both attacks, no demon made any attempt to target us. At the camp, they went after the goblins first, and in the tournament, it was a general melee. If the eggs were for us, the demons should have made turning us into corpses their first priority. Even with as much as we know, that knowledge still leaves us with no clue as to why they're appearing."

"I must, sadly, agree," Sierva said. "I'd hoped that a key to understanding the attacks would be buried in your observations, yet it seems this mystery remains unsolved. All we can do is continue searching for answers. I do thank you for your time, at least. I'm sorry to have imposed on you and not delivered results."

"Dinner was thanks enough," Grumph said, rising from the table. The others followed his lead and the room became a bit chaotic as hands were shaken and formal goodbyes exchanged.

When Thistle went to bid farewell to Sierva, she handed him a small bundle wrapped in burlap.

"What's this?"

"A gift, as a way to say thank you and good luck," Sierva said. Most of the others had headed into the hallway, stretching their legs after such a filling meal. The elf and gnome were all that remained in the room of nearly-empty plates.

"I cannot accept it, you've already been too generous," Thistle objected.

"Please, I insist. You've shown us a great deal of trust when you weren't obliged to; this is merely a token of my appreciation. Besides, we have to look out for others of our kind."

Thistle tilted his head a few slender degrees off center. "Our kind? We're clearly not of the same race, so I take it you mean you're actually a paladin?"

Sierva said nothing at first, merely standing back to her full height and looking down at Thistle with a smile.

"Your story hangs together well, but remember that real adventurers would brag more about the kobolds they slayed, adding detail and embellishment whenever possible. Don't fault yourself for making a misstep; it takes practice to get accustomed to such deception."

With that, she was gone, leaving Thistle alone in the room, gripping his gift with uncharacteristic intensity as he watched her gather up the rest of her party and head back toward the stairs. Were one exceptionally perceptive, they could make out a few muttered words passing his lips just before he left the room.

"Aye. *Our* kind."

*   *   *

Russell stretched his back, a series of small pops echoing from his vertebrae. He took a moment to remove his glasses and wipe them on his shirt. They were ill-fitting, and his eyelashes would begin smudging them the moment they were donned. This resulted in the Sisyphean task of endlessly cleaning them, an annoying activity that Russell privately regarded as excellent training for dealing with tabletop players. Minor comfort and vision attended to, he resumed his role as GM and began the narration.

"After many hours of pitched battle, you finally manage to tear through the last of the ogres in the encampment. I'll roll up loot later tonight and let you all decide amongst yourselves how to disperse it. Your characters can take a rest in the now corpse-filled enclosures, and we're going to call the game here for the night."

"Come on, just roll us loot now. We want some of that sweet, sweet gold," Terry egged on. His plump hands clutched a mechanical pencil, one that was practically vibrating in excitement as he spoke. He loved loot like the rogue he'd rolled; any delay in receiving his payout was deemed unacceptable.

"Calm down, it's not going to be a lot," Russell informed him. "This was a watch post, filled with scouts and messengers, not guards. Why do you think you were able to beat them so easily?"

"Because we know how to bring the pain!" Glenn leapt up from his chair, thrusting his fist into the air to illustrate his point. For someone who'd only managed to throw a few paltry sleeping spells in the battle, he seemed to have no problem laying claim to what he considered his share of the glory.

"That's bullshit," Mitch piped up. Russell had been wondering how long it would take for him to find something to object to. "You're just trying to keep us gear-starved by nerfing the loot. We took out a whole ogre post, there's no way they don't have at least a few magical items."

"If they had powerful items, wouldn't they have used them on us?" Tim's eyes studied the map, a serious expression on his slender face, replaying the battle in his head with exceptional detail. "We're not that high of a level, and we tore through them without taking much damage, so it sure seems like they wouldn't have very good equipment."

"Stop being a GM kiss-ass," Mitch snapped. "Clearly, the good stuff is hidden away, awaiting conquering adventurers to find it."

"Yeah! There has to be a cache of items somewhere. Maybe we could all roll our own independent searches and see what we come up with." The greedy glint in Terry's eyes spoke to the discrepancy in what his character would find versus what would be reported to the party.

"If not weapons, then maybe a few more ogres still hiding from the fight that we could finish off," Glenn suggested.

Russell took a deep breath, then gathered every scrap of composure he could muster and addressed the group. "Listen, we've been over this again and again: the module is a realistic setting. That means, among other things, no random loot rolls. If you want to find gear from a fight, it's going to be used against you first. These ogres didn't have much; they were a paltry scouting outpost that likely would have surrendered if you'd even tried a bit of diplomacy. They had little and you killed them, so now that little belongs to you."

"What about the tournament we could have gone to?" Tim asked, his voice filled with genuine curiosity rather than wheedling discontent, a rare and wonderful change for the GM.

"Yes, the Appleram tournament had lots of gear, not to mention gold you could have won," Russell confirmed. "But you all decided to ignore the invitation and go a different path, set on hunting in ogre lands."

"Oh, whatever. Like the tournament would have been any fun," Mitch said, adding a derisive snort at the end of his sentence. "You said it was all competition, no killing. Why the hell would we go in for that?"

"How about you just give us the loot we would have gotten from the tournament?" Terry suggested, nodding his round head enthusiastically at the mere thought of the idea.

"Forget it. This is the path you chose, and these are the consequences of that choice. You find what you find. End of discussion." Russell might have been a bit more forgiving if he hadn't so been looking forward to running the tournament. It was, hands down, one of the coolest parts of the module he was using. But instead, the party had decided that competition without killing was stupid and had gone off in a whole different direction.

It really was a shame. He had hated having to scrap the tournament.

17.

Mayor Branders might have been a cunning politician, and a bit ruthless when it came to organizing tournaments, but no one could say he didn't keep his word. When Eric rose two days after the tournament, a little ahead of the others as habit from his old life, he found the mayor already waiting outside their door. The sizable man had a single bag slung over his shoulder, one with arcane runes etched into the fabric. With him were five attendants, all still rubbing sleep from their eyes while trying to pretend they were wide awake and ready to go. Eric felt for them; they must have risen hours before dawn to be waiting when he emerged.

"Mayor," Eric greeted, clasping the rough hand of the town's overseer and shaking it. "Pleasure to see you this morning."

"Pleasure is all mine." Mayor Branders took care not to press too hard on the smaller man's fingers. He wasn't so arrogant that he thought he could easily injure an adventurer; however, he didn't want to give insult by trying. "If you'd be so kind as to rouse the rest of your friends, I've come by to deliver the goods you requested."

"Certainly." Eric headed back into the storeroom where the others slept and quickly pulled them out of their dreams with gentle, yet firm, shaking. In moments, he had everyone more or less up and ready to greet the world, though Gabrielle retained a grumpy expression even as the mayor and his attendants entered.

They took a seat at the table where breakfast would be served while the party stayed on their beds. Seating in a place like this was a matter of finding a spot to plop down at; there was no sense of formality to be found.

"I won't beat around the bramblebush," Mayor Branders announced, undoing a clasp on the strangely-designed bag and pulling open the top. "As you all know, I've come to make good on my promise and equip you with suitable gear. My attendants are here to help everyone get into their armor, as well as provide any other assistance you may need. Now, the bulk of your supplies and transport are outside being watched over, but I wanted to bring in the weapons and armor personally to make sure everything fit."

"Very kind of you, Mayor." Thistle avoided pointing out that the attendants would also serve as witnesses to his good deeds, no doubt with instruction to spread word throughout the town. He did this because it would have been in bad form to say something, and, more importantly, because the equipment they needed had yet to be doled out.

"First, the axe-wielder," Mayor Branders announced. He reached into the rune-covered bag and pulled out a small round shape. It was like a ball of fog clutched in his mighty hand: indistinct on the edges and shifting through the center. The mayor set the ball onto the ground and then quickly backed away. A loud *pop* filled the air, startling everyone save the mayor, who'd clearly been expecting it. Suddenly a set of armor was sitting where the ball had formerly been.

It was gorgeous stuff: red scales woven together to form interlocking plates. As Gabrielle studied it, she was struck by just how familiar the red color was. She'd seen it recently. It was associated with a memory that would haunt her until the day she finally died and perhaps for some while after.

"Is this... demon scale from the giant?"

"It is." If Mayor Branders felt any shame or strangeness at presenting her with the flesh of a monster that had turned fellow adventurers into corpses, it wasn't evident on his bearded face. "It's tough, pliable, and damn hard to hack through with anything short of a blessed object. The crafters in town have already been snatching up every bit of the scale they can get their hands on. Trust me, that armor will keep you safe."

"I do like the color," Gabrielle admitted, lifting the heavy gift from the ground to study it more closely. "Definitely adds a bit of intimidation."

"From what I've heard about you on the battlefield, you hardly need the addition." Mayor Branders allowed a rare smile to fall on his lips with that statement, then immediately turned stoic once more. "If it's acceptable, my attendant can help you get into it."

"Yes, yes, I think I'd like to try it on." Gabrielle's own face wore a sly, understated grin as one of the attendants hurried over to assist her. The blonde in blood-red armor. She rather liked the image that evoked in her mind. If reality could come close, she'd be quite content with her new ensemble.

"Next, the wizard's request for a weapon." Mayor Branders pulled out another misty ball from the bag, although this time, he set it on the table rather than the ground.

The popping sound was far more diminutive, a pleasant break for the adventurers' already abused ears, and then a blade sat on the table. It was somewhere between the length of a dagger and a short sword, bone-white in color and slightly curved toward the tip. Grumph rose from his seat and ambled over, studying the weapon with intense scrutiny as he did.

"Small demon's tail blade," he announced, picking up the weapon and turning it over in his hands.

"Quite right. You've seen firsthand how sharp and deadly those tails could be. Thought you might like to be on the giving end of that instead of the receiving," Mayor Branders explained.

Grumph gave a noncommittal nod, still turning the blade over in his hand. After a moment's more examination, he gripped the handle carefully and raised the bone-blade overhead. With one mighty swing, he brought it blazing down on the corner of the table. It passed through easily, seemingly without effort, and a small chunk of wood tumbled unceremoniously to the ground.

"Good blade," Grumph announced, pleased with the gift. "Thank you."

"It was well-deserved," Mayor Branders assured him. He reached into the bag once more and produced a sheath, which he handed to Grumph before turning his attention to Eric. "Now, you were a bit trickier."

"Do I not get demon armor, too?"

"I thought about it, I really did. The hide from the clawed ones is darn thick; it will make excellent armor. However, that material gets a touch inflexible when dried, and you wanted movement above defense. Thankfully, the glut of adventurers in my town means the tannery had been stocked to the brim with every kind of hide one can imagine." Mayor Branders pulled another mist-ball from the bag and put it down on the ground in front of Eric. "That included veilpanther flesh."

The ball popped away, revealing a thin, grey set of armor. Eric picked it up, shocked at how soft and pliable the fabric was. It felt more like cloth than armor, which wouldn't do him much good against more demons.

"Soft as it is, veilpanther hide is roughly as strong as toughened leather," Mayor Branders informed him. "Not useful for anyone who prefers chainmail or stronger, but a fair sight better than just the tunic on your back. Besides, veilpanther armor still holds of a bit of the monster's magic. It blends with the shadows perfectly and makes no more noise than a whisper when moving about. Perfect for someone who likes to get into places without being seen. Places like the tournament storage sheds, for example."

Eric jerked his head up in surprise, but the mayor gave him a small wink of reassurance. It seemed he knew Eric was the one who'd broken into the site, and he wasn't going to hold it against him. It was a small kindness, given what Eric's unlawful entry had accomplished, but it was still one he was grateful for.

"Your kindness is greatly appreciated. I'll try it on right now."

As Eric was set upon by a single attendant, Mayor Branders looked at the central reason for his outpouring of generosity, the small gnome who had been sitting there patiently while the others received their equipment. The mayor had trouble getting much of a read from Thistle, though whether this was due to the trademark stoicism of a paladin, or the slightly misshaped nature of his face, Mayor Branders was uncertain. What he did know was that the unassuming body this gnome had been given belied the courage and intellect housed within it. In another time, under different circumstances, he'd have tried with all his might to convince Thistle to stay and work as his right hand. The mayor didn't know it, but his mind and courage were among the set of traits that had endeared Thistle as a minion to countless other wielders of power.

He was also loyal, capable, and small enough to kick if he got uppity.

"Finally, I have armor and daggers for the savior of my children. I presumed that, as a paladin, you might not feel comfortable wearing demon armor or weaponry."

"Thank you for the consideration," Thistle replied. "While I'm not certain Grumble is too particular about those sorts of things, I'm happier not trying to chance it."

Mayor Branders pulled out three mist-balls this time, setting each one on the ground in succession. The first two turned into daggers: long, sharp tools that were well-made and honed for killing. The final ball made a loud *pop* before revealing a set of gleaming steel armor, sized perfectly for one of Thistle's stature and proportions.

"The armor has been mildly enchanted. It will offer a slight increase in resistance but, more importantly, it should conform to the nooks and bends of your body like fitted cloth. The daggers are mundane, but the finest I was able to procure."

"Your generosity overwhelms me," Thistle said, hopping from his perch and hobbling over to examine the wares. The daggers felt exquisite in his hands, second only to the ones he'd borrowed from Sierva. Polished, balanced, and actually made for hands his size, these would be true weapons when he wielded them, not mere slapdash tools of defense. The armor was also notably well-made, so much so that Thistle felt he'd look ridiculous wearing it. Who had ever heard of a gnome, a minion at that, in plated steel? Well, the kingdom of Solium would, once they arrived to serve the king. Best to get comfortable with the idea now; soon enough, he'd have to be selling others on it.

"I'd like to get suited up, if your people would be so kind as to assist me," Thistle announced. "We have a long ride ahead of us and the roads are perilous. Best to be ready for anything."

"Of course." Mayor Branders gestured and the remaining two attendants hurried over to help Thistle don his armor. "The remainder of the supplies you need have been loaded onto horses outside. When you're ready, you are all free to ride out of town."

"We cannot thank you enough," Thistle insisted, knowing full well that by the time they were ready to go, the town would be bustling with adventurers, all getting an eyeful of the mayor's kindness as they left.

"No, good paladin, I cannot thank you enough," Mayor Branders replied, knowing the same things as Thistle, but one thing more. He knew that, pageantry aside, he truly did intend to make good on his word and turn Appleram into a haven for well-meaning adventurers. He didn't begrudge these people the twinkles of doubt in their eye, even as they accepted his gifts. Mayor Branders was a man who came from working stock and considered himself one of them. He understood that actions, not words, proved the merit of a man.

This was a good start, but he had a long road of his own ahead of him.

* * *

The four adventurers who left Appleram that day, amidst the stares and curious whispers of adventurers and townsfolk alike, could scarcely have been recognized as the same foursome who'd traipsed along the road only days prior. For one, they were no longer dirty or road-weary; instead, they held themselves tall and proud atop their strong horses. For another, they were no longer clad in filthy clothes and clutching meager belongings. Whether it was the wild-eyed blonde in the blood-red scales, the tiny gnome in the gleaming plate, the stoic half-orc with the book clutched under his arm, or the lean human who made eyes water if stared at for too long, they were each an impressive sight to behold.

They encountered no resistance as they made their way out of Appleram, save perhaps for the occasional nod or wave from a fellow adventurer. Some of these were superfluous, but many were gestures of recognition, gratitude, or respect. In the melee of the demon's attack, there had been no time for formalities such as name exchanges, greetings, or even words. Still, when one was saved from a monster by a fellow warrior, that face tended to stick about in one's memory.

Despite lingering about long enough for breakfast and taking a slow, trotting exit out of town, the four travelers passed the last of Appleram's outlying farms before midday. With that, they were officially on the road, subject to the whims of the wild, and facing the possibility of danger at every turn. Even so, it was another hour into the ride, when the sun hung directly overhead and bore down on them with relentless intensity, that the first words finally exited their mouths.

"Think it's safe to slump down a bit yet?" Eric asked, his tone terse as the spasms from holding his spine in place threatened to make him yelp in pain.

"A bit more," Grumph instructed. "We need to leave strong."

"I know, I know; we want to be high-profile and easily recognizable in case anyone checks our story. I'm just not used to riding like this and it's killing my back."

"Hey, one of us is wearing much heavier armor than you and managing not to complain," Gabrielle piped up. "I think you can pull it together for another few miles."

"Says the girl who has more experience than any of us riding and holding proper posture," Eric replied, pain making him a touch more snappish than he might normally allow himself to be.

"We'll be on a proper forest road soon," Thistle said, pointing to the large patch of green in the distance. "Once we're in there, I think we can get more comfortable. If nothing else, there are wild animals about, and I'd hate for us to die on the road because we were too stiff to react properly, especially after coming all this way."

"That's actually something I wanted to bring up." Eric bit his lip a bit, this time not from the pain but from uncertainty. He wasn't quite certain how to broach this topic, yet he felt like it needed to be addressed. Better to do it clumsily than not at all. "After everything we did in Appleram, building up our profile and the like, is it possible that Maplebark might already be safe? I mean, we definitely made a name for ourselves, and no one will go looking for dead adventurers in Maplebark when they were fighting demons days later in Appleram."

Thistle nodded, causing a beam of sunlight to bounce off his new helm and momentarily blind Grumph, who snorted in annoyance. "I hit on the same conclusion yesterday. You're right; for all intents and purposes, we've probably removed Maplebark from being a potential target of the king's wrath."

The road filled with the sound of clopping hooves as Gabrielle abruptly jerked her horse to a halt. "Wait, what? If we saved

Maplebark already, then why are we going to Solium? We did what we set out to do."

"Please note, Gabrielle, I said we *probably* succeeded. That means we have very good chances of our families and friends not being killed if we die on the road. But there is still a measurable chance. Is 'probably' good enough when it comes to the lives of people you love?"

"Oh." Gabrielle squeezed the horse with her thighs and it began to move once more. "Sorry, I misunderstood."

"It's fine," Thistle assured her. "But I want to pose a question to you, something to ponder on this last leg of our journey. If we make it to Solium, pass off our deception, and complete whatever task King Liadon assigns us, what comes next?"

"Obviously, we'd go home," Gabrielle said.

"I'm not sure I want that." Eric's voice was clear and audible, yet somehow softer than they were accustomed to hearing. "My life back there was… unfulfilling. I'm not saying I want to be an adventurer — these last few days have been beyond terrifying — but I don't think I can go back to being the laughingstock of the guards. That's assuming your father would hire me back."

"My father would… you'd get a job." Gabrielle trailed off as she spoke, the full realization of what she was proposing hitting her. If she went back, the tug-of-war would begin anew. This time, it would be even worse, actually, because her father would spare no expense on keeping her safe. No more goblin vacations to help keep her mind steady. She'd be stuck in her prim and proper role with no release, no escape.

"Bear in mind, this all hinges on us actually surviving," Thistle reminded them. "A very thin possibility. I merely wanted to bring up the idea because, if nothing else, it will give us all something to hope for. Sometimes, on these journeys, having a dream at the end of it all is the only thing to keep you going."

"Sooner or later, you have to tell us how you know so much about adventuring," Eric said.

"Soon, but not now."

"After Solium." Grumph's rough voice surprised them all; they'd been lulled into a peaceful state by the conversation and sound of hoof beats.

Thistle stared at his old friend for some time before deigning to give a nod. "Aye, very well. If we make it through Solium, I'll tell you my whole story. Don't get too excited, it's not all that fascinating."

"Then why work so hard to keep it secret?" Eric asked.

"It's not secret; I don't really care who knows my past." Thistle turned his eyes away from his friends and set them on the path before them. "I just hate talking about it. Reliving it all is too… there are painful memories that I don't like to dwell on. But Grumph is right: if we make it through this, that's the least I can do. After Solium."

They rode in silence after that, intently listening for warning sounds and to the worries echoing in their own minds.

18.

The city of Solium announced its presence long before any traveler stepped through the mighty gates in the stone wall that encircled the city. It could be seen in the upkeep of the roads, how they were flat, clean, and showed few signs of wear. It showed in the increase of soldier stations positioned along the way and the decrease in wild animals or bandits that was a direct result of those stations. It could certainly be perceived in the increased road traffic, wagons and caravans and riders of all sorts commuting to the grand city. One could even see it in the farms they passed, all flying banners with the city's crest atop their house in a fervent attempt to let those that passed by know they were proud of where they lived.

Of course, the most obvious way Solium announced itself was with its massive towers jutting into the sky, visible from over a day's travel away. Legend said that the three towers had been fashioned by wizards of untold power ages back. This was true in that the wizards had fiddled with gravity enough to permit them to stand and added a few hidden dimensions inside, but, as with most things, the real work had been done by underpaid peasants who were immediately removed from the story. Glory and legend belonged to those who seized it; at least, they did in this kingdom.

By the time the shadow of the gates fell across Grumph's brow, his party was more than ready to be done with riding and also a touch sick of seeing the damn towers on the horizon. As weary as they were, even the travel-hardened four felt their eyes bulge a bit as the gates gave way and they entered the true city of Solium.

This was not just another large town; it was an entity all its own. The whole place seemed to have been made from stone: the roads, the buildings, even some of the signs directing travelers to assorted locations. The only wooden items in sight were the stalls that ran the length of the entrance road, each housing a vendor shouting louder than the last. Various wares hung from hooks in their stalls: weapons, shields, glowing gems, bottles filled with colorful liquids clearly intended to be potions. Most travelers were road-wise enough to know that real magical items weren't bandied about by street vendors looking to make a quick gold, but every day enough folks got swindled to keep the trade profitable for the vendors.

The other thing that amazed the adventurers from Maplebark was the amount of people packed into this city. Being from rural areas, they were accustomed to having plenty of room to move, even when in town. Here, the people skittered about, bounding through the roads with no concern for the horses or carriages bearing down on them. More than once, the adventurers would tense as an impending collision threatened to flatten a peasant, only to let out a sigh of relief as the pedestrians emerged unscathed, having darted aside at the last moment.

"Please tell me you know where we're going," Gabrielle said, looking over to Thistle. "I really do not want to try and navigate these streets longer than I have to."

Thistle nodded and pointed up ahead of them. "Our missive said to report to the castle. Judging by the large shape looming in the distance, and that sign we just passed, if we stay on this road, we'll come right up to it."

"Now we just have to try and avoid trampling anyone along the way." Eric jerked his horse to the side, narrowly missing a small, half-elf child who scurried between the horse's legs.

"First of many hurdles," Grumph replied. From the way his sharp, yellow teeth were showing, it seemed like he was either trying to threaten everyone or just make a joke. Perhaps it was both.

"All too true," Thistle agreed. "But we've made it this far, and I think we should be proud of that fact. We only need to receive our task, try and survive it, and get out of this town."

"He makes it sound so easy," Eric said, winking at Grumph.

"Oh no, we'll probably die in the process, but since that's been the situation for so long now, it hardly seemed worth mentioning," Thistle said.

His words rang true — truer than they'd been intended, likely — and the others had to admit that the constant threat of death was such a persistent companion, it almost felt like they should get it a horse. Regardless, they'd managed to get this far despite the odds. Perhaps luck would hold and see them through the final leg of their journey.

* * *

About a mile behind Thistle, Grumph, Gabrielle, and Eric, another foursome of adventurers traipsed along the road to Solium. These were far less reserved in their discussion as they rode the worn and weary horses that had been stolen from a peaceful city to the south. In fact, their voices were the loudest things audible halfway to the horizon. The other travelers gave them a wide berth;

adventurers in bad moods often led to sacked caravans or beaten townsfolk.

"I can't believe we had to run from the stupid guards," Mitchzelin complained, kicking his horse for no reason other than to feel the impact of his heel on flesh. "We lost half our traveling gear from that crap." He was adorned in armor made from bear and wolf hide, a single-bladed axe strapped to his back. First game be damned, he was going to play a barbarian.

"We stole from their town," Timuscor reminded him. "Which we didn't need to do. They only wanted a little bit of gold to trade, and we had more than enough after the ogre camp."

"Why would we buy what we could take?" Terriora asked. If there were ever a motto for rogues, that would have been a quite viable candidate. "Besides, you shouldn't care if we stole: you're a knight now. That's why we didn't let you re-roll a pally."

"I can still try to be good." Timuscor's defense was half-hearted at best; he'd grown weary of protesting the others' actions. It was easier just to let them do things their way. That was why he'd been a knight, instead of a paladin, this time: knights weren't obliged to speak up against moral injustices. Even when they really wanted to.

"At least I got to smoke a few of them with a fireblast," Glennvint said, gleefully reminiscing about the innocent guard's incineration.

"That was smart," Mitchzelin told him. "Last thing we need is them sending a rider ahead to get us in trouble with Solium. That's something *Russell* would totally do just to be a jerk." His acidic emphasis on Russell's name left no doubt of his sentiment toward the young man.

"That seems less jerky than it does us reaping the consequences of our actions," Timuscor pointed out.

"Kissass," Terriora mumbled, very much over his breath.

"Shut up. Look, do we even have a plan for when we get to Solium? We aren't exactly invited guests anymore," Timuscor said.

"This is the one time where *Russell's* emphasis on realism comes in handy," Mitchzelin said. "The missive our last group had still exists; the king is still expecting someone to show up. All we have to do is present ourselves and say we lost the scroll. No big deal."

"But what if he's already discovered our characters are dead? Or found someone else to do the job?" Timuscor asked.

"How would he already know about us dying in some shithole tavern half a kingdom away? That would be stupid. But yeah, he might have hired someone else to do the job; that seems like the kind of bullshit *Russell* would pull on us. Even that problem is easily solvable, though."

"How do you figure?" Terriora asked.

"Simple; we just find them, and work out a nice little compromise with diplomacy. Well, Glennvint's style of diplomacy, anyway." Mitchzelin let out a laugh at his own wit, one that was quickly echoed by Terriora and Glennvint as the meaning of his words sunk in. Timuscor tried to muster up a small chuckle, but it was pretty pathetic.

The other travelers, already a distance away from the adventurers, moved a bit further still.

* * *

The castle of Solium, home to King Liadon and central capitol of the kingdom, was an impressive sight to behold. Like the city itself, the castle was ringed in an outer stone wall with only a single set of gates to enter through. Along the walls stood a variety of soldiers with bows, staffs, and swords, clearly braced for any sort of threat that might present itself. The grounds leading up to the wall were covered in grass — the first bit of it Eric and the others had seen since entering the city — with only a single road leading up to the gates. Despite the lush greenery, not one person set foot on the grass surrounding the walls. Given the number of soldiers lining the road to the gates, it seemed a fair bet that walking on the grass was taboo, and earned a swift enough punishment to discourage even the most daring.

The four adventurers led their horses carefully along, taking their places in a line that ran down the road and up to the castle's wall gate. It seemed today was a popular day to visit the castle, or perhaps this was the routine and they had mismanaged their expectations. As they waited, Eric took note of the exchanges at the gate. It seemed a guard would interview one person in the group, that person would either talk or display a document, and then the guard would open the gates.

That pattern held until the fourth group, when the guard snatched the paper away, tore it in half, and beat the traveler across the shoulder with his polearm. The group was sent hurrying back up the road, past the other waiting travelers, and heading in the direction of Solium's gate.

"What do you think that was about?" Eric asked.

"Probably a forgery," Thistle said. "I'd wager the guards are checking for people that are known, expected, or have scrolls that authorize them to enter the castle. That fellow was likely trying to get in with fake papers."

"All that just to enter? Seems excessive," Gabrielle said.

"Perhaps, but it is the capitol of an entire kingdom. And it's not like there aren't ample folks with reason to sneak through the gates. Plenty of money to be made and havoc to be wreaked inside a castle, after all."

"Has it occurred to anyone else that we have no clue about the authenticity of the scroll in our possession?" Eric asked.

The group fell into a moment of dumbstruck silence before a snort of laughter from Grumph broke the spell.

"That would be funny," Gabrielle said.

"Aye, if we'd done all this and it turns out we're dealing with a forgery, that would be quite a surprise. A nice one, though, since it would mean our job was done."

"It would mean our job never needed doing," Gabrielle corrected. "And that we just wasted weeks of our lives."

"I wouldn't go that far. If nothing else, we got some nifty new equipment out of the bargain," Thistle reminded her. "That has to be us coming out ahead."

"Grumph burned down his bar," Eric reminded him.

A small frown ran along Thistle's shrunken face. "Aye, that part slipped my mind. Well then, I suppose we're back to hoping the scroll in my pack is the genuine article."

"From the looks of things, we'll find out in about three groups," Eric said, gesturing to the clusters of people ahead of them.

"Do we have a plan if it is a fake?" Gabrielle asked.

"As in, where do we go from here? I don't think so," Thistle said.

"No, as in, how do we get out of town without the guards trying to beat us?" Gabrielle clarified.

"Oh, that." Thistle paused for a moment and mulled over the idea. "I suppose 'run like hell and meet outside the gates' seems as viable a plan as we're going to get."

"Good plan," Grumph complimented.

*   *   *

King Liadon sat in his throne room, watching through the window as the procession of travelers made their way past the castle gates. He wasn't perched on the actual throne; that thing was far too uncomfortable. High-backed, forged from gold, and adorned with jewels in every conceivable nook or cranny, the throne had been fashioned with the intent of impressing all who laid eyes upon it, not providing lumbar support to the man who rested his ass upon it. Instead, he was seated on a small stool with a round, red cushion atop. Among the throne room's flowing, silk tapestries, white marble walls and floors, and golden trim, it stuck out like... well, like a stool in a throne room. It was comfortable, though, so the king kept it tucked away nearby when there were visitors and pulled it out when he was alone and in need of a seat.

Almost alone, at any rate. Next to him, standing well above the king even if he hadn't been seated on his stool, was Ardel, his most trusted advisor. Ardel was a half-elf, but the court tried not to hold that against him, mostly because he was also smart, capable, and unwaveringly loyal. The last part mattered more to Liadon than the others. Loyalty was rare, at least when dealing with other royals and aristocrats. He'd take a loyal dunce over an unfaithful genius any day. Thankfully, in Ardel, the king hadn't had to choose just one trait.

"We'll soon have enough adventurers for another expedition." Ardel's voice was soft, gentle, unassuming. It hid well the pools of dark resourcefulness concealed in his mind.

King Liadon nodded, his shoulder-length, blond hair catching on the long elven ears that stuck out from his head. "What does this make? Eleven?"

"Thirteen, sire." Unlike the king, Ardel kept his muddy brown hair trimmed short, almost the length of a soldier's. It drew attention to his ears, the short things that stuck out just a touch and ended in a misshapen-seeming roundness. His ears had none of the human simplicity, or the elven grace. It was for this reason that many half-elves kept their ears concealed, and it was for *that* reason that Ardel left his plainly on display.

"Thirteen, eh? That's a good number. Not as good as seven or eleven, but those expeditions didn't turn out any better, so perhaps thirteen is what we need. Have any failed to show up?"

"According to the guards at the gate, the next to last group checked in a few minutes ago: some adventurers who won their missive by slaying kobolds."

"Kobold slayers?" The king gave a sad shake of his head. It might have knocked his crown askew, had he been wearing one. It, like the throne, was suited for appearance, so it rested on the throne when Liadon didn't feel a need to impress anyone. "I almost pity them. That group likely won't make it past the entrance."

"Likely not," Ardel agreed. "But one never knows who the hands of fate will guide."

"Of course, of course; that's why we're grabbing all we can. What's the deadline on this last batch of missives, anyway?"

"Tomorrow at sunrise," Ardel said. He had no need to double check a scroll or notebook to recall this information. It was his duty to be abreast of all things his king might need to know.

"Very good. We'll do the briefing at noon. Oh, and have some riders ready to go if the last group doesn't arrive," King Liadon ordered.

"The usual instructions, sire?"

"Of course. If they failed to come, kill them. If they fell while en route, kill everyone responsible. Maybe a few extra too, just to send the message. Can't have the peasants getting ideas about killing people in royal employ. Adventurers are too useful." King Liadon turned his gaze back out the window, his eyes charting the movements of various riders. After a moment of observation, he spoke again.

"Oh, one more thing. Is the next batch of missives drawn up?"

"Yes, sire. They'll go out as soon as the thirteenth expedition starts."

"Send them out today," King Liadon instructed. "Lucky numbers aside, no sense in not getting expedition fourteen off the ground as soon as possible. We both know, odds are, these adventurers will likely be corpses before the next new moon."

"Yes, sire."

*   *   *

Despite their worrying, the process of getting through the castle gates had gone quite smoothly. Thistle handed a guard the scroll they'd acquired only a few short weeks ago, the guard had looked it over, then handed it back, and with that, they were ushered through onto the castle's grounds.

More grass ran along the landscape, but now, it was broken up into sections, with roads and various buildings in between. These roads ran in a complex, circular pattern with the castle standing at the center. It was a squat, grey cube of a building, almost aggressively unremarkable. It was certainly overshadowed by the presence of one of the three great Solium towers within the same grounds. To some, it would seem that the builders had no eye for aesthetic details. To those gifted with a bit more intelligence, they would understand that the castle was not meant to awe with ostentatiousness; it was meant to impress by being fortified and impregnable.

As Grumph and the others made it past the gates, they found themselves almost immediately greeted by another guard. This one wore less-imposing armor than the others, and actually permitted himself to smile a bit as he stopped the adventurers from moving forward.

"Good day," he greeted. "What business have you at the castle?"

"We were given a missive to come see the king for a task," Thistle told him. "You see, we defe—"

"Right, more for the expedition." The guard jerked his thumb to the left, pointing to a large, stone building further down the road. "Go over there and talk to the guard out front. He'll put your horses to the stables and set you up in a room. You should get your instructions sometime tomorrow. Until then, there's food, beds, and a training ring out back. Try not to break anything."

Eric opened his mouth to ask a follow-up question, but Thistle shook his head. The guard was done with them, already walking over to the next group coming through the gates. Eric pursed his lips, but kept silent, keeping pace as they headed over to the building where they'd been instructed to go. It was a bit insulting, to be treated so dismissively after everything they'd gone through to get here. Eric calmed himself by keeping in mind that they weren't coming in as heroes of Appleram, having helped thwart a demon invasion, but as mere kobold exterminators.

As they drew closer to the building, the sounds of battle reached their ears. From their perch on the road, they could make out several figures behind the building, swinging various weapons at one another. Many were using wooden implements; however, several had real blades in their hands as they attacked their opponents. From a glance, it appeared there were at least ten to fifteen people out there.

"Right then, so, a building full of adventurers," Eric surmised, words breaking free at last.

"Seems that way," Thistle agreed.

"Why, though? Another tournament?" Gabrielle asked.

"They don't need adventurers for a Solium tournament; that's where royals show their stuff," Thistle said. "I'd wager it's for a task too difficult or dangerous for a single party to handle."

"Or for competition," Grumph added.

"Aye, that might be it too, having us all compete for the same goal so that the king only has to reward one party."

"Is everyone out to screw adventurers?" Eric muttered.

"Seems that way," Gabrielle agreed. If it occurred to either one of them that only a short time ago they'd have laughed off such practices as what the troublemakers deserved, they both chose not to comment on it.

The party soon reached the building where, just as they'd been told, another guard was waiting out front. He helped them down, then called some attendants to bring their horses to the nearby stables. After checking their missive for confirmation, he directed them into the building to get settled.

Whatever it was being used for now, this place had clearly been constructed as barracks; the cold, grey floors, lack of decoration, and abundance of bunk rooms made that obvious. The guard showed them around. There was a communal dining area, where food would be served to them, a small stove for cooking if they felt so inclined, and three bathrooms, two of which had been designated for women. The training ground out back was expansive, an area of hard-packed dirt littered with wooden weaponry. When the tour was complete, which took so little time their horses were still standing outside, the guard showed them to a bunk room and told them to settle in.

It didn't take much encouragement for the adventurers to comply. Sparse and worn as the bunks were, they were still an incredible luxury after so many days of sleeping on hard ground beneath the stars. Add in that they wouldn't have to split into guard shifts, and slumber became such an exciting prospect that they almost bedded down right then and there. Almost, but not quite. Cushy as this was, it merely represented the last bit of peace before things grew dangerous once again.

Soon, too soon, they'd have to find out why the king wanted this many adventurers. With little discussion, each took up their weapons and headed out to the training ground. An afternoon of effort was highly unlikely to make any sort of real difference in the coming task. They would only improve by a fraction.

Still, if it was a fraction or nothing, each of them would take the fraction.

*   *   *

Later that day, a small caravan entered through the gates. It was manned by a slender grain farmer and his wife who had come to the castle to sell their harvest of rare Abstanial Silver grain to the royal brewers. The farmer was a regular at the castle, and if he looked a bit more nervous than normal when speaking to the guard, they thought little of it. After all, he was a small man in a big world. Fear likely overwhelmed him at every turn.

It was only after he had come through and had gotten directions from the greeting guard that the reason for his worry presented itself. Or, rather, themselves. From out of the back of his wagon emerged four adventurers, knocking his precious cargo from their armor as they set foot upon the ground. The last of them to emerge, a robe-wearing elf with a vicious gleam in his eyes, held a spellbook in his thin hands and kept his eyes locked on the farmer, waiting for the slightest hint of provocation.

"I told you we'd get in," Mitchzelin announced, spitting to get the taste of grain from his mouth.

"And all we had to do was threaten an innocent man," Timuscor said, his voice as heavy as his armor. He did his best to scoop the grain from his chestplate into the cart, but it was a losing battle.

"He's just an NPC, it doesn't matter." Glennvint's long, nimble fingers twitched against his spellbook, the desire to blast bucking against his limited restraint.

"Don't even think about it." Timuscor took a step over, putting himself between the farmer and Glennvint.

"Think about what?" Glennvint's attempt to feign innocence was so bad, it might as well have been a critical failure.

"Think about torching these two. They did everything we asked and got us in. You're not allowed to hurt them." Timuscor rested his hand on the hilt of his sword and locked eyes with the wizard.

"Timuscor, cut that paladin shit out. You're a knight. Glennvint, reign it in. We can't have fiery explosions or corpses raising suspicion." Mitchzelin finished cleaning off his armor and pointed to the couple on the cart. "They can run off, as long as they know we'll be coming after them if they say a word to anyone. And I highly doubt they want to see us again."

The farmer and his wife agreed whole-heartedly with that statement. As proof, the farmer whipped the reins on his horses and hurried away, desperate for distance lest they change their minds.

"We could've nuked them," Glennvint whined as he watched his targets escape.

"Forget them. We have bigger fish to fry," Mitchzelin instructed. His gaze fell on the stone building across the castle's courtyard, where several forms could be seen training and dueling against one another.

"Or, should I say, bigger adventurers."

19.

When the sun rose over the barracks, it found an empty practice field. The wooden weapons were stacked neatly against a stone wall, untouched since the day before. Inside, the various adventurers rose slowly, taking time to stretch, read spellbooks, or say prayers to their gods. Breakfast was served up in the dining hall, met with appreciative, yet silent, eaters. When the food was gone, the process of donning armor began. There was little discussion in any of the rooms, and no mention of doing some training before the sun grew too high. Today was not a rest day. Each party, even the newest among them, understood that. Today, they received their orders, and they needed to meet that challenge with preparation and readiness.

As the adventurers finished equipping and wandered out into the main area, they found the guard who'd shown them around waiting quietly. Taking the cue, they gathered near him and waited as other parties joined them. Soon, the entirety of the barracks had arrived and only then did the guard speak.

"Today, you will be addressed by our king," the guard said. He began walking as he spoke and motioned for the others to follow. They complied wordlessly.

"His majesty has seen fit to grace you with a royal task. You are all fortunate beyond words, and I can scarcely contain the envy that burns in my chest." Nice words aside, he didn't seem particularly jealous as he opened the barracks' door and led the way onto the castle's outer grounds.

"However, with such blessings also come responsibilities. As recipients of a royal task, it is your duty to see it fulfilled, even at the cost of your own life or the lives of your friends. The king has personally selected you out of the whole kingdom; it would be a far kinder fate to die while attempting success than to return a failure." The grounds were warm in the mid-morning sun, the last traces of dew already evaporating away in the burgeoning heat. They walked down a road that had been full to bursting the prior day yet now was utterly deserted. The only people they spotted lingering about, aside from themselves, were occasional guards dotting the landscape. Not that the groups were looking around too hard; nearly all of them were focused on the upcoming task they'd be handed.

Perhaps this is why, after walking through a narrow corridor between two buildings, no one noticed that the group of adventurers suddenly increased by four.

"You will all wait here," the guard informed them, gesturing to a circle of stone in a small moat of grass. Above the circle, perhaps twenty feet in the air, was a small balcony jutting out from the castle proper. Such a structure was far from regal enough or removed enough, to house a king giving orders to his subjects; however, for addressing a relatively small group, it was perfectly suited.

"The king will arrive soon. You will listen attentively as he gives you your orders. When he has finished deigning to speak with you, I will return to show you to the next phase of your journey. If you have any questions, you may ask them of me at that time. Under no circumstances are you to interrupt or ask anything of our king." The guard turned to leave, then swiveled halfway back to look at the adventurers. "Once more, I commend you on your good fortune to have been chosen by our king for this task."

That said, he finished his turn and headed back the way he came, leaving the parties awaiting the start of their next adventure.

*　　　*　　　*

King Liadon sat on the edge of his sprawling bed and fussed with his crown, trying to find an angle where the hard, golden edges didn't dig into his scalp. The first king of Solium had been human, and thus the royal accoutrements had all been crafted with a human in mind. For a human, with their thick skulls and coarse hair, the crown was just fine. Those brutes were so unaware, Liadon doubted the first king had even known when he had the damn crown on at all. Elves were gentler, more sublime creatures. They had keen senses and noticed things like hard metal digging into their fair skin through the barrier of thin hair.

Ardel watched his king fuss, knowing it was not a matter of him finding a comfortable way to wear the symbol of his leadership but merely of waiting until he wore himself out from trying. Royals were like toddlers: it was often a more prudent use of time and energy to simply let them tire themselves out than to try and intervene. They had the time, thankfully. The one good aspect of being an attendant for the king was that he was never late. Whenever the king arrived, that was when he was meant to be there. It was a benefit Liadon used frequently, since he felt little obligation to keep track of things so peasanty as "time."

"Are they gathered?" Liadon asked, finally letting his hands fall away from the crown in frustrated acceptance.

"Yes, sire. The guard brought them out to the southeastern grounds, by the far wing's balcony. They eagerly await your royal presence."

Liadon snorted in a distinctly un-kinglike, or elflike for that matter, way. "I'm sure they do. Just chomping at the bit to face the man handing them their execution papers. Somehow, I doubt even adventurers are that foolhardy."

"Then you overestimate them. The more dire the circumstances, the faster they rush in. Presuming the reward is right, of course."

"I'll never understand that lot. They treat life as if it's disposable, like they can go get more from a vendor once a dragon's fang has run them through."

"Some are more prudent than others," Ardel said. "And it certainly helps us that we've kept all word of the failed expeditions quiet. I fear we might see a higher desertion rate if word of the cumulative body count were to slip into public knowledge."

"Then, we'd just have to add those deserters to that body count," Liadon said. "It matters little. Sooner or later, one of these groups will get it done. We just have to keep throwing them at the problem until it's resolved. Standard kingdom procedure."

"Yes, sire. On that topic, have you given any more thought to the rash of demon attacks currently plaguing the lands? We're up to six confirmed so far, with several more suspected."

"One thing at a time. The citizens are a hardy lot; they can fend for themselves. Expeditions are our first priority."

"Very well, sire. Does that mean you are ready to address them?"

King Liadon rose from his bed, examining himself in the mirror. He was fully dressed, long purple cape flowing from his shoulders, down past his regal clothes and stopping inches above his fine leather boots. The crown sat atop his head, gleaming in splendor despite the discomfort it caused. He looked every inch the part of a king, which was eighty percent of what it took to be a king.

"I'm ready, but let's take our time getting there. It does adventurers good to sit and stew on occasion. Keeps them reminded of who they really work for."

"Yes, sire."

*　　*　　*

The sun climbed through the sky, nearly reaching its zenith by the time there was finally movement on the balcony. Adventurers quickly scrambled into position, pulling themselves up and taking a respectful stance. The king's blood-soaked reputation had reached all of their ears, and none were keen on receiving an arrow through the eye for perceived transgressions.

King Liadon emerged from the shadows of the castle and stood prominently on the balcony. He stared down at them wordlessly, face stoic and eyes hard as he assessed this fresh crop. Whether he found them impressive, or wanting, was anyone's guess, because as he began to speak, it was in a flat, neutral tone that betrayed no more about his thoughts than his stone-faced expression.

"I welcome all of you, brave warriors who have earned my attention through your heroic deeds. Truly, your reputations precede you, and I consider it a fine day to have such folk as my guests at the castle. Today, however, is not a day of celebration or boasting. Today I have summoned you here to serve your kingdom, a privilege so few citizens are ever given the opportunity to do. You are greatly blessed, for you have the rare chance to attempt to repay me for the protections and benefits reaped from living under my rule."

King Liadon paused, half-watching his marks soak it in, half-waiting to see if anyone would be dumb enough to speak up. When no one did, he continued, and the archers waiting unseen in various shadows allowed their bows to slacken just a touch.

"Some time ago, a group of citizens located a dungeon that had been hidden away by time. This was brought to my attention, and I undertook its investigation. After endless magical reconnaissance, we have deemed it to be ready for actual exploration. Now, there are various monsters and traps entombed there, which is why I have decided to send only the mightiest of adventurers to handle the task."

Again, King Liadon paused, and again, the crowd remained silent. He was impressed; most of the other groups had lost two or three loud-mouths by this point.

"Your task, upon entering the dungeon, is to retrieve a highly potent magical artifact from a room at the direct center. Our wizards have been able to glean its existence and location, but nothing more. Anything else you find is yours to keep; however, the artifact should be your primary goal. The group that brings it to me will be gifted with land, titles, and gold far exceeding anything you might find in some paltry dungeon."

King Liadon saw the greed shimmering in some of their eyes, twinkling like gold coins amidst a dragon's hoard. That should keep them properly motivated. A few did not seem enticed by the promise of riches; however, Liadon didn't spare much worry for any of the adventurers' motivation. Whatever had drawn them into the adventuring lifestyle would compel them forward on their path, with or without his promise of gold at the end. Of course, the threat of death should they stray was also an effective way to keep things moving along. King Liadon was a fan of using both the carrot and the stick, when possible.

"Remember, be wary in your exploration. We've confirmed the presence of many monsters that could present a danger even to those as powerful as yourselves. It is your goal to see the artifact returned and your king pleased, not to die for no purpose in musty dungeon corridors. So go forth, and make your king proud!"

With a sweep of his purple cape, King Liadon slid back into the shadows of the castle corridors, leaving a large group of adventurers wondering why a guard couldn't have just told them all that hours ago. So many were watching the now empty balcony that they didn't notice the return of the guard who'd led them here and jumped in surprise at the sound of his voice.

"Now that our king has graced you with his voice to give you your orders, it is time for you to begin." The guard motioned for them to follow and once more headed off, already beginning to speak as he anticipated their following. It was with a clatter of armor and hurried steps that the adventurers kicked into movement and gave pursuit.

"The dungeon his majesty mentioned is many weeks' travel from here, so we have decided to send you to the location by magic. You will be teleported to a camp just outside the dungeon's entrance, where you will receive a quick meal, some provisions, and a scroll with all the information we currently possess about the dungeon and the artifact you are to retrieve. From that point on, you will all enter the dungeon in whatever groups or intervals you like, provided you've all stepped in by sundown. Anyone who sees the night sky will be considered to have deserted their mission, and I trust there is no need to elaborate on what happens to deserters?"

There was no need indeed, as the adventurers quickened their step to keep pace. It was well known what King Liadon's stance on people disobeying him was. Even if this dungeon were a hundred levels deep and filled with nothing but dragons, it still provided a less certain death than going against the king's orders.

From the moment they'd set foot on the castle grounds, there had never been an option of backing out.

*   *   *

The teleportation was a quick affair; some wizards had set up a circle of glowing runes at the far south end of the castle grounds. Once an adventurer stepped onto the circle, they were transported to the camp outside the dungeon's entrance, so within minutes, all twenty-eight adventurers, along with a few guards, had arrived at their destination.

"Not much to look at, is it?" Gabrielle said. She wasn't wrong; it didn't appear to be some fearsome dungeon as much as a cave whose mouth stuck out of the side of a mountain. There was a clear slope downward, then all vantage was lost to the cave's shadows.

"Don't let the looks fool you. Anything dangerous enough to gather this many of us is bound to be worth looting." The speaker was another adventurer, a dwarf in plate armor with a set of crossbows on his hips. He gave Gabrielle a respectful glance, no doubt entranced by her fiery red scale armor and sizable axe, before tottering off to join his own group.

Most of the adventurers milled about, testing their blades or doing some light stretching. One or two from each group had gathered at the makeshift tent where the guards were set up, finding out what supplies were available. Simple observation told them they wouldn't be getting much more than a pack with dry rations and a single scroll.

"He's right," Eric said, stepping next to Gabrielle. "We should assume any number of untold dangers await us in that dungeon."

"They're not all untold," Thistle interrupted, walking back from the tent area. No one had even noticed him leave. This wasn't because he was particularly stealthy or quiet; it was merely due to the fact that he was a gnome amongst a group of larger races. "I gave the scroll a glance and it looks like they've got a fair bit of the place mapped out."

Thistle finished walking over to his group and laid the scroll out on the rocky ground where they stood. The whole area around the cave was littered with gravel; likely the kingdom had been excavating a mine when they happened upon the dungeon. Within forty feet or so, there was soft grass, but it was close to the line of the forest. No one wanted to be seen as making a run for it, so each group did their plotting atop the rough terrain.

"Mostly the outer layers," Eric noted. The dungeon they were entering seemed to be structured in a ring-like fashion, with each path providing ways to move to a path closer to the center at irregular intervals. It was impossible to say how many rings this dungeon had, as only the outermost seven were drawn on their scroll. Everything further inward was a black blob, void of information, save for a red point dead in the center. No doubt, it was meant to mark their goal.

"I'm still impressed with how much they have," Eric said. He pointed to a spot on the scroll with tightly-clustered handwriting and a crude drawing of spikes. "Look, they've even got the locations of known traps marked."

"And a few expected monster types," Gabrielle added. Sure enough, there was a small key near the bottom that listed off monsters they were likely to encounter. "It tells us quite a bit."

"It actually tells us even more than I believe they meant it to," Thistle said. His voice was quieter than the others', intended for his friends alone. "This map tells us that regardless of what the king may have indicated, we are in no way the first adventurers to try and crack this dungeon."

"How do you… because if they got this by magic, they'd have mapped the whole thing," Eric said, realization striking.

"Precisely. My guess is that somewhere in this pack of rations is a magical relay program that tells them what we encounter," Thistle surmised.

"So, the reason it only goes seven paths deep is that…" Gabrielle trailed off, not eager to reach the conclusion right before her.

"Farthest anyone has got." Grumph's harsh voice was low as he completed her thought. It was quite disheartening, especially when one considered that seven rings probably was only halfway through the dungeon, given the density of the black blob area. Halfway through at best.

"Most likely, each group does a little better than the one before, thanks to the information they've been provided, and when they die, their encounters are added to the map," Eric said.

"Couldn't have said it better myself," Thistle agreed. He rolled up the scroll carefully and tucked it in his pack. "But sadly, it really changes nothing for us. Our current choices are certain death and slightly-less-certain death. All we can do is press on, and hope the gods are watching over us."

"Says the only one of us with a direct line to a divine being," Gabrielle noted.

"While Grumble seems pleased with my service thus far, I'm not so sure of his favor that I expect to make it through here alive. At the end of the day, I'm just one paladin, and Grumble has a tremendous amount of minions begging for his attention."

"Didn't you just say we should hope the gods are watching over us?" Eric asked.

"Aye, but there is a key difference between hope and expectation."

Their conversation was interrupted by a loud cheer from the other adventurers. It didn't take long to suss out the source of the excitement: one of the parties had gathered at the cave's mouth and was about to embark into the shadows. The still-preparing adventurers raised their fists or weapons in salute and those departing mirrored the gesture. Once it was done, the group of five turned toward the mouth of the cave, brought their weapons to the ready, and carefully crossed the threshold.

"And with that, the task is officially started," Gabrielle said. She watched the mouth of the cave, as did many others, half-waiting for a spray of blood to break into the light. Nothing came, though, neither blood, nor shrieks of terror, nor even the sounds of battle. It seemed whatever lay in wait for them was further inside the dungeon's walls than right at the entrance.

"We should get ready." Eric complied with his own order by adjusting his armor a few degrees and making sure his sword was in a position to be drawn easily.

"Take your time," Grumph disagreed.

"He's right; now that we know the score, it makes more sense to be one of the last teams in," Thistle explained. "We're not really in a race; we're in a contest of survival. The more people who go ahead of us, the more traps they trip and monsters they slay."

"That's a pretty heartless stance for a paladin," Gabrielle pointed out.

"I'm a paladin for the god of minions. Do you know what minions do best? Lay low and try not to die." A curious look suddenly darted across Thistle's face, as though his words had shaken something loose in his brain.

"Got an idea?" Eric asked.

"No; more a thought to mull on. I'll let you lot know if anything comes of it."

"If we're just standing around anyway, then pull the map back out," Gabrielle suggested. "We can get familiar with the layout of the first few rings, choose our paths, and be ready for any traps that we know are coming."

"Good idea," Grumph said, patting her gently on the back. Well, gently for a half-orc.

"Agreed," Thistle said. He reached into his pack and produced the scroll, but his fingers snagged on a brown paper package as well, which came tumbling onto the ground.

"What's that?" Gabrielle asked.

"Oh. A gift from Sierva. I meant to open it, but I got… distracted." Thistle hadn't told them about the implication that Sierva and her people were like them, frauds who had picked up the adventurer title. Until he was sure what it meant, he didn't want to worry the others unnecessarily.

"Now seems like as good a time as any to open it," Eric urged. "Might come in useful."

"Perhaps. I suppose it is worth checking." Thistle carefully tore away the brown paper to reveal a white belt with a pair of dagger sheaths on it. Unlike the one he'd borrowed from Sierva, this had clearly been made with Thistle's size in mind. It was a fine bit of craftsmanship, dyed leather stitched together immaculately.

The most striking feature of the sheath-belt was not the style, or the skilled assembly: it was the small set of arcane runes glowing faintly on each sheath. Thistle examined them closely, but their complexity exceeded the limited magical knowledge he possessed. Carefully — as careful as one should be with unknown magical items — he lifted the belt up and showed it to Grumph.

"Well, old friend, any idea what these might be?"

Grumph stared at it, trying to match the symbols with anything he'd managed to understand in the spellbook. There were a few bits he could put together, but a complete comprehension was beyond his reach.

"Not sure," Grumph said after several minutes of study. "But probably not dangerous."

"'Probably' seems pretty risky when dealing with unknown magic," Eric pointed out.

"Aye, but one must consider the source," Thistle replied. He lowered the white sheath-belt to the ground then set about the task of unfastening the lesser one currently strapped to his waist. "Sierva was a friend, one who helped save my life, so if Grumph says the magic is probably not dangerous, that's enough for me."

As Thistle worked to change out his belt, the area around the mouth of cave grew crowded once more. Now that the first team had broken through, other adventurers were making their own entrances, lest they be left behind.

*   *   *

"Okay, you've entered the dungeon. Since the paths form rings, you have two directions you can go; which one do you want to choose?" Russell stared at his group with a worried expectation. Getting them to the dungeon had been hell on earth; now that they were finally in, he just knew they were going to find a way to screw things up.

"Which way did the others go?" Terry asked. He'd been rolling checks to evaluate as much of the other adventurers' equipment as possible.

"You can only see the two other parties who entered at the same time as you," Russell said. He picked up the module book to double check the information he was about to dole out. This one had a lot to keep track of, so he didn't want to mess anything up. "Each one went off in one of the two directions."

"How many are still outside the entrance?" Mitch asked.

"Let me see. The first one went in a while ago, then you guys entered with two more, so that makes four, leaving two more groups outside for a total of six parties." Russell's eyes flicked down to the book on instinct and he realized he'd made an error. "Wait: seven parties. There's one more group that still hasn't entered."

"Way to fuck up," Glenn said. "I think it's GM retcon. He just wanted to add another team to up the competition."

"Glenn, I misread something, that's all." It was strange, though; Russell had carefully gone through this book when he started and he was certain there had only been five parties besides the one that his group would be playing. Luckily, it was an easy enough mistake to fix, as long as none threw the kind of tantrum Glenn looked like he was gearing up for.

"Don't worry about it, Glenn. This is actually a good thing," Mitch said. He was leaning over the map carefully, examining the small figurines representing their characters. His eyes darted along the drawn bits of the map, eagerly drinking in every detail.

"How is it a good thing? You know Russell will try and make one of them get the artifact first."

"It's a good thing because one more party means one more set of loot," Mitch explained. "We're not going to do like these other guys and try to wade through the dungeon for treasure. Our party is going to take a far more proactive approach."

20.

"It's cleaner than I was expecting." Gabrielle's eyes wandered down the spacious stone walls and floors, all of which were easily visible thanks to the presumably magic light-casting gems embedded in the walls at regular intervals. Despite purportedly having been lost for time untold, the dungeon showed no signs of dirt, degradation, or disrepair. It was like the whole thing had been built only days before.

"Magic," Grumph surmised, eloquently explaining the entirety of the situation quite well.

"Aye, but it must be powerful magic for it to have persisted for so long. We'd best be careful."

The party had waited until the sun was dipping low on the horizon — long after the other teams had taken the plunge — before finally entering the dungeon. In truth, they might have pressed their time a bit more, but the guards were starting to get fidgety and keep their weapons close at hand. Once in, the act of making their way through the dungeon had been fairly easy. Thanks to their knowledge of the dangers, the small dart trap and explosive runes along their path were easily skirted. The route they'd chosen had evidently been infested by monsters, but judging by the giant vermin corpses they passed at irregular intervals, the other adventurers had already seen to that particular challenge.

"What do we have coming up?" Eric asked. He was at the head of the line, his attentive stare sweeping for any indicators of unexpected obstacles. Yes, they had forewarning on the traps, and the monsters should have all been killed, but he wasn't one to discount the possibility of pure bad luck assaulting them.

"Spike pit," Grumph said. While they'd all studied the map, he'd clearly retained the best mental impression of it. "After next corner."

"A spike pit, you say?" Thistle ran his hands along the seam of his new belt as his mind whirled furiously. This idea he had, this theory, it was utter madness. The dungeon he was in had been crafted ages ago, built with such precision that no adventurer had made it further than halfway through. There was no possible way his hunch could be accurate... except... except...

Except that minions, whether now, then, or in the future, would always be minions. And Thistle knew how minions worked.

"When we get to the spike pit, there's something I want to do," Thistle announced.

"Got some trash to dump?" Gabrielle asked, the smile on her face a stark contrast to their grim surroundings.

"Not quite. Do you recall earlier, when I said I had an errant thought? Well, I think the time has come to put it to the test."

"Could you possibly be more cryptic?" Eric said.

"Sorry, just don't want to say it out loud and jinx it," Thistle replied. "But, before we get there, everyone open your packs. We're going to need a fair bit of rope."

"There are just so few ways this can possibly be a good thing," Gabrielle said. Still, she pulled her pack around and opened it up, just as Grumph and Eric did. Caginess and odd requests aside,

Thistle's ideas were a key part of what had gotten them this far. They weren't about to start ignoring them now.

*   *   *

As Thistle's group grabbed rope, another team was clutching onto hope. In the third ring of the dungeon, the first team of adventurers had encountered a pack of barghests that were tearing through them. Their pugilist was down, as was their knight. The only ones still standing were the wizard and the archer, though standing didn't come easy as their clothes were already slick with blood from their wounds.

"What the hell, why can't we land a damn hit?" the archer swore. "This is such bullshit."

"I know, the odds against this are nuts," the wizard agreed. "I think the dice are cursed. But I've got a plan: can you buy me two rounds?"

"Maybe; I'm pretty low on Health Points. What are you going to do?"

"I've got one good spell left, and the hit difficulty for it is so low I'm sure to connect, even with our shitty rolls."

"Fine," the archer agreed. "It's the best option we've got so far." With that, he took off in a charge, firing arrows at a rapid clip. Despite his skill and proficiency with the bow, each arrow went wide, nowhere near making contact with the beasts. The only saving grace was that his effort succeeded in drawing attention away from the wizard. The dog-like monsters surged forward, closing in around him.

As quick as the barghests were, the wizard was still able to begin his conjuration in the time it took them to attack the archer.

He pressed his hands together, words of power slipping from his mouth like audible gems as he condensed and directed the magic within him. A purple glow formed around him, crackling magical energy surging over each part of his body. The wizard's eyes sparked with energy as he parted his hands and stuck his left palm out, putting every ounce of his focus on the barghests. One final word echoed from his mouth as he spoke the phrase of activation, completing the spell.

In another world, one with five people sitting around a dining room table, a young girl rolled her twenty-sided die. Upon seeing the roll, her friends shook their heads and whispered the words "critical failure." She was forced to roll again, but this time, the result of her roll filled the room with tension. It was the same as what she had gotten before. A young man with wavy dark hair with a screen shielding his part of the table nodded at her wordlessly. With trembling hands, the girl picked up the die and rolled it across the table one last time. It bounced and tumbled along the surface, nearly knocking over a small figurine of a male elven wizard, before finally coming to a stop.

Its outermost face, for the third time in a row, showed the number 1.

The wizard's heart exploded as his magic misfired, killing him instantly. The magic continued to surge, however, erupting from his corpse in an explosion of arcane power. Within moments, there was no sign that the wizard had ever existed, save for the scorch marks along the walls, marks that were already beginning to fade as the dungeon's own magic cleansed them.

Nearby, the barghests looked up from their meal momentarily, then set back into it. Within seconds, the archer's pain-filled screams had faded just like the wizard's scorch marks.

* * *

"All right, we've got the ropes secured and enough slack to feed it halfway back to Solium. Now will you tell us what this about?" Eric asked. The last of the preparations were done, the team having run the ropes together and tied them off on various points in the dungeon's walls. This left them with an exceptionally stable length of rope that would allow them to lower someone down into the spiked pit magically concealed directly in front of them. What they lacked, however, was any understanding of why they'd want to do such a thing.

"I suppose we've come along far enough that the jinx is a bit of a moot point," Thistle said. He produced a small hunk of dried meat from his pack, walked calmly up to what would be the lip of the pit, and tossed it. His aim was true, striking one of the many magical sensors that would open the pit if touched. Immediately, the ground in front of them dissolved, revealing a wide pit with jagged spears poking up from the ground.

"This is one of the secrets of minions, one we keep as close to the heart as our own true loves. Whenever constructing dungeons — which we do, because obviously, your average tyrant or mad wizard can't be bothered with grunt work — minions always include secret tunnels and burrows. These tunnels are to allow the minions who have to work in the dungeon to get around, navigating all the traps and monsters that would easily tear us to shreds. The reason we guard this trick so fiercely is that if it got out, we'd no longer be able to do it."

"Wait, I thought people found secret doors in dungeons all the time," Gabrielle pointed out. "We've heard people talk about it in the tavern."

"Oh sure, we hide a few obvious ones for people to discover. Oftentimes, we stick our tunnel entrance in those rooms, since no one ever thinks to check a secret for another secret. But, make no mistake, those are decoys designed to make adventurers think they've thoroughly explored an area. The real tunnels are far more useful, they allow a minion to scamper safely to almost any point in a maze, even the heart of it."

"And you think one of those tunnel entrances is in the spiked pit?" Eric asked.

"Early, easy access, simple traps surrounding it... makes sense," Gabrielle said.

"Precisely. If I were building this dungeon, I'd stick the entrance at the bottom of the spiked pit. No adventurer ever goes combing about on the floor of those; in fact, they barely pay them any attention at all."

"Hiding in plain sight," Eric said. "That's damned cunning."

"It's damned cunning if I'm right," Thistle replied. "Otherwise, it's just a silly notion. Now then, you lot ready to lower me down?"

"We can handle it," Grumph assured him, grasping hold of one section of the rope. Eric and Gabrielle followed suit, everyone getting a firm grip. Light as Thistle was, it would only take a small mistake to send him tumbling onto those spikes.

"I'm sure you can, old friend. Remember, two tugs to bring me back up, or just listen for the sound of me screaming to hurry up and pull." Thistle picked up his side of the rope and stuck his right foot through the loop they'd fastened at the end. With extraordinary care, he lowered himself off the ledge and into the pit.

His friends didn't let him down; they doled out slack at a slow, constant pace. It took him over two minutes to descend the entirety of the pit's forty feet, but eventually, Thistle was able to thread himself between the spikes and find a clear section near the wall. He stepped out of the rope's loop, careful not to give any tugs that might make the others think he wanted it pulled back.

The floor of the spiked pit was like the rest of the dungeon: clean and maintained. There should have been a few skulls, or perhaps a bit of dried blood decorating the area. Instead, it was pristine. The tips of the spikes even looked as if they'd been recently polished.

Moving about was a tricky task. Thistle was small, but his armor was cumbersome and heavy, compounding the poor dexterity his warped form already imparted on him. What Thistle did have on his side was experience. He'd been forced to navigate tight quarters on countless occasions in his tasks as a minion, so he understood that it was all a matter of staying calm, keeping focused, and making each move deliberate. It wasn't the fastest method of exploration, but it was something.

As he made his way through the pit, worry cast a dark shadow over his heart. So far, he'd seen no signs of a tunnel entrance. If his idea didn't pan out, they were stuck going through the dungeon the normal way, an almost certain death. He didn't realize until he was hunched down amidst the spikes just how much hope he'd put in this theory, and how crushed he would be if it wasn't so.

Thistle was nearly at the point of giving it all up when his eyes noticed something, a mark etched into the base of one of the spears. In any other dungeon, he'd have taken it for wear and tear, but in this unmarred environment, it stood out like a beacon. He worked his way over to it carefully, winding through the forest of spears. When he finally came close enough to make out the mark, a small smile bloomed on his misshapen, gnomish face.

It was not a random mark, nor was it wear and tear. No, it was a rudimentary carving of a broom with a dagger tied on top. It was the symbol of Grumble, god of the minions. Thistle reached out and grabbed the spear. It took some fumbling, but he finally found the hidden latch he'd been searching for. The pit echoed with sound as the spear let out a gentle click, and then a small section of stone along the wall shifted out of place.

Thistle released a long sigh of relief before lifting his head up and calling to his friends.

"I hope you lot don't mind doing some crawling. It looks like a tight fit!"

*   *   *

The wraith stabbed its incorporeal claws through the summoner's eyes, draining the last of her life and sending her sprawling to the floor. Around it, other wraiths had already finished the remainder of the party. These had been strong adventurers; their efforts had killed off two of the six wraiths before they finally succumbed to their wounds.

Eventually, they'd fallen, of course. Everyone fell in these halls. The closer an adventurer came to the center, the more chance turned against them. By the fifth ring, they'd be fortunate to walk without falling to their deaths. Anywhere past the seventh and even that much was an impossibility.

The wraiths ran their claws over the newly-made corpses once more, just to be certain their prey was fully drained. None paid attention to the rune on the scroll that had fallen from a barbarian's clutches. It was a small rune, positioned below a drawing of the very dungeon these wraiths inhabited. Before the party died it had been entirely invisible, but now it glowed with a dark green hue.

This was all irrelevant to the wraiths, which held no concern that information was being sent back to the king's guards. All the wraiths cared for was eating life, and they could sense that there was still some in the dungeon to be had. They'd have to hurry, though; the lives were fading fast.

Of the seven clusters of adventurers who had entered the dungeon, only four were still drawing breath.

*   *   *

"Cozy fit," Grumph muttered as he tried to ignore the sensation of tunnel walls closing in around him. He was already on his hands and knees, as was everyone aside from Thistle, inching along in the dim tunnel. Grumph, like the others, thought safely maneuvering down to the bottom of the pit would be the hard part. All things considered, he might have taken a poke from one of the spears if it meant a few inches' more comfort on his trek.

"Yeah, sorry about that," Thistle said from his position at the front of the convoy. Gabrielle was behind him, then Grumph, and Eric was in the rear, listening for anything that might try to sneak up on them. "Minions tend to be my size most of the time. Makes us easier to kick around and discipline as needed. Occasionally, we get some bigger folks — since we gnomes are shit at heavy lifting — but they're never weighed down by things like armor or weapons when they come through the tunnel."

"I don't want to hear any complaining from the half-orc not wearing armor," Gabrielle snapped. "I've got this demon-scale and a giant axe weighing me down."

"I'm very wide," Grumph countered.

"He is robust," Eric agreed. Since his armor was barely thicker than cloth, he was the least inconvenienced of anyone, save for Thistle. "Any idea how far we are from the center?"

"We've been passing exit hatches at regular intervals," Thistle informed him. "I'd wager each one exits in a different ring of the dungeons, so right now, we're somewhere between the fifth and sixth rings."

"That would be a lot more helpful if we knew how many there were total," Gabrielle said.

"Helpful, but unnecessary. If the minions built something this direct, it almost certainly will take us all the way to the center of the dungeon. We might not be right in the artifact's chamber, but we'll be quite close." Thistle put his hands on his daggers unconsciously. No matter how far they got through the tunnel, there was bound to be some monsters guarding their prize. When they arrived, there would be bloodshed. He only hoped not all of it would be theirs.

"I wonder how the other teams are doing." Gabrielle paused to reach back and adjust her axe, nearly banging Grumph's skull in the process.

"Probably bad," Grumph said. "Based on history."

"We don't know how many have gone before us," Gabrielle said. "Maybe we're the second or third expedition to attempt this.

It's always possible one of the other teams might actually make it through."

"Perhaps they will," Eric agreed. He didn't have the heart to tell her what he'd figured out. If the king was courting adventurers who had done nothing more than kill off a few kobolds, he was not looking for the best adventurers around. For something this important, there was only one reason why the king would be using the dregs of the adventuring barrel: all the good ones he could find had already failed. No, they weren't the first or second group of teams to try this. He doubted they were even in the first ten.

This place had already claimed the lives of countless adventurers. By the time the next sun rose, it would have certainly gotten the blood of more. All they could do was pray not to be among them.

*   *   *

A sickening howl filled the air as the drake plunged its teeth into the dwarf's flesh. The dwarf refused to go down easily, grabbing the short sword from his hip and stabbing at the monster currently chewing on his leg. Surely, at this range, he would finally hit. He wouldn't go down like the rest of his friends, who were all dead, or bleeding out around him. He would survive. He would hit this damned thing and make his escape.

The dwarf's howl turned into a scream of rage as he thrust the blade forward, aiming right for the drake's eye. It should have been a killing blow, but at the last moment, the drake turned its head to the side, causing the blade to bounce off its armored skull and stab the dwarf in his other leg.

"No… no. I can't have…" Whatever final words the dwarf might have been ready to utter were lost to the ages, as this fresh wound was more than he could withstand. He toppled to the ground, unconscious.

The drake continued its meal undisturbed. By the time it had finished eating the dwarf's meaty leg, its remaining victims had finished bleeding to death and were now simply dead, a set of three corpses in the sixth ring of the dungeon.

And with that, only two teams remained.

21.

No one was sure how many hours they'd been crawling on their knees; all they knew was that everyone except Thistle was sore from their shins to their toes. So when the tunnel finally opened up into a room large enough for everyone, even Grumph, to stand, it took a great deal of effort not to scream in joy at the act of getting up.

The room was simple and small, ten feet by ten feet, made of the same dark stone as the rest of the dungeon and sporting a large door at the far end. On the door were a variety of runes and symbols, each incredibly complex. Grumph took one look at them and knew he had no hope of deciphering any of it. Not that it would have changed things if he could; they'd come this far, and their only hope of salvation lay on the other side of that door. Even if it was rigged with enough magic to bring down a dragon, they still had to open it.

"We should rest," Eric said, his voice hushed. "Everyone is worn out after that trek, and who knows what's on the other side of that door."

"I'd guess an artifact, a guardian, and more trouble than any sane man would want to deal with. Aye, resting is a fine idea." Thistle also kept his voice quiet, though he showed less concern for stealth as he dropped his pack to the ground and rummaged about. He pulled out a waterskin and some dried meat for rations, biting off a large chunk that would take him ages to chew through.

The others followed suit, getting food and drink from their packs and digging in with more vigor than they'd expected. Fear, adrenaline, and pain had dulled them to the fact that it had been hours upon hours since their last meal. The first bite reawakened the voice of their biological needs, and soon everyone was devouring without a thought spared to manners.

Only as the pain of hunger was curbed did another realization begin sneaking up on each party member: they were exhausted. The simple beds of the barracks seemed years ago, and the fog of fatigue began descending on their minds almost immediately.

"How long do you think we've been in here?" Gabrielle asked, washing down the last bites of her dried meat.

"The moon is probably coming down and the sun will rise soon. So, almost a full night," Thistle said. No one asked how he made his guesses; they were too tired to care.

"That means we've been up for almost a full day," Eric surmised. "We're going to have to get some sleep if we want to be even close to good in a fight."

"That should be fine." Thistle put his waterskin into his pack then laid the whole thing down on the ground. "If anyone thought we were using the tunnels, they'd have killed us ages ago."

"What if other minions are here?" Gabrielle asked. She laid a hand on the axe that rested by her side. "They might come through this tunnel and find us."

"It's possible, but unlikely. This place has no need for the sort of minions who would use these tunnels. It's self-sustained through magic, and none of the monster types listed on the scroll would be inclined to need or know about the minion tunnels. I could be wrong, of course, but we need sleep, so if anyone is too worried, we can set a guard."

"Forget it." Eric pulled off his own pack and set it on the ground. It would prove to be a very uncomfortable pillow, but it still would be better than the stone floor. "At this point, getting killed in our sleep almost sounds like a pleasant option."

"It is pretty strange to be sitting here, knowing that when we open that door the things on the other side are likely to kill us." Gabrielle lifted her hand off her axe slowly, as though the act were causing her physical stress.

"Adventurers sometimes call this 'the calm before the storm.' Never did know why. Usually, before storms, there's lots of wind whipping about and clouds in the sky, but they say it, anyway. I suppose it refers to the calm we get, the chance to take a breath and prepare before all hell breaks loose." Thistle ran his hands along the new belt once more, his mind miles away from the dungeon enclosing them.

"That's a pretty good segue to what I wanted to ask," Gabrielle said. "We're going to face almost-certain death in the morning. So, before we go to sleep, why don't you provide us with a bedtime story, Thistle? The one about how you have so much knowledge about adventurers."

A dark smile slithered onto Thistle's face. "I thought you might poke for that. Well, I did say it would be after Solium, and we've left the city, so fair is fair." He leaned onto his pack, letting it support his lower back and trying to find a position that was actually comfortable.

"My tale isn't a very grand one, not compared to the other tales that live in our world. I was born as you see me: hunched, crooked, and misshapen. That might not have been so bad, however, I also had no talent for magic, and among gnomes such a condition is a far darker curse. I made my living as a worker for the local church of Mithingow, the god of the gnomes. While they had clerics and priests and wizards aplenty, there was still always a need for someone to clean rats out of the basement, or sweep the rafters. Those were my duties and I did them happily, for I was thankful to have a source of income at all, and I was always pleased to serve my god."

"Wait, you follow Grumble," Eric interrupted.

"Aye, but this was before I even knew of Grumble, or many other gods at all. I knew a few from the legends where Mithingow tricked or triumphed over them, but in a gnomish community, there was never any need for more gods. No, I would still be working in that church to this day, polishing the pews and sweeping the floors, if a group of adventurers hadn't stumbled into our foyer one sunny afternoon."

Thistle paused to take a drink from his waterskin, carefully soaking his throat.

"They were on their way to a nearby forest, where a lingering curse from an ancient necromancer was prone to turning deceased animals into undead monsters. I hid the first time I saw them, shameful as it was. I was terrified; they were so strong, so powerful. The adventurers requested aid; they only knew a general location, no real information about where the curse reigned. Our clerics decided that, for a healthy donation to Mithingow, they could spare some guides. One of their younger apprentices, who they felt could use the experience, as well as a gnome who was known to frequent areas near the forest on his days off: me. So it was that the adventurers set off the next morning with two new additions: myself and... Madroria."

The gnome halted his story, this time, not because of a need for water. He pressed his hands together gently, willing back the tears that tried to form in his eyes. He couldn't let the emotions break through now, not when the hard part still lay ahead in the story. At last, he succeeded in pushing away the sorrow and continued his tale.

"Madroria was roughly the same age as I, but she was not cursed with my crooked body, nor my lack of skill when it came to wielding magic. She was, in fact, perfect. Perfect to me, anyway. I'd loved her, silently and sorrowfully, since the first day she came to the church. As scared as I'd been of the adventurers, the idea of walking with Madroria, of speaking to her... I shook with terror all night and barely found the courage to go with them in the morning."

"It's hard to picture you like that," Gabrielle said. "You're usually so calm and clear-headed."

"Well, this was decades ago, and I've gotten to do a lot of growing up since then," Thistle reminded her. "Anyway, we set out on the road together. At first, it was quiet and awkward, but over time, I began speaking with the adventurers, getting to know them. It was actually quite funny; despite her beauty and power, Madroria was too shy to make much conversation with our strangers, while I soon gave way to my natural eloquence, surprising even myself. I'd never had much opportunity to talk with people, and I'm sure they assumed I had nothing worth hearing. It was a pleasant shock to discover I could hold the interest of these amazing people. Of course, it might have been because I asked endless questions, giving them the chance to talk about themselves."

"Is that how you know so much?" Eric asked.

"Not quite. That was merely the appetizer that whetted my curiosity. By the time we arrived at the forest, we were all something akin to friends. I could even speak to Madroria without growing so fearful I stumbled over my own words or feet. In the forest, however, the monsters were far greater in number and power than the adventurers had predicted. It was horrible: giant undead beasts, eyeless sockets and snapping jaws, the stench of death snarling through our nostrils. In the end, they uncovered the necromancer's lingering spell circle and destroyed it. However, it came with a cost. One of their own was killed, and Madroria was skewed through by the tusks of an undead boar."

"Oh no." Gabrielle put her hand to her mouth. "Did she…"

"No. She was horrifically wounded, but we were able to stabilize her. The real danger was the rot that began to destroy her from within. Left unchecked, it would devour her life force and leave her as one of them, the undead. We retreated from the forest and rushed back to the temple of Mithingow. It took two days, two days that I spent always at her side. She drifted in and out as the fever grew stronger, but she held on. My Madroria was always a fighter. Then, on the day we knew would be her last, we finally reached the temple. I was crying as we burst through the doors, certain her salvation was close at hand. We brought her up to Mithingow's altar and screamed for the priests to come out. When I saw them, I collapsed in relief, certain she would be saved."

"She should have been," Grumph said, giving a small nod.

"Wait, they didn't save her?" Eric asked.

"Couldn't, they said. The priests told me the curse was too powerful, the magic beyond their capacity to undo. I lost my temper at that point, demanding they try. When that failed, I sat on the altar and screamed right at Mithingow himself, making promises, threats, and just plain begging for him to save Madroria. It was foolish, overly emotional, and accomplished nothing, but to this day I think I'd do the same if I were in that position again."

"So, Madroria… she died?" Eric had his hands gripped to the side of his legs, clutching them in anxiety as he listened to Thistle's tale.

"It seemed that she would. The clerics said the only thing they could do for her was to cut off her head and spare her the indignity of returning as an undead. I lost my mind at that, socked one of them right in the jaw. Crippled as I was, I don't think it ever occurred to him that I might have some fight in me."

"That sounds more like the you we know," Gabrielle said.

"Thank you. After that, the adventurers had to pull me away, and that is when they told me of the last hope for Madroria. On one of their previous excursions, they'd come across a magic elixir that could heal any wound, lift any curse, cure any disease. It could reverse the ravages of all but death itself. They'd neglected to tell me about it because it was precious beyond value and was not something they would use lightly. As fond as they'd grown of Madroria and me, it was still an item they hesitated to relinquish."

"Greedy bastards." Gabrielle spat in the dirt.

"No, I don't begrudge them their reluctance. These were people who saw danger every day. They would need that elixir themselves, sooner or later, and giving it away could mean the death of one of their own. It was a great kindness of them to even make me a deal, which they did. Madroria and I would serve them, follow as their guides, pack mules, whatever was needed, paying forth our portion of all treasures found until the elixir had been purchased. Needless to say, I leapt at the opportunity. The wizard of their group, a willowy woman with silken hair, produced a bottle that resembled stopped sunshine and poured it down Madroria's throat."

Thistle's eyes grew moist, the battled back tears finally breaking through. He let them this time, for he was now to the part of the tale that filled him with joy. Thistle had no qualms about crying happy tears for his wife; he only avoided those of sadness.

"Save only for the day we wed, many years later, I have never seen Madroria so beautiful as when the magic enveloped her, healing her wounds and driving the undead rot into oblivion. She glowed, not just with magic, but with life and vitality. Had the gods taken me in that moment, there would have been no heaven that could have equaled my joy. Then, as always happens, the tab came due. Madroria and I left the temple, our home, and put to the road with the adventurers. It was a very long time before our debt was paid, and perhaps we journeyed with them for a while longer. Those years with them, my first real job as a minion when I think about it, are how I have such knowledge about adventurers."

"That does explain quite a bit, but there's one thing I was hoping to hear about that you didn't touch on," Gabrielle said. "You constantly refer to Grumph as old friend, and I'm pretty certain you two knew each other before Maplebark. Where does he fit in with all that?"

Thistle and Grumph exchanged a short glance, and Grumph gave the barest of shakes of his large, half-orc skull.

"A story for another time," Thistle replied. "My obligation is fulfilled, and we need to sleep while we can. When we rise, there is a very real chance it will be for the last time."

"Thanks, Thistle, that's not going to give me nightmares or anything," Eric sighed. He laid his head on the bedroll anyway. Nightmares, at least, were illusionary, and therefore better than the terror waiting for him on the other side of the red-rune-inscribed door.

"Strangely, I think you'll find that's not true at all. When faced with near certain death, the mind has more than enough real fear to occupy it without conjuring up more. Usually, in times like this, I have the happiest dreams I can ever recall," Thistle said.

"Agreed," Grumph chimed in.

Gabrielle shot him a look, still clearly curious about his friendship with Thistle, but said nothing. The truth was that they did need rest. Whether it was filled with horror or happiness was irrelevant; they still had to get some. She laid her head on her pack, wondering how she would actually fall asleep in such a place and under such odd circumstances.

Within moments, she had passed out, snores gently joining into a chorus that the others had already begun.

22.

"Everyone ready?"

"Ready," Thistle called, daggers out and anxious to be hurled.

"Ready," Grumph said, magic spell firmly in mind as he stared at the door.

"Ready," Eric said, hand resting on the hilt of his short sword.

"Then, let's do this." Gabrielle grabbed the handle of the door and jerked it open, surprised at how easy the motion was. Given the stone material it was constructed from, she'd expected it to be heavy and awkward; but it took almost no effort to move. It made sense, when she stopped to think about it: minions were usually small and weak, so a heavy door would be a big obstacle to them.

As soon as the door was ajar, everyone sprang into motion. They'd discussed the best strategy while eating the remains of their rations for breakfast. She would fling the door open, since her armor was the strongest and most likely to ward off any trap that might be on it. Eric would race through quickly, getting a lay of the land and hopefully finding a place he could hide. Grumph and Thistle would lead the charge, since they could handle monsters at a range or in close combat, and Gabrielle, if still alive, would follow and use her axe for any melee needs.

Eric dashed through the open door into the dull, crimson light streaming through. He leapt into a long hallway and took a good look at his surroundings. Eric was ready for anything — undead, demons, perhaps even a dragon — but what he found was nothing like he'd expected.

"Hey... um, you guys should probably come take a look at this."

The others trickled in slowly, weapons at the ready, and then stood in dumb wonder at what they found.

There were no monsters, or demons, or beasts of any sort. The room was made of the same material as the rest of the dungeon, but here, they finally saw signs of filth. It was not dust or wear that met them, though; instead, there were half-eaten plates of food everywhere, dozens of bottles that had once held wine, and a rough mattress with sheets that were strewn about. The red light that enveloped the small room came from a small lantern shaped like an ale mug and the color of old wine.

"It looks like my cousin Eldreb's place," Gabrielle said. "He's unmarried and lives by himself. We tend not to visit when we can avoid it."

"Thistle, is this more minion stuff?" Eric asked.

"I highly doubt it. Minions rarely get luxuries such as beds, and we are never given indulgences like wine or decent cooking." Thistle turned to look at the door they'd come through and found that on this side it looked like nothing more than a section of wall behind a chamber pot. The chamber pot had, thankfully, slid with the wall and was not turned over. Definitely a minion access point: no adventurers ever went rooting around near the toilet.

"We should go." Grumph pointed down the hallway that led out of the room, toward a turn that curved to the left. There was more light coming from down the hall, soft and inconstant, flickering about. The others nodded in agreement and shifted back into ready stances.

Eric took the lead, moving quietly, thankful as the red lantern's light faded and he was once more amidst darkness. He didn't notice the way his veilpanther armor seemed to shimmer with shadow and cloak him; all he knew was that he felt safer when he was harder to spot. Eric rounded the corner carefully, silently, and motioned for the others to follow. This hall led to a room where the light was brighter, and as his boots moved softly across the stone floor, Eric slowly pulled his short sword from its scabbard. When he stepped into the light, it would be almost impossible to hide. He needed to be ready to strike, quickly and efficiently, against anything that might be waiting. With a darting stride forward, Eric closed the last of the distance and peered around the corner into this new room.

Staring right back at him, mere inches away, was a set of pale-yellow eyes in a wide, round face, topped off by a set of long and pointed ears.

"You know, there's a ward on that door that sounds whenever you open it." The voice was male and lower than most elven voices; even the men usually sounded like singing flutes. It belonged to an elf wearing long, red robes that didn't fit his expansive stomach and holding a wooden staff with symbols carved across it.

Eric braced for attack, but instead, the elf turned around and walked back into the room. "Come on then, may as well chat for a bit. I haven't had any company in ages. Tell your friends they're welcome, too."

Eric swallowed hard, trying to gulp down his nerves and uncertainty at the oddness of this situation. "Aren't you going to demand we sheath our weapons or something?"

"Why? It's not like they'll do you any good."

Briefly, Eric considered testing that theory and rushing the elf. It was only the robes and staff that made him hesitate. That was the garb of a wizard, and if he knew they were coming, he'd had ample time to cast trap or protection spells. Only fools and gods fought a prepared wizard.

"My name is Eric." He sheathed his blade and motioned for the others. Strange as this was, no blood had been spilt yet, and he wanted to see if that trend could continue.

"Good to meet you, Eric. You may call me Aldron. Please, take a seat. It will be nice to have someone to talk to for a bit."

For the first time, Eric noticed the rest of the room. It was large, expansive, filled with bookshelves along the walls. In the center were various workbenches, along with a table that still held scraps of meal on it. In one corner sat several large chairs, each filled with cushions and appearing quite comfortable. At the far end was a small stove and cabinet, presumably filled with food, next to a low table with various cooking tools atop it. Beside the kitchen area was a large wooden chest that hosted no lock, and directly across from the chest was a pedestal. It was carved from some sort of white marble, inscribed with all manner of runes to the point where it practically glowed with magic.

Sitting atop it was a strange object, misshapen to Eric's eye, yet beautiful. It was forged from crystal and clear as day, save only for a design on the top that he couldn't make out. Unlike the pedestal that supported it, the object gave off no glow or light, yet

Eric found himself unable to look away. It didn't present its magic like the things he was accustomed to seeing. No, this object somehow spoke to a part of him he'd never known about before, whispering that he was looking at a piece of the world beyond his comprehension. This artifact was not powerful. It *was* power.

As soon as his eyes fell upon it, Eric knew he'd found what the king sent them after.

"Quite pretty, isn't it?" Aldron said. He had taken one of the soft chairs and was sitting comfortably in it. "Of course, someone like you can't appreciate the real beauty of it. That's a privilege reserved for folks purely of our world."

"Of our world?"

Thistle's voice snapped Eric out of his fugue, and he realized the others had caught up to him while he was gazing at the artifact. He turned his gaze away from the pedestal and the prize it held, determined to keep his wits about him while dealing with this mage.

"Yes, of our world. Didn't expect me to know about that, did you? My time with this magical object — The Bridge, I've come to call it — has opened my mind to many of the secrets normally veiled from our kind."

"Oh, and what sort of secrets might those be?" Thistle walked over and took a seat of his own. Gabrielle followed, but Grumph and Eric stayed standing. Pleasant as the atmosphere was, it wouldn't do to have them all clustered together in an easy target.

"The Bridge has whispered to me of countless things since I discovered it all those months ago. But the most important one is that I know you people, adventurers, are not truly beings of our world. Sure, you may look and feel like flesh from this plane, but the spirit guiding you is separate. It dwells in another place altogether." Aldron pulled out a pipe and lit it with a flick of his wrist.

"The magic crystal told you that, did it?" Gabrielle didn't bother keeping the incredulous doubt from her face.

"It isn't a crystal," Aldron corrected. "Truthfully, I'm not entirely sure what it is. All I've discerned in my time is that it is a piece of a larger whole, an artifact of untold power that will finally allow us to fight back."

"Why don't we back up a bit," Thistle suggested. "Just who are you, and how did you come across this Bridge, as you call it?"

"I was a wizard working under the king's thumb, aiding the excavation team that first uncovered this dungeon. The others scampered off to report their findings, but I was tasked with exploring and mapping duties. After several days, I eventually made my way to this chamber, where I found The Bridge. From that moment on, I've lived here, provided for by the dungeon's magic, tirelessly studying the effects and power of this magnificent artifact."

"Bugbearshit. There's no way one wizard fought through this entire dungeon," Gabrielle said. "Not when countless adventurers have died trying to get past the halfway point."

"Ah, silly adventurer, there were no monsters when I came through. It was my discovery of The Bridge that led to the dungeon's reawakening. The dungeon and The Bridge were in states of dormancy… they were sleeping. I awoke one, which roused the other. That is how I made it here unscathed." Aldron rose from his comfy chair and ambled across the room, stopped at a table and picked up a half-full glass of old mead.

"As to why none of you can press through the dungeon, I did tell you already, The Bridge allows us to fight back against you invaders."

"Fight back how?" Eric asked. His eyes were on the artifact once more. He could hear it, a keening note that filled up his soul. It was almost as if it was speaking to him, yet he knew not the language.

"Your world pushes into ours like a river flowing into a lake. The lake has no recourse; it must accept what the river sends. The Bridge changes that. It allows our world to push back. Not much, in its incomplete state, but enough to render adventurers in its proximity powerless. The term I believe you use is 'critical failure'. None of you can so much as a land a blow on me right now; The Bridge is calibrated to cause catastrophic results from all but the most mundane of actions." Aldron finished off his glass of old mead and set the empty container down on the table. "Does it terrify you, brave adventurers, to know that the river no longer flows in a single direction?"

"More intrigues us, really," Thistle replied. "So all adventurers come from this other place, and your crystal there can make it so nothing they try to do succeeds. It's a neat trick, but it seems a bit limited in its capacity."

"I'll give you that, but remember, this piece of The Bridge is just that: a piece. When fully assembled, there is no telling what havoc we can wreak on your world." Aldron's face fell a bit, his elf ears drooping slowly. "Even if there is cost to our own."

"Cost?" Grumph asked. In his mind, he began calling up spells. As a fellow wizard, it was his job to knock out as much of the magical might of their attackers as possible.

"Yes, horrible cost, not that you care." Aldron shook his head slowly. "The Bridge is not perfect, not yet. For using its power, there are repercussions in our world. I've tried to keep them minimal; unfortunately, a few have slipped through. The cost of altering the world of the adventurers is that it compounds the repercussions of adventurers meddling in our world."

"Forgive me, I don't quite understand," Thistle said.

"Of course, you don't." Aldron's sadness seemed to evaporate, replaced by a bubbling sense of anger. "You act as if our entire realm exists purely for your amusement. It would never occur to you that some of the monsters you see are neither of your world nor of ours. The Bridge links more than one world, and using its power causes them to bleed together, often in horrible, bloody ways."

Gabrielle rose from her seat, hand already on her axe. It took every ounce of self-control she'd managed to muster not to draw the weapon and charge. As it was, she wouldn't be surprised if her grip left fingerprints in the wooden shaft of the axe.

"The demons... it was you. You're the reason the demons have been popping up all over the kingdom."

"Yes, that was one side effect of using so much of The Bridge's power," Aldron admitted. "A terrible price that had to be paid. They slip past the world's barriers, sent to unleash death upon areas where adventurers frequent, though even I don't know who directs them."

"What do you mean, 'one effect'? What others did you unleash?" Thistle asked. His own ire was rising as well, his mind filled with memories of bloody bodies falling at his feet. Even if this mad wizard were actually right, no one deserved the sort of death Thistle had seen served up by those beasts.

Eric wanted to ask questions too, but he couldn't quite make his tongue move. The artifact's hold on him was growing. He felt as though his teeth were rattling from the vibrations of its song echoing through his body.

"Nothing as grand as the demons," Aldron said. "I've only charted a few oddities, to be honest. The Bridge has not only blessed me with true enlightenment, but it has also given a lesser freedom to the minds of those in the realm. Adventurers seem shrouded by a magic that allows them to pass in our world without us realizing their foreign nature. The Bridge has shaken that magic, permitted a greater freedom of thought. Not enough to make everyone see the truth of what you are, but a little."

"Just to be clear, you've unleashed unknown hordes of demons in exchange for what, exactly? Protection from adventurers, and a theoretical freeing of the kingdom's minds?" Thistle got to his feet, hands resting on the hilts of his daggers. "You'd trade countless lives for that little? I think I speak for all of us when I say that your madness cannot be allowed to stand. Surrender now and pray the gods find a way you may seek repentance."

"I was wondering when it would come to this," Aldron said. "It was inevitable. You adventurers, you only know one way to live: through blood and blade." The carvings on his staff began to glow a pale yellow, the color of his eyes. "But I am shielded by The Bridge, my mind suffused with the magical wisdom it has imparted. Go ahead, attack me uselessly. If you manage not to kill yourselves, I'll happily finish the job. By all means, give it your best shot."

Thistle, always one to oblige a host, yanked free a dagger from his belt and whipped it forward. It whirled through the air and sank right into the wizard's fat gut.

Aldron looked in shock from the dagger to Thistle, to The Bridge, and back to the dagger. When he next raised his eyes, all jovial disdain was gone, replaced by pure, naked hatred.

"How... what are you?"

23.

Confused as he might have been, Aldron didn't waste any time reacting to the new knowledge that he was no longer entirely protected by his Bridge. The hefty elven wizard lifted his staff overhead and slammed it down on the floor, releasing a shockwave that sent all but Grumph to the ground. It also conjured a hefty burst of smoke that clouded the area, watering eyes and obscuring vision.

"How did you hit me?" Aldron's screams pierced the choking clouds and bounded off the walls. "Was it luck? Some artificial power? Tell me!"

"Just that good, I guess," Thistle called from his nearly prone position on the ground. Though normally skilled at scrambling to his feet, the armor was slowing him significantly. As it was, he'd barely made it back to standing when a bolt of lightning zipped out and struck the floor where he'd been. The magical charge cleared away some of the smoke, giving him a clear visual on Aldron's face, now flushed red with fury.

"You will tell me what magic you used to cheat The Bridge." Aldron raised his staff and another lightning bolt shot toward Thistle. The gnome was almost able to dodge: almost, but not quite, as it struck his right shin squarely. Sheer force spun him through the air, and he landed in a heap. He was still conscious, albeit barely.

Aldron might have pressed the attack if not for the large axe swung at his head by an angry young woman in armor the color of blood. He deflected it with a raised hand, calling a near-transparent magical shield into existence just in front of him. If Gabrielle even noticed it, she paid no mind, pounding forward like a hellhound set on dragging some soul to the pits. As Aldron readied another spell, he felt the sting of ice strike his shoulder. A quick glance confirmed that the half-orc had cast a cold spell at him.

Eric crept up behind Aldron, staying as silent as he could, which was impressively so. The blast had partially snapped him out of the trance he'd fallen under when gazing at The Bridge. He could still hear it, still *feel* it, really, humming and pulsing like the blood in his veins. It was there, but it no longer overwhelmed him, meaning he could focus on things like aiding his friends. With every inch, he readied himself more, keeping his breathing steady, shifting his sword to his left hand so that he could stab from a better angle. He was drawing close to Aldron, only a few steps away from being able to sink his blade into the wizard's ample flesh, when his whole body vibrated with a command from The Bridge.

Stop

It wasn't a word, wasn't a sensation, wasn't a command; it was a fundamental aspect of existence. Eric could no more have disobeyed the order than he could have halted a sunrise. His entire body froze in place, and just in time.

Aldron, tired of fending off Grumph and Gabrielle, slammed the butt of his staff to the ground once more. This time, the concussion was not just force; it was ice and darkness as well. It blasted the area around him, coming only inches away from Eric before the magic subsided. Gabrielle was on the ground, bleeding from several wounds, and Grumph had been hurled into a wall. He was on one knee, and from the way his head bobbed about, it was evident he'd gotten a bell-ringing.

Quickly surveying the room, Aldron realized that Eric was still standing, locked in place mere inches outside the blast zone.

"How did you... you couldn't have... adventurers *can't* hear it." Aldron whipped his staff around and a surge of black chains flew from the top. Eric jumped back instinctively, but they managed to wrap around his left arm, pinning it and his sword to the ground mere feet away from the pillar where The Bridge rested. "Impossible. But better to examine you, just in case." Aldron's muttering seemed to be growing more insane by the minute, a fact that wasn't lost on any of the still-conscious party members.

Eric struggled against his shackles, trying in vain to find a way to free himself. It was no good; his arm and weapon were completely locked into place. While he yanked on the chains pointlessly, he felt a now-familiar surge in his body as The Bridge's melody called to him. It was telling him to do something again. Eric understood the request, but not the reason behind it. Then again, the last order it gave had probably saved his life, so he reasoned it might be best to give the magical artifact the benefit of the doubt.

He pressed his hands to the ground, the hard stone pushing on the knuckles of his left hand where the sword's hilt was chained in his clutches, and shoved himself upward. It wasn't a lot of lift, and in seconds, Eric would crash back to the ground, but in that brief moment where his hind quarters were in the air, Eric had a slim window for action. He took it, striking out with his right leg and kicking The Bridge squarely off its pedestal.

"No!" Aldron yelled as it flew by, inches from his grasp. The gleaming artifact sailed through the room, seemingly destined to crash into the stone floor. Eric was doubtful that such a powerful item could be so easily destroyed, but with magic, one never knew. Perhaps fragility was the price for housing such overwhelming power. Whether it would have shattered or not was a question Eric would have to wait to learn the answer to, for it didn't land on the floor.

The Bridge was snatched out of the air by a hairy, green-skinned hand belonging to a half-orc wizard who'd been pulling himself back up when a gleaming crystal came rocketing at his face. Grumph had barely enough time to register what it was he'd actually grabbed before he felt The Bridge break into his mind.

It was as if the whole world dissolved and then reformed, now made out of the same shimmering material as the artifact clutched in Grumph's sizable fist. He could see the flow of magic running through the air to Aldron's staff, to Thistle's belt and armor, and to his own hands. He could sense the way the magic fit together, seeing it as not a series of symbols and gestures, but rather as an art meant to encapsulate the intangible. He could feel a pulse thrumming through the entirety of existence, a single undulating harmony that seemed to stretch back before time, and forward beyond the infinite. Grumph could also see the adventurers in the world, and Aldron was right: they were different. Something unnatural ran to their bodies, threads that reached past the veil of their reality and into a place that was strange and foreign. All of this Grumph experienced in less than a fraction of a second and then it was gone.

He realized two things upon coming back to himself: first was that it was no wonder Aldron had gone mad. Just that sliver of a moment had weakened Grumph's grip on reality. The second thing

Grumph realized, was that he was no longer confounded by the fifth spell in his book. His free hand swept through the air, carving symbols in the ether beyond mortal sight as words of power tumbled unbidden from his lips. With a final flourish, Grumph stuck out the palm of his hand.

"Rouse!" A blinding flash strobed from Grumph's hand, forcing Aldron to hurriedly rub his eyes. As the word bounced around the room, the magic burst forth, flowing not at Aldron, who'd been braced for an attack, but rather to Thistle and Gabrielle's slack forms on the floor. Their eyes leapt open as new energy poured into their bodies, and in seconds, both had scrambled up. Grumph knew it was only a temporary measure, not nearly as potent as Thistle's healing. It would bring them back into the fight, though, and right now, that would have to be enough.

"Did I miss anything?" Thistle asked.

"Crazy wizard. Artifact gave him power. And I'm tapped." Grumph struggled to keep his words steady even as a slight shake rippled through his body. That spell had taken a lot more power than he'd expected, more than he suspected he possessed. It was likely The Bridge had bolstered him a bit, but the aftereffects were already showing themselves. Grumph still pulled his bone-sword free with his off-hand. He might be out of magic, but he still intended to fight. The thought of magic reminded him of something else he'd noticed with his magic sight.

"Thistle, call your dagger," Grumph instructed.

There was no time for further explanation, as Aldron's vision had finally cleared, and the wizard wheeled around, staff at the ready. Fortunately, Thistle trusted his friend enough to take a few things on faith, so without hesitation, he let out the same quick call he'd used back in the arena. The dagger wedged in Aldron's gut glowed briefly, then reappeared in the sheath of Thistle's belt.

"Now, that is a handy gift." He pulled the dagger free, along with its twin, and began circling, looking for an opening in Aldron's defense.

"I don't know how you're all doing this, but I promise you'll pay for it," Aldron spat. He eyed the half-orc warily. The Bridge was hearty enough to withstand some rough handling; however, its power was both tremendous and unpredictable. As long as it was in an adventurer's hands, there was no telling what effects might spill forth.

Aldron was so focused on Grumph that he nearly missed the red-armored blur racing toward him. As it was, he barely called up his magical shield in time to halt Gabrielle's axe as it drove toward his face.

As soon as he halted the axe, Aldron felt a sharp pain in his back. The damned gnome had hit him with another dagger. On his left, the half-orc rushed forward, odd-shaped sword at the ready as he charged. It was clear Aldron wasn't going to be able to beat them if he worried about The Bridge, so he closed his eyes, called forth a spell, and hoped it would all work out for the best.

Grumph saw the elven wizard shimmer as he approached, but he kept on coming. If he stopped every time a spell was cast, he'd never get anywhere. The half-orc swung his blade with every bit of strength he could muster, hoping to take the wizard's head in a clean blow. Instead, the blade rang and produced sparks as it struck a tough, rocky exterior.

The first blow hit Grumph in his gut, taking his wind and remaining energy in a single strike. A second attack knocked the bone-blade from his hand, sending it clattering to the stone floor and nearly impaling Eric in the process. Grumph pulled The Bridge close as he sank to his knees, determined to keep it from Aldron for as long as possible.

"I'm sssssick of you," hissed the seven-foot-tall monster that had once been Aldron. Its flat, serpentine head jutted out from a pair of broad shoulders, shoulders that, like almost all of its body, were coated in a thick, black armor that resembled stone. His form was humanoid, even though his arms did hang so low they nearly reached his knees and a thick tail sprouted from his rear.

Thistle lost no time hurling both of his daggers at its head, the only spot that seemed not entirely encased in armor. The first one managed to leave a gash on Aldron's cheek, but the second bounced off a segment of armor near his brow.

A sharp ringing filled the air as Gabrielle hammered blows on the monster's rough hide. The head of her axe chipped with every attack, yet she refused to relent, hitting again and again with everything she had. Aldron swept his claws at her; what had once been hands were now fingers ending in blades that begged to be coated in blood. She parried many of the blows, but a few landed on her torso. The demon-hide armor buckled against the force of the attacks, though it held intact. Whatever Aldron had turned into, it definitely didn't carry the sort of blessing needed to easily rend demon flesh.

As their exchange continued, a careful, silent, human hand crept along the floor, grabbing a forgotten weapon in its desperate clutches.

Aldron switched tactics, slamming Gabrielle with his strength, rather than trying to cut through her armor. The axe-wielding girl managed to dodge several times, but unfortunately, Aldron had time and size on his side. Despite the constant peppering of daggers from Thistle, the monster kept on task and eventually broke through Gabrielle's guard. He struck her square in the chest, sending her hurtling through the air and slamming into a wall.

As she hit, another blow was struck, this one not against Aldron, Gabrielle, or Thistle. The slight sound went unnoticed in the comparative din of her impact.

"Now that jussssst leavessss you, little gnome," Aldron hissed. He leapt across the room, powerful legs carrying him over half-destroyed furniture. The landing left him a few inches short of Thistle, but Aldron merely leaned forward and grabbed the small paladin with his massive hands.

Thistle struggled valiantly against the claws pinning him to the floor. A wave of sour breath washed over him, and he realized Aldron's face was mere inches from his own.

"You adventurerssss are all the same. Bold. Sssstupid. Carelesssssss."

Thistle wasn't certain if the serpentine "s" sound was intentional, or just a side effect of the form. Either way, it certainly wasn't something that boded well.

"Us? You're the one killing people by letting that crystal pull demons into the world!" He struggled as he talked, but even his enhanced paladin strength was no match for the monster's size and power. It looked like he'd be seeing Grumble again soon.

"A sssssmall price to pay. Sssssoon, I will find the other pieces. Sssssoon, I will free our world from your kind. And it will be eassssssy, because you are all ssssso sssssstupid. You even forgot the firsssssst rule of combat: never take on a wizard in their lair."

"Actually, you're the one who forgot the first rule of combat." Eric's voice came only a twitch of a hand before the attack. Thistle saw the tip of the blade, Grumph's bone-sword, burst forth from Aldron's left eye. It had been run through the back of his head, skewering his brain in the process. The monster that had once been Aldron slid limply to the side, clearly dead.

"Never, but never, take your eyes off the rogue." Eric smiled as he spoke, a weak expression on his pale skin. Thistle looked up at his friend, overwhelmed with joy to see him. It wasn't until he noticed the rapid sound of dripping that the gnome realized something was wrong.

The dripping was blood raining onto the stone floor from the stump where Eric's left arm had once been. Thistle glanced across the room to see that the appendage was still chained to the ground, short sword clutched in its grip.

"Hey, Thistle, I know I'm not much of a minion, but do you think you could put in a good word with your god for me?" With those words, Eric collapsed to the floor, body as limp as the monster he'd given up his arm to slay.

24.

Eric's eyes fluttered open as the smell of fresh stew reached his nostrils. He pulled himself up gingerly, then realized that his body wasn't in any sort of pain. In fact, he felt great. Standing up, Eric noticed two things: his left arm was attached to his body, and he was standing in Grumph's tavern, the very tavern that had been burned down only a few short weeks ago.

"So, heaven is a tavern," Eric said, voice echoing off the empty tables. "I suppose I owe my drunk Uncle Jerry an apology for laughing at his theory."

"Sorry, kid, you're not in heaven, at least, not yet." The voice came from a squat kobold that appeared on top of the bar. Had Grumph been here, he'd have been livid at someone sitting on his precious bar top. "Think of this as a way station. It's where most gods hold our meetings with those who are either fresh off, or still on the mortal coil."

"Meaning I'm either still alive, or I just died," Eric surmised. "Which is it?"

"Well, that's sort of complicated. You want an ale or something?"

"Please."

The kobold snapped his fingers and a frosty mug appeared on the table next to Eric. The former guard pulled out a chair and took his seat, then drank deep from the mug. This was Grumph's brew, no question about it.

"Okay, I'll bite," Eric said after a few more gulps. "How is it complicated?"

"For starters, you're on the bubble, life-wise. Chopping off your arm with a demon-bone sword took a lot out of you, and the darkness spreading through your blood isn't helping the situation any. Thistle only has so much healing magic in a given day, and even if he ignored the others completely and tried to save you, there's no guarantee it would work."

"Right then; so I'm looking at probable, if not certain, death." Eric nodded and took another drink. He wasn't sure why none of this bothered him much. Perhaps it was because he'd known the price when he took the sword to his shoulder.

"That's just part of it. See, normally, in this situation, you'd just pass on and that would be that. But at the moment, there's a bit of a debate over ownership regarding your soul. Since your last prayer was to me, even as inadvertently as you made it, that gives me a certain amount of claim to you. However, Tristan, god of the rogues, is kicking up a mighty shitstorm over that. Seems your performance was respectable enough to warrant his attention."

"Other gods were watching us?"

"Being a god can get kind of boring. Lots of us look to mortals for entertainment," Grumble admitted, shrugging his scaly shoulders. "Besides, you were fighting over an artifact with a kind of power even we deities don't fully comprehend. That's the sort of thing that draws a viewership."

"Makes sense." Eric drained the remainder of his mug and set it on the table. "Let me see if I've got this: I should be dying, but if I do go, then it creates a headache between you and another god. I take that to mean you're thinking of letting me live?"

"Thistle is a paladin of mine, and as such, it's well within my divine rights to give him an extra boost of healing magic. Thing is, you aren't really a follower of mine, at least, not yet. That means if I'm helping you, there has to be a price."

"Had a feeling that was coming," Eric said, leaning forward a bit. "What do I owe you?"

"It doesn't work like that. We're gods; you can't just pay us off with gold. No, for something as hefty as a second chance at life, you're going to be given a divine task. I tell you to do something, and you have to do it, or die trying."

"Let me guess: you want me to assemble the rest of the artifact," Eric said.

"That would be great, but no, I'm not that cruel. The artifact is something that exists beyond all known magic; it can't be located by any known spell unless it's actively being used. Not even gods can sense the pieces of it; they have to be discovered in person. It's been centuries since the last one was found, so you'll likely be long dead before the next one comes around. Your job is a much simpler one: don't go back to Solium with the artifact. Right now, your group is on the border of Alcatham. Take the artifact, leave the kingdom behind, and never return."

"Won't the king send people after us?"

"Only if he knows you're alive," Grumble pointed out. "You're a smart little group, I'm sure you'll think of something."

"But, never going back would mean…"

"Yes, Eric. Your old life is gone. That's why they call it a price. Today, no matter what you choose, Eric of Maplebark, former guard of the mayor's daughter, dies. Whether you rise again as an adventuring rogue, or simply rot in the ground, is your choice entirely."

Eric pressed his hands to the surface of the wooden table, a table that no longer existed in his world. It had been eaten by fire, along with the rest of Grumph's tavern. Yes, they'd abandoned their family and friends expecting to die on their quest, but now… now, they were so close to getting out alive.

"It shouldn't be my choice. This impacts all of us. It's wrong for me to tell everyone else what to do."

"A wise sentiment, but a misguided one," Grumble said. "This is your task alone, Eric. If the others want to go home, they can. Only you can never return."

"Oh." That single word stretched on in Eric's mind as he realized the weight of this choice. If the others wanted to go home, then he would be an outcast, walking the world by himself, possibly for the rest of his life.

Then again… what would he be going back to? A life as a terrible guard, protecting a girl who didn't need protection in the first place? Yes, he would miss his mother, but was that alone reason to go back to a town where he was a joke?

"I've got two questions," Eric said at last. "First, does this have anything to do with the fact that I seem to hear The Bridge in a way the others don't?"

"A little bit," Grumble replied. "Like I said, being a god can get boring at times. We don't really know what the resonance you have with it means, but we're certainly curious."

"A fair, if vague, answer. Second question: why do you even want me? My last prayer was, like you said, an indirect technicality. Wouldn't it be easier to let the god of the rogues have me?"

"Partly because, in your guard days, you were a minion, even if you didn't know it; partly because I like reminding the other gods that I won't be pushed around into caving on demands; and partly because I think you're interesting. You and Thistle are both oddities in my world of followers: brave, determined, self-sacrificing. These aren't qualities a lot of my worshippers have. I'm not so keen on giving up one of the exceptions."

"So, it's half desire, half just wanting to piss off the other gods?"

"More or less," Grumble said, flashing a toothy, kobold smile.

"Good enough for me." Eric rose from his seat and stretched, enjoying the sensation of having his left arm while he could. "I accept your divine task. For the rest of my life, I will never again willingly set foot in Solium. Any divine guidance before I go back?"

"Always tip the bartender more than you think you should, be nice to the people who know where you sleep, and beware the bush with red flowers." Grumble raised his hands, and his scaly body began to glow.

"All right, Thistle, you've prayed hard enough. Time for me to give you an answer."

*   *   *

Thistle was on his knees, hands clasped, mere inches from Eric's bleeding body, when the surge of divine magic hit him. It exploded outward, too much for him to even dream of directing, pouring from his small body and soaking the entire room in a soft glow of white light. The vast majority of it fell on Eric, whose flesh began to knit together even before the blood stopped flowing. Within seconds, the light faded, leaving Thistle's head feeling as though he'd tried to run a mile after chugging dwarven whiskey. A slight stirring occurred below him as Eric's eyes weakly pulled themselves open.

He looked up at the gnome's worried face and gave a smile. "Grumble says hi."

Thistle grabbed his friend in a hug, trying to show his emotion without opening any of the freshly healed wounds.

"You're a gods-damned madman, did you know that?"

"Oh sure, everyone else charges monsters and it's brave; I do it once and I'm a madman."

"Let's all try to avoid monster charging as a general rule from here on," Thistle said, relinquishing his grip. Across the room, Gabrielle and Grumph were pulling themselves to their feet. No one was fully healed, but at least they could move under their own power.

"That might be easier said than done," Eric whispered to Thistle. He got up carefully, uncertain how his body would balance with his arm missing. It was actually quite effortless, as though his body hadn't been shorted an appendage at all. A quick glance to his left explained why very quickly.

"Did my… is that my arm?" He wiggled the fingers carefully, finding each responsive. This appendage was identical to his old one, save that it lacked many of the scars he'd acquired over his years of training as a guard.

"No, that's your arm." Thistle pointed to a severed appendage on the ground, still clutching a short sword. "That, I'd guess, is a gift from Grumble."

"Less of a gift than a trade," Eric replied. "Maybe a bonus is the right way to put it."

"Suckered you into something, aye?"

"That he did. I'll explain everything once Grumph and Gabrielle are back up. Better to handle it all at once."

"Just tell me it was worth it," Thistle said.

"I think so," Eric replied. "But I guess I won't really know for what I hope is a long, long time."

"One of those?"

"One of those."

* * *

It took around a half hour to catch Grumph and Gabrielle up on what had happened after they'd passed out, then another half hour more for Eric to explain the deal he'd struck with Grumble. By the time he finished, his throat was getting a bit parched and he wondered if the mead Aldron kept had anything dangerous in it. When he was done at last, it was Grumph who spoke first.

"Where are we going?"

"I'm heading to Alcatham with The Bridge," Eric replied. He'd set the gleaming crystal in his pack for the moment. Even though he could no longer see it, he could still feel it humming softly through his veins. "The rest of you are free to go home. If we can sneak past the guards, then no one will ever know we didn't die in here. The king will keep sending teams of adventurers, trying to recover an artifact that isn't there."

"Except he will know," Gabrielle said. "He found it with magic, he's sure to keep checking in."

Eric shook his head. "The Bridge only shows up to magic when it's being actively used, the way Aldron was employing it when adventurers came. I'd bet there were plenty of times the king couldn't sense it. Even if he does realize it's gone, I don't intend to keep it active, so we should be able to disappear."

"You're not a mage, Eric. How do you think you can control that thing?" Gabrielle asked.

"You'll just have to trust me on this. I can't explain it, but the artifact and I are... synced up, I suppose. It helped me during the fight."

"Makes as much sense as anything else about that thing," Thistle sighed. "But that still leaves the question of where we're going, once we hit Alcatham that is."

"Only I have to—"

"Eric, stop. Do you really think I'm going back to Maplebark?" Gabrielle touched her armor delicately, feeling the strength of the hide press back on her flesh. "I can't be that version of myself anymore. Going to balls, minding my manners, being silent and proper... that Gabrielle is gone. I don't know if this is who I really was supposed to be, but I like it. I'm happy like this. And I'm damn sure not going to let you wander off into unknown wilds without me watching your back."

"Agreed," Grumph said.

"I'm a paladin now," Thistle reminded him. "We go where we're needed; seems to me that helping a friend on a task for my god falls well into the job description."

"You all don't have to do this," Eric protested.

"We do, actually. Gabrielle said it best: there's no going back for us. Had you died on the floor, we'd have certainly taken a different path, but none of us would have returned to Maplebark," Thistle said. "Each of us has said our goodbyes to the life we left somewhere along the road. Only you could have returned; that's why Grumble made you choose. For better or worse, we're all adventurers now."

Eric stared in silence at his comrades. They were battered, burned, and covered in blood, yet each wanted to come with him on a path that would only lead to more. He was lucky beyond blessings the gods could give; he had found a party of true friends.

"Well then, as adventurers, our next task is clear-cut. How do we want to handle the guards?"

25.

Russell was impressed in spite of himself. When the party said they wanted to sneak out of the cave and kill off the guards, he was certain that would be the end of them (again). The stats on each guard should have proven more than enough to wound, if not kill, any given character. However, it seemed the dice were on their side. They managed to circle around and cut the throats of several guards, despite Tim's objections, before the whole thing dissolved into a full-blown battle. When the blood settled, everyone was still standing, even if Glenn was nearly out of spells and Terry had only a few points of health left.

Russell pulled out the module book, almost certain that their efforts would have been for nothing. He was pretty sure that all the other parties in the dungeon were supposed to wipe, meaning all his players had done was murder a bunch of innocent guards only doing their jobs.

"Well?" Mitch demanded. He rolled his D20 through his fingers, anxious for more battle.

"Well what?" Russell knew damn well what Mitch was asking, but he saw no reason to make it easy on him.

"Is someone coming with the artifact or not?"

"You don't know that," Russell reminded him. "All you know is that you just killed a bunch of guards. If you want to see if anyone else completed the dungeon, then you'll have to wait around and watch."

"Maybe this time we could try talking first, if anyone comes out," Tim suggested. "It's possible other characters gave up too, and don't have the artifact."

"But they have other things," Terry said. "Gold pieces, weapons, magic items, all things that can belong to us if we kill and loot." At present, his character was rifling through the pockets of a guard who had only a few trinkets on him and whose entire net worth was less than a single gold. The rogue stuffed his bag with every item the still-cooling corpse held.

"Ignore him, he's been a buzz-kill the whole campaign," Mitch said.

"Yeah, he tried to get us to talk to the guards," Glenn reminded everyone.

"I just thought they could be reasoned with. They were people with a job; maybe a little gold could have made them look the other way." Tim rolled his own D20 along the map, avoiding eye contact with the others.

Russell continued digging through the module book, ignoring the sniping going on around him. Tim was actually right; the guards were all poor and could have been bought off for the right amount. That was information the party didn't have, however, because everyone who could impart it was already dead. As his hands danced past the page with the guards, he found what he was looking for. There it was: which characters succeeded if the adventuring party failed. He was positive he remembered it being no one, but it never hurt to double check.

"Hmmm." His eyes scanned the page, only moderately surprised to find the entry different than he recalled. Russell had misremembered so many things, it was almost like the book was purposely changing on him.

"What does 'hmmm' mean?" Mitch asked, impatience evident on his slightly flushed face.

"It means, tell me what you each are doing." Russell set the book down and looked at his players. "Like I said, if you want to see if anyone is coming, you have to wait."

"Oh, we'll wait, all right," Mitch replied. He glanced at the others, flashing a wicked grin which all but Tim returned.

*   *   *

Eric poked his head out first. Even though they'd decided to take the diplomatic route and see if the guards responded to a bit of gold, there was no guarantee they wouldn't immediately shoot at anyone exiting the dungeon. As the spryest of the party, plus the only one fully healed from their encounter, Eric was the natural choice to test the guard's willingness to listen. He surveyed the landscape, watchful for arrows coming in his direction, but none appeared. There also didn't seem to be any guards about, though his keen eye did catch splatters of blood on the grass near the guards' tent.

"I think something might have happened to the guards." Eric motioned for the others to follow him then stepped fully from the dungeon's cave entrance. Putting his hands together, he cupped them in front of his mouth and let out a loud yell. "Hello! Is anyone about?"

The only response was silence and a soft rustle of wind through the forest trees.

"Maybe there was a monster attack?" Gabrielle pulled her axe free of its sheath, wincing slightly as she did. Aldron's last blow had torn something in her shoulder, and until Thistle regained his magic, she'd have to muddle through the pain.

"Too clean." Grumph had no magic left, but he gripped his bone-sword tightly. He'd come too far to go down easily. "Monster would have shredded the tent."

"Aye, you're right, old friend." Thistle pulled his daggers free, twirling them once in each hand. "What we have here are signs that another party also wanted to leave the dungeon, and did so over the guards' protests."

"Then, shouldn't there be bodies?" Eric asked.

"Could have been moved. Could be scavenger monsters. Lot of options," Grumph grunted.

"So... is this just a free win? No guards, no one to deal with?" Gabrielle was a bit relieved at the idea of getting through this without combat. She'd hoped the guards would take the bribe, but if they hadn't, the only option remaining was fighting. That would have been exceptionally risky since everyone in the group, except Eric, was already halfway dead.

"It looks that way," Eric agreed. His eyes swept the forest once more, and he noticed a slight rustle in one of the bushes. It was tiny, likely a rodent or the wind, and he would have dismissed it as just that if not for the flowers blooming in its viridian depths. They were a brilliant scarlet, as though they'd been dipped in flaming blood.

"Red flowers." Eric pulled his short sword free as he stared at the bush.

"Beg pardon?" Thistle asked.

"Grumble told me to tip my bartenders, be nice to people who knew where I slept, and to watch out for a bush with red flowers. Those flowers are definitely red, and I think I've seen it move twice since I've been watching it."

"I was really hoping this would be a free win," Gabrielle sighed, bringing her axe to the ready. She'd just gotten it into position when the four figures burst forth from behind the bush.

*   *   *

"This is bullshit! We totally should have been able to surprise them!" Mitch had actually stood from his seat at the table and was glowering at his D20, resting lazily on the number two.

"You got a two on your Sneak roll, and they have a high Vision," Russell said. "You fail to surprise the party, so no bonuses."

"Don't worry about it. We can take them, anyway," Glenn said. "I've got first in the turn order, and I'm going to let loose with my last spell: *Blazeferno*. I'll cover them in fire so hot, it will melt the flesh from their bones."

"Just don't let it destroy any of their gear," Terry protested.

"Let's see if you even succeed first," Russell said. It was a pointless exercise; the roll for Glenn's min-maxed wizard was ludicrously low, but the rules demanded it. "Roll your Casting check."

"Gladly." Glenn tossed the green D20 across the map, where it rolled between the figurines without disturbing a single one. It slowed down, clearly showing a nineteen on top. Then, at the last instant, it moved just a touch more, and a new number stared up at the waiting players.

"I got a one? No, it was on nineteen, you all saw it!"

"Bad rolls happen," Russell replied. He might not have taken quite such joy in it if the group hadn't been such a relentless pain throughout the entire campaign. "You fail to cast *Blazeferno*, successfully and no harm comes to the other party. Now, roll again to see if you hurt yourself with that critical failure."

*   *   *

The thrum that filled Eric's body nearly knocked him from his feet. As soon as the enemy wizard began to cast, Eric could feel The Bridge awaken, power surging outward. He could almost see it happen before it occurred: first, the wizard was calling forth magic, then, the spell was about to convalesce into a hellish spell of flaming death, and then, at the last moment, *something* shifted. The fiery blast meant to destroy them was gone; instead, the wizard was struggling to put out his now blazing robes.

Grumph, Gabrielle, and Thistle didn't hesitate to capitalize on the momentary advantage, pressing forward with an attack of their own. Eric tried to join them, but the sensation surging through him made even the smallest of movements difficult.

"What... what are you doing?"

The Bridge didn't answer him in any tangible sense, nothing as clear as the "stop" he'd gotten in the fight with Aldron. Instead, he received a vague feeling of certainty and relaxation, as though whatever was going on was well in hand; all he had to do was play his part. Without even realizing he was doing so, Eric had reached into his pack and pulled out The Bridge. It shone in the sunlight, or perhaps the sunlight shone in it; such distinctions grew fuzzy when Eric clutched it in his hands.

"Okay, tell me what you want me to do."

*   *   *

"Come on... come on... come on... GODDAMNIT!" Glenn jumped up so hard that his knee knocked the table, spilling a bag of chips that had been resting on the edge. "How does she keep hitting me?"

"You're wearing robes for armor, she's a barbarian, and the dice are working against you," Russell said. "You were at three Health Points, and she does nine damage, meaning your character is knocked out, bleeding, and almost dead."

"Someone get me a potion!"

"We got our own trouble to deal with," Mitch replied. "This fucking gnome keeps pinging me with daggers, meanwhile, I can't roll shit." He tossed his D20, which proved his point excellently by landing on a three. "Another fucking miss?"

"The dice really are against you guys in this fight," Russell said. He checked the order and found Tim was up next. It was a shame; if anyone in the party didn't deserve to wipe, it was Tim. But the dice were the dice, and a game without risk wasn't really worth playing.

"Tim, you're up."

"Come heal me," Glenn begged.

"I can't, remember?" Tim stared across the table with unmasked exasperation. "I'm just a knight. I wanted to roll a paladin again, but none of you would let me, so now, we don't have any healing in the party besides a few weak potions." He turned away from Glenn and looked at the map. "I guess I'll go after the half-orc."

"Roll it up," Russell said.

*   *   *

The tall, blond man in the shining armor took a swing at Grumph, but stumbled at the last moment, sending his blow wide. Grumph didn't miss the opportunity, stabbing him cleanly through a gap in his dented breastplate with the bone-sword. Grumph's opponent let out a light whimper and fell to the ground.

Grumph turned back to the smaller man on his left, probably a rogue by the look of him. He ran toward Grumph, daggers at the ready, only to trip on a rock in his path and fall down. No sooner had he landed than blood began pouring out from under his torso. Judging by the amount and the angle, it appeared to Grumph that the man had fallen on his daggers and seriously injured himself. Just to be sure, Grumph drove his own blade through the man's skull. There would be no getting up from that blow.

With a slight twist, he moved to check on the downed knight's status and found Eric already perched over him.

"Go help the others," he called. "I'm supposed to be here."

Grumph noticed the glowing artifact clutched in Eric's hand but said nothing. He'd been under its thrall briefly; he understood the clarity it could provide. If Eric felt he should deal with the knight, then Grumph would trust him. Besides, the last of their enemies, a barbarian with an axe even bigger than Gabrielle's, was proving a real bastard to put down.

On his way over, Grumph paused by the form of the unconscious wizard. It was weak, but the body was still breathing. With a quick chop of his sword, the wizard's head went rolling past Grumph's feet, and that breathing came to a halt.

*   *   *

"Why won't any of them die?" Mitch threw his D20 again, unsurprised to find another low number staring up at him. No one had rolled higher than a five in this entire battle. Nothing worked: not changing dice, not blowing on them for luck, nothing. He couldn't even accuse Russell of using overpowered enemies; most of the damage the party had taken was self-inflicted.

"At least you're still alive to try," Terry grumbled. "Glenn and I are already dead, and Tim's not far behind."

"He's not dead yet," Russell said. "But Tim, when the paladin and barbarian are done attacking Mitch, be ready for a roll. The sword already nearly killed you outright, and it also has a blood-poisoning effect. If you don't save against it, your character will die."

"I understand." Tim held the blue D20 in his sweaty hand, staring into its swirl-patterned depths. As much as he hadn't cared for the way his party did things, Tim didn't want his character to die. He liked Timuscor the knight, he liked the game, and he didn't really want it to end. Tim suspected that if the party wiped again, no one would want to play anymore, and finding another group was a prospect he had no idea how to tackle. When he rolled, it wouldn't just be for Timuscor: it would be for his whole future of gaming.

*   *   *

Eric stood over the unconscious knight, aware of a growing warmth coming from The Bridge. As it heated, the knight's eyes fluttered halfway open. He stared at Eric in confusion, as though he were drunk, gaze flitting from the glowing artifact to Eric and back again.

"Whroo... yu..." The knight's words were slurred and only halfway intelligible.

Eric gave him what he hoped looked like a reassuring smile and pressed The Bridge to the dying man's chest. "I have no idea what's supposed to happen now; I'm only following orders. Let's just hope it isn't boring."

The Bridge did not disappoint.

As the enemy barbarian's death cry echoed across the field, The Bridge's glow intensified. It seemed to envelop the knight, seeping over him like spilled jelly. The air around them began to ripple, first lightly, and then with such intensity that it was all Eric could do to hold on. Even with his eyes closed, he could see the ripple, feel it rattling his very bones. It grew stronger still, and just when Eric was certain he could hold on no longer, the energy seemed to snap.

It surged outward, inward, and all over at once. Eric felt like everything had been burned away and rebuilt thousands of times, all before he could draw a single breath. Then, just as suddenly, it was over.

He carefully opened his eyes, uncertain of what would lay before him.

* * *

"With Mitch dead, Tim is the last one still breathing," Russell said. "Roll the dice, and see if you survive another round."

Tim nodded, touched the D20 for luck, and then sent it tumbling across the map. Usually, it would roll for a few seconds before unceremoniously stopping on a number. Sometimes, it would strike an object, and very occasionally, it would be rolled too hard and would tumble off the table, necessitating a re-roll.

None of those things happened this time.

The D20 rolled twice then stopped in an impossible position, resting on one of its corners. Before the players could comment on the strangeness of such an event, it was overshadowed. The D20 began to spin in place, moving with such fierce speed that a whistling sound filled the air. Small wisps of smoke began to rise from the map below it, and the die's blue facade seemed to throb with light. Then, without any slowing down as warning, the D20 stopped spinning. It shook once, the barest of shivers running through it, and crumbled into countless pieces.

Everyone in the room stared at the now-destroyed die, dumbfounded into silence at what they'd just seen. It was Tim who finally spoke. Tim the rookie, Tim the newbie, Tim who was willing to turn to his GM and ask a question, inane or insane as it may seem.

"So... what does that mean?"

*   *   *

The knight's eyes opened slowly, the stabbing pain in his head making exposure to all but the faintest bits of light an unbearable pain. He found four people standing over him: a gnome in shining armor, a woman with an axe, a half-orc in robes, and a smiling human male clutching an object that shone with a fading glow.

"Who are you people?" He tried to sit up but found his body stiff as a dragon's talon. The throbbing ache from his stomach made him brave the discomfort to check it; thankfully, there was no wound that he could see.

"We were going to ask you the same thing," the gnome replied.

"I'm..." His voice trailed off as he plumbed the depths of his mind. Surely there was an answer; it was such a simple question. Yet it eluded him as he bore the pain in his skull and searched about. Who was he? He was... a warrior, yes, that felt right. A knight? No... a knight for now; his true dream had always been to become a paladin. The pain receded as these details and more came to light in his mind. He'd been stuck working with a group of... well, assholes, to try and progress his goals. He was here on a mission for the king, and his name was...

"Timuscor," the knight replied at last. "My name is Timuscor, and I'd like to take this chance to apologize for the way my cohorts treated you. They were unscrupulous men, and I'm happy to be free of them."

Everyone looked at Eric, who gave them a small nod. He carefully tucked the object he'd been holding back into his pack and looked down at Timuscor.

"Well, Timuscor, how do you feel about travel?"

Epilogue

Russell and Tim were the only ones left in Russell's house, the others having left as soon as the game ended. Only Tim had stuck around to help clean up. In fairness to the others, after what they'd seen the D20 do, it was hardly surprising that they'd wanted to put some distance between themselves and dice.

"I guess we're not going to play *Spells, Swords, & Stealth* anymore, are we?" Tim had held back this question for some time, but as he deposited the last soda can in the trash, it seemed he needed to ask now, or lose the opportunity.

"It doesn't look likely. Dice weirdness aside, I don't think the others liked my new game-running style very much."

"Well, that's their loss." Tim yanked the trash bag out from the container and tied the edges together.

"You liked it?"

"I thought it was a lot of fun. Sure, keeping track of meals and stuff got a little tedious, but it also made it feel a lot more real. Honestly, the only part I didn't like was how the others kept making their characters act."

Russell silently mulled Tim's words over for a moment, scooping some unattended sour cream into the sink. He was so distracted he nearly let some spill onto one of his mother's Rodrigo romance novels left on the counter, a sin that would have earned harsh punishment. "You know, there are other gaming groups out there. I bet if we hit up the comic shop, we could find more than enough people to put a new group together."

"Really?" Tim almost dropped the trash bag. "I mean... are you sure you want to run another one, with everything that happened?"

"Shitty players are part of the package that comes with GMing. As for the dice thing, I have absolutely no idea what that was, but weird stuff happens all the time. I heard on the news that last week, a whole bunch of birds fell out of the sky for no reason, and I've got a cousin that still swears up and down he met an actual god on a vacation. There's tons of unexplained crap out there, and I'm not going to give up my favorite hobby because of one weird incident."

"Count me in," Tim said excitedly. "I can hardly wait to make a new character. Any idea what the next game will be about?"

"Nothing offhand, but there are some really cool modules at the comic shop. There's one I've had my eye on by the same company who made our last campaign: it takes place in a kingdom neighboring Solium."

"There's more than one kingdom?"

"Way more than one," Russell confirmed. "This one is called Alcatham."

*   *   *

Thistle walked over to the campfire where Eric sat on a fallen log. The Bridge was in his hands, shining in the firelight. Eric's eyes seemed lost in its depths, but as Thistle approached, he looked up to greet his friend.

"How's it going?"

"He's settling in all right," Thistle replied. "Got more than a few gaps in his memory, but genuinely seems not to be put off about us killing his comrades."

"I doubt he remembers more than their names and skills," Eric replied.

Thistle sat down on another log, keeping his gaze away from the artifact resting on Eric's lap. Whatever it was, whatever it did, Thistle didn't need to make a connection with it. Grumph had only held it for a few moments, and now, he was resting under a tree, writing out new spells. Eric had heard the thing speak without laying a finger on it, and when he finally did touch it…

"Have you figured out what happened? Did it wipe his mind or change his disposition or something?"

"Or something," Eric whispered. He turned The Bridge over once more, then stowed it in his pack. "I have… let's not call it a theory yet. Maybe a suspicion. Do you remember what Aldron said about adventurers being influenced by people from another world?"

"Aldron said a lot of crazy things."

"Yes, but that doesn't necessarily make him wrong. Let's assume, just for a moment, that he was right. Real adventurers, not fakers like us, are influenced, connected in some way to another world. Their world flows into ours, shaping the actions and choices of the adventurers."

"That would be the gist of Aldron's claim, aye."

"Then maybe The Bridge broke that connection, severed the influence. Maybe it made Timuscor like us, an adventurer who isn't ruled by some foreign magic. After all, The Bridge is supposed to be able to affect their world; why not the connection from theirs to ours?"

"If what you're saying is right, and I am in no way jumping on ship with that idea, that would mean everything we know about our world, about magic, about life itself; all of it is bunk," Thistle said.

"Maybe, maybe not. Maybe it means there's more than we realized. Maybe we've only scratched the surface, and what remains is sheer wonder. Of course, if we want any real answers there's probably only one way to find them."

"You want to look for the other pieces, don't you?"

"As you'd say: aye. The longer I think about it, the more it feels like what we're supposed to do. Besides, it's not like we have anything else planned."

"I had a healthy amount of 'not-dying' all lined up, but I suppose, for a paladin, that's a crazy dream anyway." Thistle leaned back and looked up at the stars. They looked the same as they had in Solium, which made sense given that they were only a few miles from the border. Perhaps, as they traveled deeper into Alcatham, he'd see new constellations. That'd be something to tell Madroria about when he finally saw her; she'd always loved the stars.

"Aren't these pieces supposed to be impossible to find?" Thistle asked.

"Nightmarishly so."

"There might be others searching for them, as well," Thistle reminded him. "Perhaps agents of the king; he's apt to realize we lived once they find the guards' corpses."

"Almost certainly," Eric agreed.

"And if we do find any, which is beyond a long shot, they'll be guarded by dungeons and monsters as bad, if not worse than, this one."

"Stands to reason."

"So, you're proposing we go on an impossible quest, facing unknown enemies and certain death, all for nothing more than the slim chance finding a few magical baubles?"

"Certainly," Eric replied. He stood up from the fire and looked across the plains to where Gabrielle and Timuscor were sparring, and Grumph was furiously writing in his spellbook. "Didn't you get the message yet, Thistle? This is what we do. We're adventurers now."

The gnome hesitated for only a moment, then rose from his own seat as well.

"Aye; that we are."

About the Author

Drew Hayes is an aspiring author from Texas who has now found time and gumption to publish a few books. He graduated from Texas Tech with a B.A. in English, because evidently he's not familiar with what the term "employable" means. Drew has been called one of the most profound, prolific, and talented authors of his generation, but a table full of drunks will say almost anything when offered a round of free shots. Drew feels kind of like a D-bag writing about himself in the third person like this. He does appreciate that you're still reading, though.

Drew would like to sit down and have a beer with you. Or a cocktail. He's not here to judge your preferences. Drew is terrible at being serious, and has no real idea what a snippet biography is meant to convey anyway. Drew thinks you are awesome just the way you are. That part, he meant. You can reach Drew with questions or movie offers at NovelistDrew@gmail.com Drew is off to go high-five random people, because who doesn't love a good high-five? No one, that's who.

Read or purchase more of his work at his site: DrewHayesNovels.com

Printed in Great Britain
by Amazon